MW01713845

J. E. D'Angelo

Blueprints for Love

DOLCE PUBLISHING INC.
Dolce Publishing Inc.
~ 2005 ~

Blueprints for Love

Published in 2005 by Dolce Publishing Inc.

First edition
National Library of Canada Cataloguing in Publication
J.E. D'Angelo
Blueprints for Love

ISBN: 0-9734656-2-X
PRINTED IN CANADA

Dolce Publishing Inc.
60 Winges Road, Suite 1, Woodbridge, ON L4L 6B1

Dedication:

To my father, the greatest storyteller,
the one to first open my eyes to the arts.

In appreciation:

I'd like to thank my friends, whose encouragement and best wishes mean so much.
In particular, a heartfelt thanks to those of you who have endured my endless phone calls, acting as my sounding boards, in order that I may finally achieve the finished product.
Daniela D., Laura M., Linda B., Linda P.
Thank you all for listening, thank you for helping, and most importantly, thank you for your friendship.

I have the love and support of my family, near and far, and for this I consider myself extremely fortunate.

A special thank-you goes to my husband for his support, confidence and unwavering determination to see things through. You gave me the courage to realize my dream. And to my son and daughter, whose pride in me shines in their eyes, only to be returned tenfold... thank you for being the best kids any mother could ever hope for.

PROLOGUE

"I have one question," she said, her voice taking on a suggestive tone. "Isn't this tie choking you yet?"

Alex looked up at her as she reached around his shoulders to undo his tie. He chuckled at her obvious tipsy state, all the while his vital signs skyrocketing at her closeness. "It wasn't."

Dispensing with the tie, Kate's arms continued their journey over his chest, snuggling her face in his neck. Alex caressed her hands as they slid across the front of his shirt, hoping to nonchalantly stop their movement.

Alex watched her, his eyes sparkling, but the feelings she was stirring in him bordered on erotic. "What are you doing?"

Kate started to unbutton his shirt, reveling in the touch of his skin under her fingers.

"What does it look like?" Her lips replaced her fingers, scattering kisses.

Okay, this wasn't funny anymore. Alex took hold of her

shoulders, lifting her from him. "Kate...."

"I love it when you say my name," she breathed, unsuccessfully trying to kiss him.

"That's your name."

"You never call me 'Kate'. You call me 'boss'.

"Because you are my boss, remember?"

"I'm not your boss right now..." she purred, undoing her own buttons, revealing the lacey white bra underneath...

Alex watched her, unable to avert his gaze, and this time when Kate cupped his face in the palms of her hands and pressed her lips to his ... this time she succeeded, she had succeeded in bringing down his defenses.

Alex returned her kiss with the same ardor, the same passion. He knew it was wrong, but he wasn't in the mood to listen to his brain at that moment.

CHAPTER ONE

The racket sliced through the air, hurling the small rubber ball across the contained room, but the loud echoing noise paled in comparison to the shriek of displeasure by one of the players.

"That's two out of three, boss," Alex boasted with his usual smile.

Kate watched her assistant through narrowed eyes. "Humph! You've been practicing behind my back, haven't you? You know you can be easily replaced," she threatened.

"Huh! Who else can put up with your mood swings?"

Kate pointed her racket in exaggerated indignation. "Just for that you're springing for lunch."

"But I won!"

"Too bad," Kate sang over her shoulder as she headed for the showers.

A smile spread over Alex Callahan's handsome face as he

retrieved the rubber ball and placed it and his racket into the black athletic bag near the door at the far end of the enclosed room. Following her to the change rooms, he forced himself not to notice the long slender legs; the swing of her hips as she pushed open the door marked 'Women'.

Kate Wallace was his boss – nothing more. At least that's what he'd been telling himself every morning since deciding to accept the position of 'Assistant to Director' of the prestigious firm of Wallace Architectural.

The hot pulsating water massaged the muscles at the base of his neck. Closing his eyes to the echoing sounds of the water in the small shower stall, inviting its relaxing effect to take over, he allowed his mind to wander.... During this last year, he had come to know his employer quite well. Kate was definitely moody and she almost always got her way. She could be ruthless, but Alex had become accustomed to her, observing her bad points as well as her good, although aside from her looks, those good points were sometimes a little more difficult to find – but they were there, he was certain of that.

The employee gym was situated on the first floor of the building. It was made available to all employees free of charge – a generous gesture on the part of his boss. The announcement of implementation three years ago was tarnished, however, by the stern advice that the facilities were made available because she expected excellence from her employees. Sound body, sound mind. She needed them at their best.

A large rotund man stood at the locker next to Alex's. He was squeezing into a pair of shorts when Alex appeared beside him.

"Hey bud! How's it going?" The man greeted, slightly out of breath.

Alex stepped into his boxers and reached for his pants. "It's going Don. How was that visit to the doctor?"

Don closed the locker door and draped a towel around his neck. "Well, not too badly actually," he shrugged and smiled ruefully. "But as you can see, this is where I'll be spending my lunch hours from now on – or at least till this ticker starts behaving!"

"That a boy."

"Yeah, I guess I'll be dreaming about the Friday night wing binge! Kate's told everybody in accounting to cut those down to once a month!" he said, shaking his bald head in disappointment.

Alex laughed. "Carrot sticks, Don. Carrot sticks!"

Don had had a mild heart attack a few months previously and was finding it difficult to change his way of life – especially his diet. "Yeah, I guess.... If I want to keep my job anyway."

"If you want to stay alive, Don! As for the boss ... you know she has to put on that strong front." Alex's eyes scanned the room. "This is for your own good, in fact, for all of us."

Don shrugged. "I suppose. I just hate to admit it, you know?" Don waved his hand and headed for the dreaded treadmill.

Yes, Alex knew what he meant. Kate was tough, but he believed under that thick skin and sharp tongue, she meant well. She did have a heart.

Regardless, Alex admired her. Eight years his junior, Kate's business savvy matched that of any veteran executive he'd ever encountered. She was intelligent and gutsy. Almost single-handedly, his boss had been able to direct the family business to achieve greater status among competitors, easily meeting and surpassing goals she'd set for herself. She was a formidable businesswoman.

Her simple beauty, which would turn heads wherever she went, was something on which Alex tried hard not to dwell. Although at times it was quite difficult. Kate was a tad shorter than average in height and slender in form. Her short dark blonde hair was highlighted with lighter shades. She kept it combed in a somewhat unruly fashion around her face, periodically tucking the loose strands behind her ears. Her large hazel eyes were bright and alert. The full lips capable of an enticing smile as well as the angered frown of disapproval were sometimes too inviting for Alex to bear. But Kate was engaged, and although her choice for a husband was one that Alex would not wish upon his worst enemy, he had to remember his place. He was, after all, her assistant; an assistant who would often take the brunt of the problems that arose, both within the office walls and in her personal life, but still, only her assistant. It was best to remember that.

Buttoning the tiny buttons under the tips of his shirt collar, Alex finally sat down in front of her at the small café situated just outside the gym.

"I ordered for you." Kate unnecessarily gestured towards his plate. "What took you so long?"

Alex sighed heavily for emphasis. "We can't all be naturally beautiful."

"No – you can't have another week off this summer," Kate told him, as she searched her salad for a piece of chicken.

Alex shrugged and draped his napkin on his knee. "Can't blame a guy for trying."

Kate looked up, an eyebrow raised, and Alex smiled at her, something that came easily to him.

"Does Tai Lee have the model ready for Gamble and Blaine?" She took a sip of her water and waved a hand toward another of her employees who had just entered the small café, stopping him in his tracks.

"Gary, I need those figures on my desk as soon as possible – like in one hour. How feasible is that?"

Gary scratched his graying head. "Kate, I have Cora working on it. I got everybody working on it," he explained, extending his arms, "you'll get it, I promise."

"I'll hold you to that." Kate wasn't being stern or ill tempered now. She was just matter-of-fact. The accounting problem having been addressed, she returned her questioning look to Alex who answered her promptly as though never having been interrupted.

"Should be ready. I'll check on it on my way upstairs."

"It had better be. Have you seen it since he 'finished' it? Last week he was missing two stories."

"Yes, I saw it yesterday. I think you'll be pleased."

"Good. That's an awfully large account. If we're awarded the contract for this building we'll stand a better chance of designing the other two in Edmonton and Montreal. And since this was a Kent property, this will mean more jobs being sent our way."

Kate stood to retrieve another bottle of water from the cooler, and Alex had to raise his voice to be heard. "I'm aware of that," he called out. "Trust me, it's great."

She dropped the required coins by the cash register and returned to her seat. "It's not your judgment I'm worried about.

Liam Gamble is notoriously picky!"

"Don't worry, you're wearing a skirt," Alex said off-handedly.

Kate looked up sharply. "What's that got to do with anything?"

"Your legs are all Liam seems to be concerned with when he comes in." Alex wished he hadn't made reference to her legs, but it was too late to backtrack now. She'd never let it go.

"What are you babbling about?" Kate's water bottle was momentarily poised in mid air.

"Come on, don't tell me you've never noticed."

His boss laughed at this ludicrous suggestion. "No I haven't, and that's because you're imagining things!"

Realizing he still had a job, Alex smiled mischievously and decided to try to peel off one of those thick layers. "No I'm not. Wanna bet he'll spend more time looking at your legs than the model?"

Kate's eyes narrowed suspiciously. How did Alex know this? How could he have noticed Liam Gamble's roaming eyes when she had remained entirely oblivious of this fact – if indeed it was a fact?

"You're wrong," Kate dismissed.

"An extra week vacation," Alex suggested as a wager.

"Forget it!"

"Okay, okay. Next Friday off."

"All right, you're on," she said pointing her finger at him. "But if you're wrong—"

"—I won't take Friday off?" Alex said tentatively.

Kate laughed. "What kind of a bet is that? No way! If you're wrong … you'll take the next business trip."

"Oh great, and where will that be – Siberia?"

"That can be arranged," she warned.

Alex retrieved the model from the art department and carried it upstairs.

The executive offices of Wallace Architectural were located on the top floor of the eight-story building. Kate had a corner office and two sides of the room were floor-to-ceiling window. Her desk was near the inside wall, giving her full view of downtown Victoria as well as the harbour in the near distance. A large tan suede couch sat closer to the window upon plush cream carpeting, as did a small coffee table and a large round mahogany conference table, four chairs flanking its sides. Kate's office also provided a private bath, as did Alex's.

As her assistant, Alex's substantial sized office was situated next to Kate's. Aside from the private door that led to the Director's office, there was a second entrance, which was more or less through Alex's office. In fact, this was the entrance Kate used; this was the entrance everyone used.

Alex preferred his desk by the large window, a credenza and lateral file of honey coloured wood to one side. The photocopier, drafting table and coffee machine were situated in the area outside the adjoining door giving Kate quick access to all. A partial wall of opaque glass allowed for privacy in his immediate workspace. The two executive secretaries, Connie and Angie, were just outside in the main offices, as were the secretaries of the structural and other architectural engineers on that floor.

Alex made his way through to Kate's office and placed the model on the table, ready for his boss's inspection. It was a masterpiece. The multi-leveled office building that they proposed to build was to be constructed mainly of steel and slab concrete. The structure's highest point was fifteen stories, scaling down three stories at a time on either side. It was to be built on six acres of prime real estate in downtown Vancouver and provided one hundred and thirty-five thousand square feet of office space, including a restaurant, two coffee shops, daycare facilities, and a health spa. Also, there would be three state-of-the-art theatre rooms in which Gamble and Blaine Advertising could demonstrate new campaigns to their clients in style and comfort.

It had been Alex's initial conceptual drawing for the building that had grasped Todd Blaine's attention. And Kate's legs notwithstanding, Alex was confident that both Todd and Liam would be satisfied with their proposal and the detailed three-dimensional model.

Kate inspected the model from every angle. Finally she stood back, arms folded in front of her. A satisfied smile lifted the corners of her mouth. "I have to admit … you did good."

The inter-office line buzzed, stopping a reply from Alex.

"Yes?"

"Mr. Gamble and Mr. Blaine are here," the secretary announced.

"Show them in, Connie." Kate crossed her fingers. "Here goes."

Alex remained standing by the model while Kate walked towards her office door to greet the two impeccably dressed middle-aged gentlemen who were being escorted into the office. "Liam, Todd, good to see you again."

"Good to see you," Todd Blaine replied, taking her hand.

His partner was quick to join in. Reaching for her hand as

well, Liam nestled it in both of his. "Kate, always a pleasure."

Kate looked over to Alex, who had arrived at her side. He greeted the two gentlemen, forcing Liam to let go of her hand, and then she gestured for them to precede her to the large table where the model sat. "Please come in."

Todd walked directly to the model, his approval apparent in his expression. Liam held back, choosing to follow Kate. His eyes, as usual, glued to her legs.

"Alex my boy," Todd sighed. "This is fabulous."

"Yes, yes, great design," added Liam, finally inspecting the model. "I was also impressed with your budgetary cost sheets. I'd like to go over some of these.... "

"Of course," she agreed. "Please sit down, make yourselves comfortable. Connie has just prepared a carafe of coffee and one of tea for you, Todd."

"You remembered Kate, thank you." Todd poured himself a cup of tea while Liam was already busy inspecting the elaborately prepared proposal folder that Alex was placing in front of them.

Kate didn't waste any time. Sitting down next to her assistant, she began her meeting. "Along with Alex's artistic rendering of the building, this also includes cost breakdowns. Here, on pages five through seven, are projected costs for windows, glazing, building material. Throughout pages eight to ten we list structural costs as well as building efficiency such as air and heat, followed by the design budget and a list of our sub-trades."

The three discussed each point extensively, reverting to the model when necessary.

"You are predicting caisson footings over the conventional or spread footings," Todd stated, flipping back a few pages.

"Yes," answered Alex. "Naturally, sub-soil investigations will have to be completed to determine the bearing capacity of the soil. Although not exactly beachfront, this particular section of Georgia Street is sufficiently close to the Coal Harbour; I'd say the odds are we won't be hitting clay. Caisson footings and in fact, caisson footings with sheet piling foundations are more common for that area."

"And sheet piling is a possibility because... " Liam tested Alex's knowledge.

"As you are probably aware, caisson footings will usually be used when the soil is unstable, and if there are other structures near the site, the new footings are to be placed lower than the existing ones. With sheet piling, corrugated steel sheets, or 'soldiers' as we often call them, are driven into the ground. That basically forms a corrugated box in which the caisson footings are then placed. This box keeps water out in case of underground springs or veins."

"And as you say, water is a probability."

"Soil testing will confirm it, but that's what is generally used for buildings along the waterfront or in close proximity."

Content with Alex's conclusion, Liam nodded and proceeded to another point. Alex explained the fabrication of the structure as well as their ideas for the different features to be installed at the different levels of the building if Gamble and Blaine awarded Wallace their contract. Todd and Liam listened attentively. Kate couldn't help but raise a smug eyebrow towards her assistant. She had yet to see Liam once avert his gaze from the model or the written proposals in front of him. It seemed he had lost the bet!

However, when she excused herself to retrieve the

preliminary structural design from her desk, Liam Gamble's eyes again followed her, focussing intently on her legs. Alex noticed immediately and was only too happy to return the smug look to his boss when Liam did not avert his gaze upon her return. It seemed Alex had been right after all.

"Very impressive," announced Todd as he gathered the proposal and deposited it into his briefcase. "Marvelous design Alex, just marvelous."

Liam stood, confirming the end of the meeting and shook their hands. "Yes, I agree. Kate, Alex, you've outdone yourselves. You know our deadline; we'd like to break ground within the next few weeks – with the emphasis on 'few'. We will require several days to go over your proposal with our team, but I'm sure we'll have an answer for you very soon."

"I'm definitely hoping we can do business," added Todd, as he too shook hands with Kate and Alex.

"We look forward to hearing from you," replied Kate.

Gazing once more towards her legs, Liam said his good-byes and followed his partner out of the office.

Kate was unable to check the grin that spread across her face. "What do you think?"

"By George, I think we've got it!" Alex exclaimed, assuming a British accent, and Kate grinned.

"Did you see their faces when they saw the model?"

"I told you they'd like it."

Kate sighed in contentment. "So you did."

"And what else did I tell you?"

"All right, all right." Kate admitted defeat, but she turned a pensive stare towards the door. "I don't know how I missed that."

"Good thing you don't notice those things," Alex said under his breath.

"Hmm?"

"Nothing." Alex rolled up their copies of drawings and gathered the papers that were scattered across the large table.

Kate glanced at her watch. "I have to meet Dorian on the Bay Street addition. I believe I might be longer than an hour. Can you handle the meeting for the Andrews job?"

"Sure."

She picked up her briefcase and shoved the necessary files into its folds. "Great. Jerry should be here soon. I asked him to attend the meeting since he's supposed to be learning the ropes. Hopefully he'll be more involved once he comes back from this trip..." she shrugged. "He'll fill me in on the particulars later."

Her assistant exhaled a slow calming breath. Jerry Kent had no qualifications, nor did it seem to Alex that he had any intention of acquiring any. Jerry's father was a successful land developer, but from what Kate had mentioned it seemed her betrothed had done nothing to help attain that success. Jerry did not interest himself in the family business. He spent most of his time at the yacht club or the gym. Recently, to Alex's disconcertment, Jerry's appearances at Wallace had become more frequent, throwing his weight and walking around as if he owned the company.

But soon he would do just that. Kate had made a deal with Jerry's father, Gregory Kent of Kent Properties, to merge their two companies. She believed that the merger would be beneficial to Wallace, and she was probably correct. Alex had been told of her decision after the fact, although either way, it was not his place to comment on this particular subject. He was aware that when Jerry married Kate he would be a permanent fixture at the office. That was Kate's wish. That was a circumstance Alex did not look forward to.

Kate draped her trench coat over her arm and headed for the door. "See you later."

"Sure," Alex said again.

CHAPTER TWO

Alex's brow was furrowed in concentration when his boss re-entered his office hours later.

"I guess I didn't make it back, did I?" she announced unnecessarily, drawing her assistant's eyes from the computer screen in front of him.

"No, I guess not."

"Jerry still here?"

Alex nodded towards the adjoining door to her office. "He's inside."

Kate didn't scurry away to greet her fiancé. She was much more interested in an update – an accurate one. "Any problems?"

Alex pushed his chair away from the computer and leaned an elbow on his desk. "Claude Sorensen wants to meet. Maybe you can check your schedule."

"Claude Sorensen?"

"The site super for Andrews," Alex explained.

"Right. What's wrong?"

"He wants to go over the designs again. He's concerned with one unit in particular – the bank. He was questioning the heat and air vents from the roof and Mr. Andrews may have changed his mind about including the mezzanines for the majority of the other units."

"Why?"

"He didn't have time to get into it. We'll have to meet. It's imperative we get a decision out of him soon. We've wasted too many hours on redesigning, not to mention all the meetings, and we still don't have a definite go-ahead to build. We've been ready to go for months."

Kate's attention was drawn to the young window cleaner hanging perilously outside Alex's office. She returned his smile. "Okay, I'll set it up," she promised, walking through to her office.

A while later Jerry emerged from Kate's office. Kate was directly behind him.

"I'll see you later?" he purred as he leaned towards her.

Alex made certain to make himself busy. Watching the two kissing was not at the top of his list of things to do.

Jerry did not say good-bye to Alex when he left the office. He never did and Alex was more than happy to ignore him as well.

Kate walked over to his desk, and, clearing a corner, sat upon it, bringing Alex's eyes to the shapely thigh clearly in view from the raised skirt. "I spoke to Claude Sorenson," she said, and Alex averted his eyes to meet her unsuspecting gaze. "This strip plaza is becoming more cumbersome than a fifty-story building. Hubert Andrews can't make up his mind. Claude just told me Andrews decided again that the mezzanines are a go." Kate shook her head.

"And I thought Liam Gamble was annoying because he's picky! Anyway, I told him we'd meet him tonight so that he can sign the contract."

"Tonight?"

"Yes, why? Alex, you said yourself we've wasted time. If we have a signature we can start soil testing within the next couple of days."

"I'm aware of that, but I can't."

Kate arched an eyebrow. "What do you mean, you can't?"

"It's my daughter's dance recital."

"Dance recital? I think this is a little more important, Alex."

"Not to my daughter."

"Can't her mother take her?"

Alex couldn't help the bit of cynicism that crept into his smile. "That would be a little difficult."

"And why is that?" Her tone leaned towards the sarcastic.

"Because she died." Alex's tone, on the other hand, was very matter-of-fact and perhaps a little incredulous. He had worked for this firm for ten years beginning in the drafting department and later as one of several structural engineers on this floor before accepting his current position. Although Alex's wife had died before Kate had taken charge, his marital status was not a secret in the office. How could she not have known?

"What?" Kate's voice was barely audible.

"I said—"

"—I heard you." Kate felt herself become cold suddenly, and all colour drained from her cheeks. How could she have simply assumed? When she'd considered him for the position, she reviewed his file extensively. The box under the heading 'married' was checked off, she was certain of that – wasn't she? Kate slid off the desk and sank down into the nearest chair. "My God, Alex, I'm sorry. When? I mean … not since you've worked for me certainly…. "

"No. It's been four years."

Kate shook her head in disbelief. "I didn't know – you never told me."

"You never asked."

"No … you're right, I just assumed ... but since you've worked for me … well, you're very private…." She found herself making excuses for her ignorance.

Alex shrugged. "I don't like to bring my personal life into the office – just like I don't like to take the office home. So, I guess I am private. But my marital status is in my file."

"Alex, the little checkmark is in the 'married' box, not 'widowed'. Obviously it was never changed." Kate shook her head, starting to question herself. "Or I just didn't notice. I can't deny that's a possibility."

"Don't worry about it."

Realizing she had been staring at her assistant, she stood now to leave, but turned to him once again. She couldn't leave it alone. "It's been over four years since my grandmother left me in charge, hasn't it? When you first started working up here – how long ago was that?"

Alex shrugged. "Three and a half years – or so."

"You wore a wedding ring."

Alex laughed. "You were checking me out?"

Kate was suddenly flustered, her cheeks feeling oddly warm. She tucked imaginary strands of unruly hair behind her ear, a definite indication of uncommon nervousness. "I – no, I mean … I just noticed, that's all. That's why I thought you were married." She shrugged, hoping to sound a little less like a schoolgirl, but her mannerisms were just that.

He raised his left hand. "I haven't worn it in a while."

"Oh. Well, that I didn't notice."

Alex smiled at her discomfort. "Boss. It doesn't matter."

"I chose you as my assistant because you had the best qualifications," she continued. "Your marital status hardly mattered – I mean to your performance – I mean you're most qualified."

"You said that." Alex had never seen his boss flustered or stammering to find the proper words, for that matter. It was refreshing … sweet.

"Yes. Well … I'm sorry," she said again, regaining most of her composure, and Alex smiled. "I know you have a couple of kids because I've overheard you once or twice, but … you never made a fuss about working late or taking a business trip – who takes care of them? Do you have a nanny?"

"No. My parents and in-laws help me out. And … I don't just have a couple of kids. Actually I have four: two girls and two boys."

Her eyes rounded in surprise. "Four?"

"Yes. Why, does that surprise you?"

Kate raised her shoulders and shook her head, still trying to digest the fact that she knew nothing about him. "I … don't know. I guess few people have large families nowadays…. "

It was time to put an end to the subject, Alex thought. "I suppose. So is there any way we can postpone this meeting? I'd rather not miss the recital."

Kate watched him for a moment longer. Alex was so dedicated to his job. During the past year he had been not only an asset to the company, but also a tremendous help to her. She was aware that more often than not she had reprimanded him for others' mistakes, to which he never stormed out threatening to quit. He understood her. He knew she had to blow off steam and he was the chosen one. Unloading her personal problems onto him had become a more frequent occurrence during the last few months, but he didn't judge her; he'd sometimes give his opinion, but mostly he just listened. And now, she realized guiltily, that she had never returned the favour. Alex was second-in-command, and in fact, took over when she was away, and Kate had decided that very soon she should make it official, perhaps give him a title more befitting, as well as an increase in pay....

"Boss?" Alex waved a hand in front of her, vying for her attention.

"Hmm? Yes, I'll ... I'll speak to him, don't worry."

CHAPTER THREE

"Morning boss," Alex greeted Kate as he strolled into his office on Monday morning.

Kate was using the photocopier. "Morning," she answered, looking at her assistant as if for the first time.

Alex was an extremely attractive man. Kate was aware of that; she wasn't blind. But she thought he was married – and that fact in conjunction with the fact that she herself was unavailable forced her to become untouched by his obvious attraction. It made it easier to work with him; to speak with him at her own level without her mind wandering to his thick black hair which he combed back away from his face, its length falling over his shirt collar. His unavailability veiled his large brown eyes, which often sparkled mischievously. She never gave much thought to the fact that he smiled easily, displaying straight white teeth, nor to the laugh lines that just barely formed dimples on both cheeks. Kate's mind thought back for a moment to the shorts and polo shirts he wore during the many lunchtime racketball games the two had shared. Alex was average in height and in build, but although his body was not the mass of muscles that Jerry was so proud to possess, Alex was definitely fit, biceps and pectoral muscles in abundance and clearly visible....

She mentally shook the image from her mind and placed another letter on the photocopier. "How was the recital?"

"It was great!" he grinned proudly. Alex sat his briefcase on the floor just inside his office and came to lean against the wall next to the photocopier. "My daughter's group of dancers were the flowers in the garden...." he explained in an especially light tone.

"Is that ballet or tap?"

"This was ballet. They looked so cute in their little tutus! Half of them don't really know where they're going, but it's fabulous!"

Kate returned his smile. Alex was so proud of his little girl ... and she doubted if she'd ever have the opportunity to attend a child's dance recital – her own child's dance recital.

Her expression had changed suddenly and her assistant knew why.

"Still dodging the question?"

She looked up sharply. He read her like a book. She dissolved that unbecoming frown and shrugged, hoping that her words would not sound bitter, hoping not to expose too much of herself. "Still. Jerry simply does not want children. He conveniently introduces another topic for discussion every time I try to talk about it. I'll have to resign myself to that fact."

"You don't normally settle for less than what you want. Why would you now?"

"We're going to be married. Don't married couples make sacrifices for one another?"

"Seems to me you're the one making all the sacrifices. Unfortunately, women don't have all the time in the world to decide to have children. If having a family is important to you … well, maybe you should re-think your decision."

Kate watched him. She had no doubt that Alex was only looking out for her best interests, but so was she. "This merger has to happen. Therefore, so will the marriage. Let's be realistic," she stated, eager to put an end to this conversation. "I don't have time to be a mother."

Alex swallowed that piece of information, however disconcerting, and Kate returned to business. "I met with Mr. Andrews Friday night."

"And?"

"We finally have the go-ahead. Start soil testing as soon as you can arrange for it. Which firm were you planning on using?"

"Foresters. They're not the cheapest, but out of the three tenders, their prices are comparable and they're reliable."

"We'd be using them for Gamble and Blaine, right?" she asked, to which Alex nodded in response. "Sounds good. Get on it." Kate gave her 'okay' and retreated into her office. Only minutes later she reappeared again, a proud grin on her pretty face.

"Guess who I was just talking to?"

"Jerry."

"No. That was Liam. We got it! We've been awarded the contract," she exclaimed, slapping Alex's outstretched hand.

"All right!"

"Excellent! Call a meeting. Afterwards, call Foresters. I'd prefer for this job to take precedence if they're too busy to handle both simultaneously."

"Right boss," he agreed and reached for his phone.

Jerry made another appearance just as Kate and Alex were on their way to the boardroom for the meeting regarding this latest project.

"I'm just going in to a meeting, Jerry," Kate explained hurriedly. "Oh. Well, are you going to be long? I thought we'd do lunch," Jerry suggested, nibbling on her ear. Revolted, Alex headed for the door.

"I can't really say how long, but why don't you come along. This is an important contract. Come," she urged.

"All right. Lead the way!" Jerry agreed, surprising her.

The meeting lasted for hours, during which Jerry nodded off twice. Instructions had been compiled and jobs delegated to proper departments. Alex would engage Foresters; the geo-technical investigators to conduct the sub-soil testing, which would ultimately determine design criteria. He would review the results and inform the proper departments and contractors. From there, excavating could begin.

The meeting over, department heads and executive secretaries all scurried to their respective stations. Kate stopped her assistant at the door. "I'm going to have lunch with Jerry. I'm going to fill him in on the Andrews plaza since he wasn't here for those meetings."

It was only a few hours later when Alex received a phone call from Jerry.

"For me?" he asked Angie, his secretary.

"Yeah I know. I thought I'd heard wrong, but that's what

he said."

What would he have to say? Nothing of any importance – that was for sure. Reluctantly, he picked up the line. "Yes Jerry?"

"Alex. Have you started the ball rolling regarding the Gamble and Blaine project?"

Alex was annoyed. This was typical Jerry, trying to play boss again. "Yes. Why?"

"Who's doing the soil testing?"

"You were at the meeting, were you not? Foresters."

"Call Malcolm Fish at ESI Incorporated."

"Jerry? Who is Malcolm Fish and who is ESI?" Alex was very patient, but Jerry he couldn't tolerate.

"ESI is a geo-technical firm, obviously. I told Malcolm you'd be calling him—"

"For what? I've already given the contract to Foresters."

Jerry was silent for a moment. "What about the Andrews plaza? Kate told me that's ready to go. Who's doing the soil testing for that job?"

"I'm planning to call the same firm."

"Well don't. We'll use ESI."

"I've heard of them, but we've never used them. I'm not aware of their credentials. I'll have to check them out."

"They've already been 'checked out' – by me."

"That's comforting."

Jerry huffed. He instructed Alex to take down Malcolm Fish's telephone number and to call him immediately, but Alex didn't reply.

"Look, I'm going to be working here on a more permanent basis. I will have some say, and I expect to be heard. I hope you're aware of that."

Alex dropped his pen and leaned back in his chair. He couldn't hide his displeasure in speaking to him. "Perfectly." He would rather have said 'unfortunately!'

"Good. Well, I want to be kept abreast in all areas. I intend to work closely with Kate on these projects—"

"—Doing what, exactly?"

"Contrary to popular belief, I do have some architectural training, you know. I can be an asset."

Alex tried to hold back the laughter that was sure to threaten his job. Well … Jerry was at least part of that word. "Really?"

Jerry huffed noisily. "Yes, really. Look, Kate wants this and you know it. And while I'm at it, I think it's about time we get something straight."

"And what would that be, Jerry?" Alex asked lazily while swiveling his chair back and forth.

"Before long you'll have to learn to take orders from me as well as my fiancée. You'd better get used to that fact. I won't stand for disrespect and I'm sure neither will Kate."

Alex was silent. He feared that if he spoke again, he wouldn't be able to refrain from voicing his thoughts. Unfortunately, however, Jerry was right. Alex closed his eyes in frustration. "Fine." You immature, inconspicuous piece of…. "I'll keep you informed."

"Good. That's all on the Andrews plaza; what's next for Gamble and Blaine – I mean besides the soil testing."

"As we discussed … architectural drawings are all but complete and I've begun plotting the elevations on the site plans."

Jerry tried his hand at patronizing. "And that is?"

Alex shook his head and rolled his eyes heavenward. "I have to plot the elevations Jerry, so that the excavators know where and how deep to dig – understand?"

"Naturally. And how long will that take you?"

Alex raised his hands in exasperation. There was no way he'd be able to handle this grilling for the duration of this project. "I don't know Jerry, a few days.... "

"All right. Like I said, I'm going to be involved. Keep me posted – on both of these jobs."

Jerry hung up the telephone before Alex could reply, but then, he didn't want to reply; he hadn't wanted to talk to him in the first place. He threw the receiver back onto its hook. Alex answered to Kate and only Kate. He was concerned about using a relatively unknown geo-technical firm for the Andrews plaza. Jerry Kent's involvement and suggestions would be nothing short of an impediment on any job, but to be involved at such a crucial stage of this or in fact the Gamble and Blaine project was just plain ridiculous. Jerry was only an adornment to this firm and he doubted that Kate would entrust any part of this job to someone who was good at nothing – for nothing, he added as an afterthought.

The message on Alex's machine the next morning unfortunately said otherwise. This had to be straightened out immediately. Alex walked towards Kate as she stepped out of the elevator.

"Yes, I know," she told him, her voice stern.

"You're okay with this?"

Kate bit into a lemon Danish while trying to juggle suit jacket and briefcase in the other hand. "Yes, I am. I told you I want him involved. You know that."

Alex walked alongside her as they entered their offices. "Fine. Just what is it you want him involved with? I mean what can he do? He's barely even here – thank God!"

"Alex." Kate stopped and looked sternly at her assistant. "When he is here – involve him, understood?"

"He's instructed me to call ESI; you ever use them before?"

"No, but Jerry's assured me that they're a reputable company, and they're cheaper than the others. What's the big deal, Alex? Run a check on them and stay on top of it."

Alex sighed. "Yes ma'am, boss." He disagreed naturally, but decided to once again remember his place.

"By the way, I have a meeting with Gregory Kent about the transfer of shares once this merger is in place. I'll be leaving for Vancouver in about an hour or so. Can you hold down the fort?"

"Certainly," Alex replied curtly, something that did not go unnoticed by his boss.

Kate paused momentarily before continuing. " … Jerry will be in later…. "

A muscle began to twitch at his jaw, but he gave her a smile, albeit an exaggerated one. "I'll behave."

Alex called Malcolm Fish at ESI as Jerry had instructed, and requested references. The company seemed stable albeit small in comparison to Foresters, but they had no liens against them and no apparent problems in completing the task. Therefore, ESI was awarded the contract. Soil testing would begin within days.

While he worked effortlessly over the site plans for their most current project job, Alex couldn't help but replay his conversation with his boss. He'd never questioned her loyalty in the past, but

Jerry's self-appointment to second banana was not going to benefit Alex, to say the least. He was beginning to wonder if he should feel threatened, at least where his job was concerned. But shaking away unfounded thoughts, he returned to his task, realizing it would be best to take the drawings home for the next few evenings. The more he accomplished without having to include Jerry, the better for the job – and for his peace-of-mind.

CHAPTER FOUR

"Dad?" Stephanie waved a hand in front of her father's face as they sat around the breakfast table.

"Hmm?"

"I said, are you going to take us to swimming lessons or is Gramma Mary?"

"Sorry, I didn't hear you." Alex got up and walked over to the long counter of the large kitchen to pour himself another cup of coffee.

"Obviously," Stephanie retorted and Alex walked around the rectangular wooden table of the same shade of the light bleached oak of the cupboards. He stood by the large bay window and glanced at the dark clouds overhead that held the promise of imminent rain. He looked out to the spacious yard bordered with flowerbeds just starting to bud, and scattered with half a dozen mature trees – one of which boasted an elaborate tree house that he and the boys had built the previous summer. The grass would need cutting soon….

Alex turned to his daughter now. Stephanie was extremely bright for her age. A mass of long curly dark hair framed her delicate heart-shaped face. Stylish, reddish-brown rectangular glasses veiled her large, ever watchful eyes, although blindfolds could not conceal their attentiveness. At fourteen she was petite in comparison to her friends, but she could talk circles around any of them as well as a few adults for that matter.

"Well?" she urged.

"Yes, I'll take you. Badges are distributed today, aren't they?"

"Yes, Daddy," Leeza joined in the conversation. "I'm getting my Orange badge – maybe."

Alex smiled lovingly at the little five-year-old who held a special place in his heart. Being the youngest she had no memory of her mother; no knowledge that she was in the car that day when his wife, having just dropped off the other three children at school, was hit head-on by an oncoming vehicle. Julie had died instantly. Leeza, barely a year old, was trapped for hours. As if by a miracle, she emerged with little more than a few cuts and bruises.

"Do you think I'll get my Orange badge, Daddy?" Leeza asked her father.

Alex's fingers gently brushed the straight brown hair away from his daughter's tiny face. "Probably."

Brown hair and expressive brown eyes were consistent with all four of his children. The only difference was that Stephanie and Paul had curls or wavy hair like Alex, where Nicholas and Leeza had straight hair like their mother. Alex was proud to say that all four of his children were intelligent and conscientious.

They had gathered together when their mother died, and Alex was at least grateful that the horrible tragedy that bonded them so closely during that time, kept them a tight knit family to this day.

"You've done very well, Leeza, but even if you don't earn your badge today, you know it only means that you need a little more work. You will get your badge, if not today, another day, okay?"

"Okay."

"Dylan asked if we can give him a ride to soccer tomorrow, Dad," Nicholas announced between mouthfuls of cereal. "Can we?"

"Yes, and can you please wait until you've swallowed before you start to speak?"

Nicholas rolled his eyes. Eleven-year-olds are not concerned with manners. Nor are eight-year-olds for that matter, but since his brother was just reprimanded, Paul made certain he swallowed and wiped his mouth before making his request – it was important. "Frankie just got a puppy! Can we get one Dad, please, please, please?"

"A puppy?" Alex exclaimed, nearly choking on his coffee. "No, we can't get a puppy."

"Ohhh ..." they all whined in unison. "But why not?"

Alex had to laugh. "Because I don't have time to walk him and take care of him and you know darn well that I would be the one to be saddled with that job!"

"We'll take care of him Dad, honest!" they promised. "Please? Please?"

He couldn't get away from unwise requests recently. What was happening, he thought to himself. Was it something in the air?

"We'll talk about it later." Alex thought it best to change the subject. "Guys, I'm really busy at the office; we were just given a new job and I might have to work late some nights during the next little while.

The children knew the routine. They were never left alone when Alex worked late. "Do we stay at Gramma and Grandpa's?"

"Yes Paul. We've been lucky. I haven't had to work late in a while, but I promise it wouldn't be for long. I'll pick you up from their house on my way home as usual on the days that I have to work late. Would you mind very much?"

Nicholas and Paul were very understanding. "If you have to, it's okay with us."

"I'm going to miss you, Daddy," said Leeza sadly.

"Honey, I'm not going away. I might be coming home late a few evenings, that's all."

"Will you be home in time to tuck me in?"

Alex leaned towards his little girl and kissed her forehead. "Yes. I'm sure I will. How can I miss such an important event?"

Leeza giggled. "Okay Daddy."

"Stephanie?" Alex waited for a comment from his eldest.

"Sure, I guess."

"Thanks."

"So, how about the puppy, Dad?" Paul started again.

Alex looked at his watch. "It's late, we can't talk about this now," he said putting an end to their whining. "Got your lunches?"

The children each picked up their bags and dropped them into their knapsacks.

Since the school was closer to his parents' home, Alex would drive the children there every morning and from there they would either walk or be driven to school by either their grandmother or grandfather; they were both retired. After school they would return to their grandparents' home where they would stay until Alex picked them up.

Usually Alex would be back in time to make it home to prepare dinner for them, but on the occasions that he had to work late, the children would stay with his parents for dinner. Both his parents and his in-laws would help with the various after-school activities and the children were happy to spend time with them.

Alex pulled up onto the driveway of the grey brick bungalow where Mary Callahan waited patiently at the door. He helped the children out of the truck, and after returning for a forgotten knapsack, gave them each a kiss good-bye.

"Good morning, sweethearts!" Gramma Mary greeted her grandchildren and then turned to her son. "Honey, do you need your father or me to drive them to their swimming lessons? It's the last until summer, isn't it?"

Alex smiled at his mother. Middle age had not slowed her down. Mary kept herself fit – unable to stay still if she wanted to. At 57, her dark brown hair was still free of artificial colour and her spark and energy was that of a woman twenty years younger. She often told Alex that his children were the reason for her energy. They needed her to stay young. Whatever the reason, Alex was grateful for his mother's input and help as well as that of his father and his in-laws.

After the horrific tragedy that had struck her son and his family, both Mary and Pat Callahan as well as Julie's parents had rallied together to offer support wherever and whenever needed.

Her son had been a mess for a very long time. Overcome by despair at the loss of his wife, parents and in-laws had more or less taken over where the children were concerned. But time heals, as they say, bringing the realization that life does go on. He learned to take on the role of both mother and father, but Mary assured him that she was only a phone call away – not to mention a two-minute drive by car.

"I don't know how you remember everything," Alex told her. "Thanks, but I'll take them. Barring any problems, I should be here by four-thirty."

The children lingered and she tried to put her arms around all of them. "What about dinner? Will you be back in time to have dinner with us?"

"No. I'll just throw something together when we get home."

"The kids will be famished, you know that. I was going to make beef stew tonight; I'll just make more." Mary waved her hand. "I'll drop it off. Gloria and Dan have asked us to go bowling with them tonight. I'll tell them 'yes' then."

"My mother-in-law – bowling?"

"Hey, what else can we old fogies do?" Mary put up her hands.

Alex grinned and climbed into his truck. "Have fun – and thanks, Mom."

"Think about the puppy, Dad!" Paul had to remind him – just in case he'd forgotten! Then they all waved good-bye and ran inside, hoping to sneak in a few minutes of TV time before having to leave for school.

"A dog ..." Alex said out loud. "I don't want a dog."

CHAPTER FIVE

The day had progressed well in spite of the unwanted and untutored interrogations by Jerry. After his departure Kate and Alex worked at the table in her office reviewing cost sheets and contracts from the various labourers being used for the Gamble and Blaine job.

Alex was so engrossed in his work that he lost track of time. "Damn!"

"What?" Kate jumped.

"I promised the kids I'd take them to their swimming lessons."

"Tonight?"

"Yes," he said putting on his jacket. "I have to go."

"We need to at least finish the jobs that have to go to tender and we won't have time tomorrow. Can you come back?"

"No. My parents are busy and so are my in-laws. I don't want them to cancel their plans." Alex rubbed the back of his neck. "Look, I'll be home about six-thirty. Would you like to come by my house?"

"Your house?" Alex had never invited her to his home – he'd never even mentioned his home – or his kids – or anything, but then … why would he have?

"Yes my house," he wondered why she'd sounded so surprised, but then remembered: this invitation was a first.

"Are you sure?"

"I'd understand if you'd rather not, but it's the only solution I can offer."

"Well, I don't mind. I just don't want to intrude … "

"Don't make me change my mind," he told her, drawing a smile. "Do you know where I live?"

"You're in East Saanich – Gordon Head area, right?"

"Very good," he said in a surprised voice. "From here, take Government to Hillside to Shelbourne Street. We're near Lambrick Park."

"Thank you," Kate answered with a wry smile. "I have your address in my directory, Alex. I think I'll find it."

"All right then, be there by six thirty … you can have a bite to eat with us."

Kate raised her eyebrows, but smiled as she watched him walk out the door.

Leeza was ecstatic. She'd received her Orange badge! Stephanie had earned the Bronze Cross and Nicholas and Paul both had successfully completed the White program.

Their mood was one of elation when they returned home that evening.

"Mmm, something smells good," Alex mused when he

opened the door. "Put your bags away, and help set the table – the dining room table." Removing his suit jacket, he draped it onto the back of the sofa and paused a moment before saying the rest. "My boss is coming by tonight; we have some work to do."

"Your boss?" queried Stephanie, her displeasure already obvious. So much for her good mood! "You've never had your boss here."

Alex retrieved the casserole from the warm oven and placed it on the granite countertop. "Well, we were very busy tonight, but since I didn't want to miss your swimming lesson I asked her to come here."

"Oh great," Stephanie rolled her eyes. "Is she eating with us?"

"Is that a problem, Steph?"

"Not at all," she said sarcastically.

The doorbell rang just as Alex had finished preparing the salad. "I'll get it. Nicholas, you forgot the glasses," he called back as he crossed the dining area.

"Nicky, you better get the crystal!" Stephanie exaggerated.

"What?"

"Never mind!" his sister dismissed.

"Hey boss," Alex greeted Kate as he stepped aside allowing her to enter into his home.

"Hi." Kate glanced into the cosy living room over the half-wall separating it from the entrance. It was simply decorated; the warm colours and classic designs making it look comfortable and welcoming. "This is nice," she commented truthfully. It was strange to find herself in Alex's home, her employee's home. She was uncertain as to exactly what she was feeling except that she felt a little odd … a little out of her element.

"It's home." Alex took the piles of paperwork from her, and walking into the living room, placed them on the wooden coffee table in front of the taupe tapestry sofa.

Kate was uncharacteristically at a loss for words. "Seems like a nice neighbourhood," she said finally after a slight uncomfortable silence.

"It is. I mean it's not your Uplands, but it's quiet, all young families. We like it."

Kate sniffed the delicious aroma emanating from the kitchen. "It smells wonderful!" She left her briefcase by the coffee table and followed Alex inside.

All four children appeared carrying glasses. Stephanie nearly dropped hers when she caught sight of Kate in her fitted black business suit, with the short shirt exposing more leg than she thought necessary.

"She's your boss?" she asked suspiciously.

"Stephanie." Alex's voice was stern. "This is Miss Wallace and yes, she is my boss."

"Kate," his boss corrected. "I'm happy to meet you."

"Stephanie, you've probably gathered, is my eldest. This is Nicholas," Alex introduced, rustling his hair. "This is Paul, and this is—"

"—I'm Leeza, I'm five and you're pretty." Leeza preferred to introduce herself.

Kate was taken aback at the little girl's outspokenness, but delightedly so. She reminded her oddly of herself. "Oh my! Thank you very much Leeza. I'm Kate, I'm well over five and you are very pretty." And Leeza smiled, shyness suddenly kicking in.

"Can we eat now?" complained Paul.

"Yes we can eat now," his father picked him up and unnecessarily carried the giggling boy to his seat.

"You can sit here," Stephanie directed Kate to her own usual seat at the other end of the table, a gesture not gone unnoticed by her father, who gave her a knowing look.

The other seat, which was usually empty, was the one their mother would have occupied when dining at this table. Stephanie would not let any other woman sit there except grandmothers. Tonight it would be hers.

The first few minutes of dinner were pointedly quiet and Alex wondered if he'd made the right decision in inviting his boss. Surprisingly it was Kate who forced herself to start the conversation.

"The stew is delicious, did you make this?" Kate directed her question to Alex, but he wasn't given the chance to reply.

Stephanie was quick to assure his boss that they were self-sufficient. "My grandmother did, but Dad's a great cook. He usually makes dinner and we all help."

"I'm impressed."

"Ha!" Nicholas laughed, deciding to join in the conversation. "You should have tasted some of Dad's masterpieces!"

Alex gasped in mock indignation. "Thanks a lot!"

"Once he poured half a container of salt into the tomato sauce. Yuck! That was bad! We had to throw it out."

"So?" Alex defended himself with a grin. "It was a little salty."

"A little? It was pure salt! And how about when you burned the chicken?" Nicholas said excitedly and Paul nodded his head, trying to hide his laughter behind his little hand. "The smoke detectors were going! The whole house was filled with smoke; it was awesome!"

"I've come a long way," Alex assured her.

"Remember when Daddy flooded the laundry room?" said Paul, finding the courage to recount his own stories.

"What is this – pick on Dad night?" Alex complained, but Paul knew his father was kidding and therefore continued, hand gestures and all.

"There was soap everywhere!"

"It was like a big bubble bath!" interjected Leeza.

"All right, now you're making me look like a real klutz!"

Everyone laughed. Even Stephanie couldn't resist a little chuckle.

Kate was in awe. She'd never experienced humorous family conversation around the dinner table. It was different … it was heart-warming.

"So how did your lessons go?" she asked the children.

"Good," was the consensus. Leeza naturally wanted to elaborate. "I got my Orange badge today. My teacher said that's good because I'm only five."

"Then you should be very proud of yourself," Kate told her which earned her an impish grin.

"Are you married?" Leeza blurted suddenly and Stephanie shot her an angry stare.

Kate looked over to Alex who decided to keep his eyes focused on his plate. "No … not yet."

"Do you have a boyfriend?"

"Leeza, stop interrogating Miss Wallace," he said now.

"That's okay," Kate laughed at Leeza's innocent curiosity.

"Yes, I do. Do you?"

Leeza giggled shyly now. "Noooo!" she exclaimed.

Soon they finished dinner and after helping to clear the table, the younger children asked to be excused.

"Yes, go hit the books."

"I don't have homework, Daddy," Leeza exclaimed.

"I know, baby. You can play in your room while your brothers and sister study."

"Okay," she agreed and followed the boys upstairs.

Stephanie started to rinse the dishes that had been placed in the sink, but Alex stopped her. "That's all right Steph, go study for your math test."

"I'll help your Dad, Stephanie," Kate assured her, and after a nod from her father, she grudgingly retreated to the second floor.

"You don't have to do that, I can take care of it later."

"I don't mind," Kate assured him, realizing in the process that this would be the second time she'd ever placed a dish in the dishwasher.

"Hey, don't think this gets you off the hook for the bet you lost. You owe me a Friday."

"Yes, yes, all right, I owe you. So can I bug you for a cup of coffee?"

"I'm just getting to that." Alex spooned in the appropriate amount of coffee into the filter and turned on the machine.

Kate dried her hands and turned to her assistant. "Your kids are so beautiful, Alex."

"Yes, they get their looks from me," he boasted, and Kate scoffed.

"I don't know about that, but you have done a great job of

raising them. They're so well-mannered."

Alex shrugged as he watched the coffee drip into the carafe. "They have their moments.... They also spend a lot of time with their grandparents."

"Granted, but it stems from you," she spoke honestly. "It shows."

"Oh, I dunno.... I've tried to keep things as normal as possible – not to overindulge them too much or be too passive. But they've lost one of – if not the most important person in their lives and sometimes it's difficult not to overcompensate. Anyway," he sighed, wanting to change the subject. "Let's get to it."

Kate walked the few steps to the large kitchen table where Alex had already scattered their paperwork preparing their makeshift office. He'd set up there, he'd told her, for better light.

Alex brought over two mugs of coffee and soon they were entranced in their discussions.

Leeza appeared again some time later. Paul, Nicholas and Stephanie were close behind. "Daddy, I'm going to go to sleep. Stephanie helped me with my bath," Leeza yawned sleepily.

"Thanks Steph. I'm sorry I haven't spent any time with you tonight. Want me to come up and tuck you in?" Alex gathered his daughter into his arms and Leeza nodded. "It's late. You guys better take your showers and get to bed too or you won't be able to get up tomorrow."

Paul nodded; Nicholas headed for the refrigerator. "I want a glass of milk first."

Stephanie scanned the cluttered table with her attentive eyes. "Aren't you finished, yet?"

"No," her father told her simply. "How's the studying going, and did you finish your other homework?"

"Fine, and no, I have a couple of geography questions and I should study a little more."

"All right." Alex glanced at his watch. "Take your shower now and then go back to your work, but Steph – lights out by eleven o'clock max okay?"

"Yes, Dad," Stephanie drawled. "Good night," she directed towards Kate, as did the boys.

"Bye Miss Wallace. Are you going to come back again?" Leeza asked, and again Stephanie shot her a look that told Leeza she might like to disown her as a sister sometime soon.

"Well, I don't want to make a habit of this. Your father works enough at the office. His time at home should be with you, right?" Kate playfully poked Leeza's tummy and she giggled when once again she nodded in agreement. "Good night, sweet dreams."

"I'll be right back," Alex said and disappeared with his clan.

It was nearly midnight when they finally finished.

Kate gathered their work into a neat pile. "Alex, thanks for your help tonight, I appreciate it, and for dinner of course."

"Not exactly what you're used to was it?"

"No. It was nice. Thank you."

Alex shrugged. "You're welcome."

"You have a wonderful family," Kate told him as they walked to her car.

"Yeah, I do," he grinned. He placed the papers on the passenger seat and shut the door.

"I'll see you in the morning," Kate said. "Good night."

"Night, boss."

Alex turned off the coffee machine, switched off the lights and made his way upstairs. He checked in on the children on the way to his room.

Theirs was a large home with four good-sized bedrooms and potential for an addition over the garage. The spacious master bedroom had a sitting area as well as an en suite. Stephanie and Leeza had their own rooms, an adjoining bathroom separating the two. Another bathroom was accessible from the hallway, as well as the fourth bedroom, which was shared by Nicholas and Paul.

Everyone was fast asleep except for Stephanie, and Alex half expected this. He sat down on the edge of her bed ready for her questions.

"Why did she stay so late, Dad?"

Alex removed a forgotten clip from her curly hair. "We were working, Steph. I told you."

"When you have to work late at the office, is she there with you?"

Alex sighed. "Sometimes, why?"

"Dad?"

"Hmm?"

"She *is* pretty."

"I suppose so, but she's my boss Steph, that's all. And besides, did you happen to notice that rock on her finger?"

"How can I miss it?" she said sarcastically.

"Well then?" Alex tilted his head to a side, and Stephanie shrugged sleepily. "Come on, get some sleep. Sweet dreams."

"Love you, Dad."

"Love you too. Go to sleep!"

Alex closed her door partway and shook his head sadly. He had been served a large slice of reality. Tragedy strikes, and regardless of that horrible fact, life must go on. He had at least four reasons that proved that theory. However, his daughter had made it clear. Stephanie did not want to share his affections with anyone outside her brothers and sister. He was blatantly aware of this and he had tried to heed her wishes, but sometimes he felt almost held hostage, physically and emotionally, and that wasn't fair.

CHAPTER SIX

Alex sat at his drafting table and reached for the site plan. Soil investigations completed, expeditious completion of this next step was imperative and Alex wanted to be certain to meet his deadline so that the excavating company could proceed. Jerry had been there all morning, hovering around Kate like a vulture. Now that Kate had left for another site meeting, Alex closed the adjoining door between the offices, hoping to thwart Jerry's interrogations if only for a short time. He was tired of explaining every intricate plotting detail, every elevation and the reasons for variations. Once completed, stamped, and safely back in the protective cylinder, Alex would then 'involve' Jerry and ask him to make the delivery.

However, the long cylinder was not on the floor leaning against the wall where Alex was sure to have left it. He looked all over the office, and actually panicked before he finally remembered that he had taken the blueprints home the previous evening although he had not had the opportunity to review them one last time. Unfortunately with Kate away and Jerry roaming the office, making his annoying presence known – to everyone, Alex preferred not to leave. Alex decided to call his parents. One of them was bound to be home and able to grant him a favour.

"Alex, you just caught me. I was going to pick up Stephanie for her eye examination. What was it you wanted?"

"That's all right, Mom. Is Dad home?"

"No, he's out looking for some part or another for that jalopy of his. Tell me Alex."

"It's just that I forgot something at home. I can't leave and I was hoping you or Dad could pick it up for me and come by the office.... What time's the appointment?"

"It'll work out fine, dear. Steph and I are going to lunch before we see the doctor. We'll have plenty of time. Just tell me what you need."

Mrs. Callahan, the site plan, and her inquisitive granddaughter in tow arrived within a mere half an hour.

"Thanks Mom, you're a lifesaver," Alex told his mother, which earned him a hug. "How you doing, Steph?"

"Good." Stephanie had never visited her father's office, but after meeting his boss, office arrangements were suddenly very important. Her eyes scanned the room, noticing the two closed doors. "What's in there?"

Alex motioned to one of the doors. "There's a bathroom through there, and that's Miss Wallace's office."

Stephanie's eyes seemed to bore a hole through that door. Why did she need a door between their offices, she thought suspiciously. This didn't sit well with her.

"Okay Steph. We'd better get going if we still want to go to lunch." Mary Callahan started to walk out of the office, her arm wrapped around that of her son.

"I'll be right out Gramma. Dad, can I use the bathroom?"

"Sure. We'll be out here," Alex motioned to the outer office. "Hurry up, you don't want to be late for Dr. Weisberg."

Stephanie rolled her eyes and walked towards the bathroom. However, the moment her father and grandmother left the office Stephanie executed a perfect 'about face' and headed to the other door. She listened at first. She heard voices. His boss was there! Slowly she turned the knob, careful not to make a noise, careful to pull the door ajar – just a sliver.

Okay, she was mistaken. It wasn't his boss, but it was a woman – perhaps in her fifties, and she was speaking to a man, although Stephanie did not have a clear view of him. Stephanie was about to shut the door when she heard two familiar names. She froze. Curiosity got the better of her and she leaned closer to hear more.

The conversation was disturbing, yet intriguing at the very least. The two spoke in hushed tones, and Stephanie, her heart pounding, had to strain to hear more. Was it a plot? A plan? She could barely make out what they were saying.... Surprised, Stephanie put a hand over her mouth to stop the gasp that nearly gave her away. At first, she couldn't figure out why they'd be doing this, but suddenly, she understood the implications all too well.

This was bad! But it could also be good. It could very well solve the problem that she knew was imminent. However it could change everything – even more than she wanted. For that reason alone, she should tell her father, but the possibility of collaboration between her father and his boss against the conspirators was too great a risk. After all, she wanted to keep them apart, not give them more reason to be drawn together! Allowing things to take their course, however unnatural, would be ultimately beneficial to her. It would suit her purpose; she had to keep quiet.

CHAPTER SEVEN

"Sweets, is that you?" called a man's voice from the living room of the Wallace home, later that evening.

This endearment was starting to rattle Kate. "Yes Jerry." She dropped her keys on the glass entrance table and walked inside the wide foyer with its granite floors and high ceilings.

Kate's home was situated in Uplands, a well-to-do area of Oak Bay, which stretches westward from the city of Victoria to the coast of Cadboro Bay at the tip of Vancouver Island, near Uplands Golf Course. The vegetation in this area is spectacular. Winding, hilly roads lined with mature trees and plants made for a scenic drive any time of the year. The mansions on the street where Kate lived almost all backed onto the bay. A short drive eastward would bring her to the Cadboro Bay Yacht Club, the place that her mother held so close to her heart – or perhaps to Kate's wallet.

Hers was a large two-story home built of stone and stucco.

The property spanned nearly two acres of perfectly manicured lawns and gardens. The kidney-shaped pool and large cabana equipped with showers, kitchenette and bar, took up only a small portion of the backyard. Slate and cobblestones were arranged in a magnificent design to form a patio, which was accessible from the living room and dining room areas.

To her left as she entered was a study, its walls lined with teak bookshelves. Directly facing the door, the modernized version of the long Scarlet O'Hara-style staircase led to the second floor. The light cream and tan runner, with its specks of blue amidst its Persian design, stretched down the centre, contrasting well with the dark blue of the floors.

The living room, decorated in mostly creams with navy and gold accents, was to the right. This was where Jerry's voice emanated from. This was her direction.

Kate looked curiously at her fiancé. "What are you doing here?"

"That's a nice greeting." The tall, muscular young man gathered her into his arms. Blonde and blue-eyed, Jerry was quite fetching, although Kate had to admit that his enthusiasm for great looks and perfect body had recently become an obsession.

Kate pushed against his chest, recently uncomfortable with his advances. "I meant that I thought we were to meet at your place."

"Your mother called. She asked me to come by."

"Oh?" Immediately, suspicion took over mere curiosity. "What did she want?"

"I don't know. She's been waiting for you."

Kate was annoyed. Aside from either informing them that she was broke again or that she had found yet another husband, Kate couldn't think of any other reason her mother would have to speak to them.

Debra sat lounging on the sofa where Jerry had left her. Her diminutive dress blended to obscurity against the cream coloured sofa. The only contrast: an abundant exposure of flesh and … her hair. This week it was an alarming shade of … well … orange.

Her mother was not a natural redhead, but Kate had to admit that this shade suited her far better than her original mousy hair colour. It also fit better with her explosive personality. Debra was aware that she'd never go unnoticed when she entered a room. Her alluring green eyes – and surgically enhanced curves – had attracted three husbands so far. Her wild hair colour was an added bonus.

As usual, Kate looked down at her with skepticism. "Mother? Is something wrong?"

Her mother picked up the bottle of blood-red nail polish from the glass coffee table and held it to the light as if to properly assess the intensity of its colour. "Actually, I have news. Whether it's good or bad … well, that's a matter of opinion."

"What news?" Kate sat on the sofa facing her mother. Jerry did the same.

Debra shook the bottle and commenced to brush the liquid onto her long acrylic nails.

Kate couldn't believe her mother's frivolousness. "Weren't you at the spa just this morning?"

"So?" Debra had a gift when it came to exasperating her daughter.

Kate extended her hand to her mother's less-than-artistic abilities. "Why are you re-doing your nails already?"

"I chipped one, obviously."

"Doing what – laundry?"

The nail polish brush poised above her third finger, Debra glared at her daughter. "Really, Kate, what is your problem? Do you want to hear the news or what?" And as Kate shook her head in exasperation, her mother continued. "Your grandmother called earlier."

She had finally succeeded in capturing her attention. Kate's face paled. "Gram called? Why would she call here?" Her grandmother disliked her ex-daughter-in-law and the feeling was mutual. This was strange.

"She figured you'd be home obviously," Debra shook her head in a patronizing fashion. "Do you want to hear what she had to say or are you going to continue to interrupt me?"

"Is she all right?"

"The old biddy is still kicking," Debra said under her breath.

"Mother!"

"She's very happy to hear about your marriage," Debra explained in a slow drawl, deterring from her previous comment.

"I hadn't told her yet," Kate said quietly, which earned a strange look from Jerry who had sat quietly until then.

"Why haven't you told her, Sweets? After all, I think she'll be very happy once she learns that you and I, as well as our businesses, will become one."

Kate made a strange face. Jerry didn't normally speak that way. What had gotten into him? However, he had a point. Why hadn't she told her grandmother? She should have been happy to relay this news, but the proposal was linked to the merger of their two companies. Kate had felt compelled to accept. She was not in love with him, but she had decided it didn't matter. They were compatible – most of the time. It was a comfortable relationship and certainly beneficial for both sides, yet she was aware of her grandmother's romantic flair. She had waited, hoping lightning would strike, but it hadn't yet. Realistically, it probably never would, and she should get used to that fact.

"I've been so busy.... Actually," she said trying to think fast, "I had planned to take a little trip and tell her in person. Besides, we haven't even discussed setting a date."

"Well, I saved you the trouble," her mother nodded proudly. "I don't know why you wanted to wait to tell her. You know perfectly well that she intended to make you CEO of the company once the merger is in place and you are married – not to mention – give you most of your inheritance."

"Yes, so? It is happening, mother. What's the rush? I have no problem waiting until she's ready."

Debra blew on her newly painted fingernails. "You wouldn't," she scoffed.

"What's that supposed to mean?"

"Look, the point is that she promised you the company and it serves no purpose to wait. Cash in when you can Hon; don't be naïve."

Kate sighed. There was no use trying to discuss anything with her mother, especially if she had her mind set on something. "So what else did she say?"

"Well ... she's going to come for a visit."

"She's coming here?" Kate exclaimed happily.

"Yes. She said that under the circumstances, she wants to speak to you, and meet your fiancé of course. She might not wait until you're actually married to relinquish the company, not to mention the money." Debra turned a mischievous smile towards Jerry.

"When?" Kate held her breath in anticipation. She barely even heard her mother's ramblings.

"Thursday."

"This coming Thursday?" Her breath was let out in a long disappointed sigh. "But Jerry leaves for Africa tomorrow."

"Yes he does. So?" Debra returned the bottle of nail polish to its most recent place of origin and held out her hands to examine her masterpiece. "You can stop in Scotland when you're off on your honeymoon. What's the big deal?"

"Oh never mind," Kate said angrily, rising to her feet. "I'll call her myself. I'll ask her to postpone her trip for a few weeks."

"Kate," her mother called lazily. "I wouldn't do that. She's not well."

Kate sank back down on the sofa. "Not well? What do you mean?"

"She's old, Kate," Debra said coldly and then in a softer, more dramatic voice, "she … doesn't have much time, but she doesn't want you to know. She … says she wants to make sure you're settled before she … well, you know, before she's too ill or, or worse." Debra's cat eyes rounded for emphasis.

Kate bowed her head, her fingers making a circling motion on her temples as her brain filled with thoughts.

It had been nearly a month since she'd spoken to her last. Why hadn't she called her more often, she scolded herself. Her grandmother had been her guiding light after her father died. All that she was, all that she had become, she owed to her grandmother. Gram meant the world to her and now she was ill. How can she disappoint her?

"Jerry, can't you stay?" Kate begged.

Jerry had been working with great effort to place the key to his Mercedes onto his brand new keychain. He hadn't heard much, only just then tuning into the conversation. "What? Stay? You mean cancel my trip?"

"Yes. Or at least postpone it. Can't you go next week? Just stay long enough to meet her."

Jerry seemed to panic. "No. Everything is set. I can't ask everyone to change their plans."

Kate was appalled. "I'm not asking you to ask anyone else to do anything. I'm asking you change your plans, Jerry."

He sprang to his feet and began pacing the short distance between one couch and the other. "Look, this is a prestigious event. The boys from the club are expecting me to be there. They're counting on me; I can't let them down. I absolutely cannot cancel."

"I'm glad I mean so much to you," Kate said sarcastically.

"Now Kate," her mother scolded. "There's no need for that. You know how important this trip is for Jerry."

Kate looked at her mother in wonder. Debra was the reason the word 'contradiction' was ever formed! "You just said Gram wanted to meet Jerry."

"I am aware of that, but we can't do anything about it, can we? The important thing is that she sees how well you're handling the business. You said yourself that she was very excited about this merger. I think she'll be just as content when she meets with Jerry's father."

Jerry stopped pacing and cleared his throat. "Umm….

Remember I told you … my father is going out of town on business. He leaves tonight and he won't be back till the end of the month."

"Oh!" Debra had forgotten about that, but she was certain it wouldn't make a difference. "Well, not to worry Jerry. I'm sure the paperwork will suffice. You know … " Debra waved her hand and rolled her eyes, "whatever portfolio you've all put together. Honestly Kate, she just wants to see for herself that you're happy. Jerry doesn't have to actually be here to assure her of that fact. Don't be silly," she scoffed. "Who knows when she'll kick the bucket?"

"Mother!"

"Well? You and Gregory both have discussed the damned business with her for months. It's a done deal isn't it? She's given you her approval. It's time to give you the rest," she shrugged and Kate cringed. "She wants to see you, Kate. Would you feel better if she dies without having had the opportunity to show her how well you've done? I thought you wanted that."

"I do, but she was hoping to meet my fiancé…. "

"Show her a picture; that'll do," Debra said logically, drawing an incredulous glare from her daughter.

Jerry came to sit next to her again. "Come on, aren't we going out?"

Kate was indignant. "Out? No, I don't feel like going out!"

"Kate," his voice became suggestive. "I leave tomorrow."

"Have a good trip," she snapped, and walked towards the door.

"Kate!" Debra barked her disapproval.

"I have a meeting that I can't cancel, why don't you go out

with him?"

Debra looked over to Jerry. Her mind was visibly working overtime and Kate was disgusted with both of them.

Kate picked up her keys and briefcase and left the house. She was blatantly aware of the intensity of the ill feelings between Debra and her former mother-in-law, but that fact only infuriated Kate more. The abundance of funds that her mother so easily squandered came from the person she hated most and Debra should remember that.

Kate's paternal grandparents founded Wallace Architectural Developments in Victoria, British Columbia, fifty-two years ago. George and Abigail Wallace worked together to establish their new company as one of the largest in the province. Deciding to retire in their homeland of Scotland, they were able to pass on the successful fruits of their labour to their only son Daniel, Kate's father. But their happy golden years were short-lived. George died the following year. Unfortunately, bad luck seemed contagious amidst the Wallace family. Only a short time later, a ruptured appendix took the life of their son, too. Devastated, Abigail returned to Victoria to comfort her grandchild, knowing full well that her daughter-in-law had never known the attributes of motherhood in good times, and would do no better in bad times.

Abigail Wallace's initial thought was to close the company, but she saw the potential in her exceptionally bright teenaged granddaughter. She kept the company running, opting to take control, albeit from a distance. Debra, having been denied her husband's family business, pushed Kate to accept her grandmother's invitation to attend the last two years of university in England.

This left Debra free to spend whatever inheritance she received on the frivolous lifestyle she so desired. Just as adamantly, however, she recalled her daughter to her side when her reserves ran out.

Eventually, after having received her degree in architectural engineering, Kate did return to her home in Victoria in the company of her grandmother, who remained to prepare her granddaughter as director of the firm. Abigail retained the position of CEO even when she returned to Scotland, receiving monthly reports and statements to keep her abreast of the dealings of the company. It was her wish to eventually relinquish the title to her beloved granddaughter when Kate married and both she and her new husband were ready to assume complete control of the business. Naturally Abigail was aware that Kate might very well marry someone with a career of his own, but this didn't concern her greatly. She knew that Kate was more than capable to manage the firm solo, but Abigail was a romantic. In her opinion, working long hours, leaving little time to spend together, wouldn't make for a great relationship. If they worked together as she and her husband had done, lack of togetherness would not be an issue.

Kate was confident that she had taken good care of the family business. Since her appointment as director nearly four years ago, her abilities had been obvious, her contracts doubling and extending to two other provinces. She had succeeded because she was capable and ambitious, and although achieving status of CEO was her ultimate goal, her grandmother's approval was just as important.

Driving aimlessly around town, Kate found herself to be

truly alone. The few good friends she had were either married or disappointed in her choice for a boyfriend.

She let out a cynical laugh. At the moment she had to agree wholeheartedly with their opinions.

Her mother had introduced her to Jerry. Kate had already begun a business relationship with his father when Debra, unnaturally interested in her work, informed her that she played tennis with a young man named Jerry Kent at the club that her mother frequented excessively. Soon she would not stop praising this young man until her daughter finally agreed to meet him.

It was an attractive fact that the Kents were one of the largest land developers in Canada. The merger that was now set in motion was a logical one from a business point of view. An association with this family would bring her firm national recognition. She wanted this, and her grandmother, as well as her financial advisors, had agreed. As for Jerry, it was no wonder Debra thought so highly of him; his family was worth millions! But his net worth had no bearing for Kate. She fell for the attentiveness and the respect he seemed to have for her; the affection that her mother never gave her. However, after dating for a mere few months, the topic of marriage had begun to infiltrate the business discussions. It had become apparent that both proposals were to be treated as one. Allowing herself to be placed in a situation that left her less than completely in control made her feel as though she had failed somehow. For this reason she opted to keep her grandmother in the dark of this new development.

After pondering at length over the prospect of this joint venture, Kate admitted that the merger would be a positive step forward, a step she wanted to make, regardless of the excess baggage. Kate met with Gregory Kent and accepted the business proposal. That same evening, she had accepted Jerry's proposal of marriage.

Kate returned the respect and affection as well as patience and tolerance, but unfortunately the demand for these virtues seemed to increase with each passing day, and she was beginning to have definite doubts about her decision.

Tonight confirmed what she had feared for the past few months. This was going to be a very one-sided relationship. Jerry knew how much Kate loved her grandmother. He should have known how horrible she'd feel about the news of her ill health. He should have wanted to stay with her, comfort her, meet her grandmother, as she had wished. Kate had never asked anything of him until tonight and tonight he let her down. Tomorrow her fiancé would leave for Africa. The safari that would take him away for a month suddenly seemed hardly long enough.

The traffic light turned red and Kate stopped for what seemed an eternity. She sighed heavily. Returning home was not an option. She needed time to cool off before she said something or did something she'd regret. She didn't want to see Jerry until his return. It would be best.

Kate finally found herself in front of the glass paneled office building of Wallace Architectural. She smiled ruefully. She was home. This was where she felt most comfortable. She parked her car in her usual spot and walked to the front entrance.

The security guard unlocked the door and allowed her to enter, a concerned frown creasing his already wrinkled brow. "Is everything all right Ms. Wallace?"

"Yes, everything's fine. I have some work to catch up on, I'll be here for a while."

"All right, Ma'am. Have a good night." The guard tipped his hat to her and retreated behind the large desk.

Taking the elevator to the top floor, Kate unlocked the door of her assistant's office and turned on the light switch. Before she ventured through the adjoining door, she allowed herself to browse for just a moment. She took a few steps into Alex's office. There were no pictures of his children on his desk, no pictures of his late wife. Then something caught her eye. On the side of the filing cabinet not clearly in view was a drawing of a family: a father and four children. 'To Daddy', it read ... 'Love Leeza'. That was so sweet. She suddenly felt a pain in her heart for that little girl, for all of Alex's children who were left motherless at such a young age. But Kate could empathize. Although her own mother did not die, Kate did not feel any more loved because her mother lived....

Kate entered her office and shut her door. She let out a contemptuous sigh. How pathetic. She was a successful business-woman, even moderately attractive, she thought to herself, and yet of all the places in this city this was where she felt most comfortable. She kicked off her shoes and plopped down onto the soft suede couch facing the large windows that overlooked the harbour lights down below. There she stayed, alone in the dark until the next morning.

CHAPTER EIGHT

A familiar voice was calling her softly. "Boss? Hey boss?"

"Shh.... " Kate begged for quiet as she snuggled under the large couch pillow that she had held over her for warmth.

The rich aroma of freshly brewed coffee suddenly entered her air passages forcing her to show more signs of life. Her eyelids fluttered open, slowly focussing her eyes on the familiar form of her assistant dressed in a dark business suit, sitting on the coffee table, a cup of the steaming liquid extended in front of him.

"Morning." Alex's voice was a comforting sound.

Kate stretched her arms over her head and tried to stifle a yawn. "What time is it?"

"Twenty to nine."

"Did I take home that suit I picked up from the cleaner's yesterday?" she asked sleepily.

"I didn't see you leave with it."

"Good," she sighed. "I'll shower here then. I'd rather not go home."

Removing her makeshift blanket she slowly swung her legs off the couch. She didn't bother to pull down her raised skirt. There was only Alex in the room, and he'd seen her in less.

Kate accepted the coffee and taking a sip, she looked up him. He wouldn't ask and she didn't have to tell him, but he was the only one she could unload onto, the only one who would listen – she wanted to....

"I had an argument with Jerry last night," she began, handing the cup back to Alex who remained silent. "And my mother."

"You okay?"

"No." Kate stood now, her skirt returning to its intended length and Alex noticing. She rubbed her eyes and combed her fingers through her tussled hair. "I'm so angry with them and with myself." Still Alex remained silent. "Apparently my grandmother called yesterday."

"Here?"

"No. She called my mother of all people." Kate's voice raised an octave indicating her annoyance.

"That's strange."

"Yes it is," she mused. "In any case, she's arriving Thursday to meet my fiancé."

"Isn't Jerry leaving today?"

"Yes he is." Kate twirled around, a cynical smile adorning her face. Her disappointment had not diminished overnight. "He wouldn't cancel his trip."

"And you ... wanted him to," Alex stated knowingly.

"Yes I did," she continued with the same quipped answers.

"Gram … Gram is ill. She wanted to meet him, to assure herself that I was settled before she … before she dies."

"I'm sure she'll understand."

"That's not the point," she snapped. "I asked him not to go! And my mother, well, all my mother's concerned about is the fact that Gram is coming to give me the business – and my inheritance! I admit that becoming CEO is what I've worked towards, but I also want to grant my grandmother the only request she's made of me," Kate concluded in a quieter tone.

"The situation is out of your hands. What can you do? It's not that you've broken your engagement; he's just out of town," Alex said logically.

Kate shook her head in defeat and made her way back to the couch. She sat back down again and taking the coffee cup from him once again swallowed a mouthful of the hot liquid. "Oooh!" She burnt her tongue, causing her to distort her face in pain, and Alex smiled. "My grandmother will only be here for a few days, why couldn't he just leave later?" she managed finally.

"It's a scary thought, but maybe you should have cloned him before he left," Alex said off-handedly. He reached for the cup and took a sip as well.

Kate's head jolted up. "What did you say?"

Alex smiled. "I said maybe you should have cloned him – I was kidding."

"That's it!"

"What's it?" Alex wasn't sure what revelation she'd just made.

Kate sprang to her feet once again and started to pace. "I'll find someone to pretend to be Jerry – that's what!" she said, proud of her idea.

"Now wait a minute." Fearing his boss's mental stability suddenly, he too rose from his seat on the coffee table and walked towards her. "Listen to yourself."

"I am. I don't want to disappoint my grandmother. I don't know how sick she really is. I mean … what if she dies. He won't stay, so I'll find a substitute," she said smugly.

"Boss! Wake up! I think you're still asleep!" Alex had to suppress the urge to take her by the shoulders and shake her. "You're going to marry the guy. For starters, there'll be pictures – do you intend to paste this imposter's head onto Jerry's body? And what if she's well enough to return for the wedding? How would you pull that off? I doubt that plastic surgery is something he's willing to undergo – at least – not to change his looks."

Kate paced while Alex continued to be logical, but she was adamant. "Alex, I'm in no particular rush. If we set a date for next year—" Kate stopped herself. She realized suddenly that it almost sounded as though she expected her grandmother would be gone by that time … because her absence would save her explanations. "Look, I don't think I'll have to worry about that, but either way, I choose to cross that bridge if and when the time arises."

"Okay, fine. Where are you going to find this guy?" he asked cynically.

Kate's idea wavered for a moment. Then, that light bulb switched on again. She turned to Alex. "You doing anything next week?"

Alex's eyes almost popped out of their sockets. "Me?" Alex abruptly placed the cup on the table, spilling some of its contents, and took a few steps away from her. "No way! I can't!"

"Why not?" she asked excitedly, as she hurried towards him

in her stockinged feet, the lack of heels reducing her height substantially. "Face it, who better than you? You know me. You probably know me better than Jerry—"

"—I doubt that," he said sarcastically.

"Come on," she begged, as she tugged at the lapels of his suit jacket.

"No. I'm sorry, but no."

"Why not?"

Alex watched her in disbelief. He'd never seen her act this way. She was desperate, grasping at straws! This was ridiculous!

"Because!" Alex couldn't readily think of an excuse, although he knew there were many.

"Why not?" Kate repeated her question. "Are you involved with someone?" she asked suddenly, and before Alex could reply she continued. "Because if you are, she has nothing to worry about."

"I'm not involved with anyone," he conceded. Alex turned away from her, trying to gather his thoughts. "You may be right. I've come to know you quite well, but not that well and you don't know me. How are we supposed to pull off being engaged to each other? Up until a couple of days ago, you didn't even know that I'm a widower with four kids! And speaking of which, did you forget that I have kids? I didn't. This is way out in left field – not at all in my job description!"

"Remember that extra week you wanted in the summer?" Kate said excitedly. "I'll give you two, plus a nice bonus. You can take your family to Disneyland."

"Bribery?"

"Whatever works," she smiled mischievously.

Alex shook his head. "I'm sorry."

Kate sobered. "Alex please," she begged, but Alex wouldn't budge. "I honestly feel I have to do this. Something's telling me that I have to do this. It would only be for a few days. We'll tell only those here who absolutely need to know and as far as your kids – well, you don't even have to tell them. It's not that I'm asking you to move in or anything. You've often worked late. I know you've missed many dinners at home, something about which I now feel very badly," she added, "but that's all you'll have to do really. Just have dinner at my house; hang around a bit while Gram is here, that's all. You don't have to tell them," she repeated.

Alex continued to shake his head and Kate took hold of his hand. "Will you at least think about it … please?"

Alex moved away from her touch. That had been a first, and he'd be lying if the innocent gesture didn't stir a feeling or two, but that was part of the problem. He was well aware of his attraction towards her. How could he put himself in this position?

"Please?" she asked again.

He watched her. Her hair messy, her blouse wrinkled, mascara smudged under her eyes … yet the cover girl for the swimsuit edition of Sports Illustrated could not have looked any sexier. "I'll think about it." The words spilled out of his mouth almost of their own accord. Well, he thought with relief, at least it wasn't the word 'yes'.

The day had been a complete write-off. Neither was very constructive. Whenever their eyes happened to meet Kate would almost pout, actually bringing an exasperated smile to Alex's lips, but still he said nothing.

It was status quo when Alex left that evening. When he said goodnight she didn't answer; she gifted him with the same sad look, a smile quivering on her lips.

"Goodnight boss," he repeated, and left the office, putting much needed distance between them. He needed to clear his mind; unfortunately, Alex thought of nothing else – all evening, all night … all morning.

CHAPTER NINE

Kate was going to ask him if he'd made a decision. He'd been awake half the night weighing the pros and cons. The cons far outweighed the pros, yet the mere prospect of the illusion of being engaged to Kate was something worth contemplating. He couldn't deny secretly fantasizing about his boss. This opportunity would place him in a position that he, until now, could only dream about. Besides, stranger things have been known to happen, and who was to say that something could spark between the two and.... "Huh!" Alex laughed out loud. "Who am I kidding?" What he should be saying was that since the reality was unachievable, what would it hurt to accept her request? Well, if he used his brain, he thought, chastising himself once again, he would realize just how dangerous this could become. If something went wrong, his job, if nothing else, could be compromised and that in turn would change things between them forever. Then again, the thought of being with Kate....

Alex entered his office; his heartbeat surprisingly quickening when he realized Kate was already there. He poured himself a cup of coffee and peeked around the open door separating his office from that of the larger one occupied by his superior.

"Morning boss," he greeted as usual.

Kate looked up from the documents she was studying. "Morning. Alex, did you get the site plans to the excavators?"

"Yes. Actually Jerry delivered them."

"Oh. All right. Better call Brian from Electrical. He said he has the estimates you'd asked him about."

"Okay." Alex was about to retreat assuming she'd had second thoughts about yesterday's conversation. He should have been elated or at least relieved ... instead what he felt was closer to disappointment....

But Kate too had thought of nothing else since the strange request she'd made of her assistant. She couldn't explain where that idea had originated, just that it had entered her mind with such force that she could not and would not ignore it. As far as choosing Alex as Jerry's stand-in ... well ... there was really no one else who not only knew her or the business well enough, but who would not judge her for making the request in the first place, no matter what he decided. She was certain he would not take advantage of the situation.

"Alex?" she called, stopping him. "Have you given any thought to what we talked about?"

She hadn't changed her mind. His heartbeat accelerating once again, he leaned against the doorframe. Today Kate was not displaying the exaggerated pout. Today she simply looked sad, as if she'd resigned herself to a 'no' answer. He stepped inside and closed the door. He walked over to stand in front of her desk and placed his coffee cup down.

"I have been thinking about it."

Kate eyes rounded. "And?"

"And … I've concluded that it's a bad idea."

Kate sighed. "I know it is. I shouldn't have involved you in my problems. I apologize.

"That's not the reason I'm debating this," he said bring her eyes back to him. "I'm worried that it may backfire."

"My mother," Kate said the word with animosity, "informed me that Gram will be visiting for ten days." Then, as though what he'd said just registered, "You're debating? You're actually considering…."

Alex ignored the question. "You think you'll be able to keep her cooped up in the house for the duration of her stay?"

"Not normally … but she's not well. I really doubt she'll feel up to gallivanting around town."

"Maybe." Alex was skeptical. "But she'll want to come here; check things out … someone is bound to make a mistake."

"But I told you," Kate said, coming around to stand in front of him. "We would tell those here that need to know – those with whom she may have contact – and I'll explain just how important it is. They'll go along with it. They will or I'll fire them!" Kate tried to sound flip, but she was serious and Alex knew it.

"What about your mother?"

"Don't worry about my mother. She's to blame in all of this. She made it her business to tell my grandmother about my marriage before I could. If she chooses to make waves, I'll just threaten to cancel her credit cards!" Kate stood with her hands behind her back, her head tilted to one side. She looked like Paul asking for the puppy. "So what do you say? Will you help me out?"

"You realize you're asking me," Alex pointed at himself, "to pretend to be romantically involved ... with you."

"Yes, I realize that. Alex, I'm sure we won't even have to hold hands, if that's the basis of your concern."

If only you knew, he told her silently. Why was he prolonging this; he knew he couldn't say no to her. "I don't want to involve my kids."

"I know."

He watched her for a moment longer. "All right."

Kate stared back, unsure. "All right? All right, you'll do it?"

"Yes."

"Yes!" Kate threw herself at her faithful assistant, wrapping her arms around his neck.

Catching him off guard, Alex's hands just barely touched her shoulders, suddenly uncomfortable with this spontaneous and uncommon display of emotion.

Almost immediately Kate drew away. "Sorry." She cleared her throat. "So ... what about your kids? Will they be all right with you missing dinner with them for a few days?"

"Well, they won't like it, but at least they'll be with their grandparents. My parents keep the kids after school when I'm late."

"That's good. Thanks Alex, you don't know what this means to me."

"You don't know what this means to me," he said sardonically, but Kate didn't pick up on his meaning.

"Oh, I know what I'm asking is extremely unorthodox, not to mention unethical and downright crazy, but it'll make an old woman happy. Thank you."

"Yeah, yeah. Don't forget – two extra weeks!" he called over his shoulder as he returned to his office.

First and foremost Kate had to speak to her mother. She had to warn her of her plan. Debra wasn't home, but then she rarely was. Kate finally found her at the spa.

Debra was incredulous. "What? Are you out of your mind?"

"No Mother, I'm not out of my mind. I am using my mind! I am not going to disappoint Gram – not now that she's ill. And by God how many times can you possibly come to this place?" Debra ignored her. "But what about Jerry?"

Kate walked around the masseur so that she wouldn't be speaking to his backside. "What about him?"

"He's not going to like this one bit!"

"Is that right? Right about now, I really don't give a damn what he likes or dislikes! I asked him to postpone his trip. He didn't. And Mother, if you hadn't gone and told Gram all about my personal affairs I wouldn't feel forced to find a substitute!"

Debra raised herself from the table, undaunted by the fact that the towel did not move with her. "Give us a few minutes, will you Rolf?"

Kate watched in disgust as the young man winked at her mother and left the room. Debra covered herself now and returned her attention to her daughter. "There is absolutely no need for this at all! She can meet Jerry any time!"

"You said she doesn't have much time! Didn't you say that?"

"Well … yes, but maybe she was just exaggerating," she waved a newly manicured hand. "Why can't you just go visit her together when he gets back? This is utterly ridiculous and certainly unnecessary! She doesn't have to actually meet your fiancé in order to give you your inheritance!"

"Stop griping about my inheritance. I only want to make her happy! I'm doing this, Mother! Get used to it!"

"Fine! But if you absolutely must resort to such lengths, I can think of four or five much more suitable candidates – just off the top of my head! Alex Callahan is your employee!"

"He's my assistant, my right hand – almost literally at times. You'd know that if you'd ever listen to me. There's no one better for this. I don't want to hear about your candidates! Alex has already agreed and that's that!"

Kate left her irate mother repeating the word 'but', and returned to the office.

Second on her list was to inform key personnel of the events which were about to take place. Kate called a meeting for all department heads, executive secretaries, receptionists for the executive offices, and in fact anyone who had any contact with Jerry during the few short hours that he appeared in the office. Alex was by her side as usual.

"All right," Kate began. "May I have your attention …" Kate drank a sip of water. She looked into the faces of her loyal employees. More than half of them were already working there when she took over as their boss, but she had been accepted from the beginning and that fact did not go unnoticed. "I've called this meeting to inform you that my grandmother, Abigail Wallace will be arriving tomorrow. It seems that her health is deteriorating and she wants to come and see for herself how well we've handled her company, before she … before she's too ill to travel. Normally her visit would not be a problem, but those of you who met her when she was here last, know how thorough she is. This is short notice, but I'll need all departments to be prepared." Kate's secretary distributed memos listing information that was required. "All forecasts from the various departments must be compiled and financial breakdowns and monthly assessments must be calculated or updated immediately. This takes precedence. I want all documentation ready for my grandmother's perusal, if she so desires; if she's up to the task." Kate took another sip of water. "She has another reason for visiting … and that is to meet my fiancé." Kate looked around the room and suddenly she felt uncomfortable. She was aware of Jerry's lack of popularity. "As some of you know, Jerry will be away for a few weeks…. "

Someone whispered, "Thank God."

Kate ignored the comment. "I don't want to disappoint my grandmother. Since she will not be staying long and since her ill health will probably keep her confined to our home, and in fact might prevent her from making another visit and will probably never meet him," she rambled, "I've decided to … reinvent Jerry … in the form of Alex Callahan."

"Wooooie! That-a-boy Alex!" Someone called. "All right Alex!" called another, and Alex just shook his head and smiled.

"All right, that's enough people," Kate said in a stern voice and the catcalls subsided. "Alex is to assume Jerry Kent's identity for the duration of my grandmother's visit. The success of this … transformation … is extremely important to me. Think of it this way, although I'm only doing this to grant her wish, if my grandmother discovers I've been lying to her, we all may very well be out of a job. Our futures will depend on everyone's ability to follow these instructions. Are there any questions?"

"Kate?" Tony Picaro raised his hand. "I was just wondering … I'm sure I speak for everyone when I say that we'll do whatever we have to do to help you with this … situation, but what about our clients? Obviously you're thinking probabilities here, and as such, a visit from Mrs. Wallace is a definite probability right?"

"I have to cover all the angles. I don't want to leave anything to chance."

"Well, that's what I mean. It's probable that a client will come in unannounced and ask for Alex." Tony said logically.

Kate looked at Alex, and Alex raised his eyebrows.

She turned to the receptionists, Elaine and Dora, for the answer to Tony's question. "That's where you come in. 'Alex' will be on vacation. Clients will be directed to either myself, Tony or Kevin."

The girls nodded and Kate looked at the two men. "Is that understood?"

"Yes, yes, perfectly," they both returned.

"But you'll be around?" Tony asked Alex.

"Yes, I'll be here, just that you'll have to refer to me as Jerry in front of Mrs. Wallace." Tony nodded in agreement.

"I know this sounds crazy and I regret having to place you all in this predicament, to involve you in my personal agenda, but I feel I have to do this. Hopefully we can pull this off. Anybody else have any questions?" Everyone shook his or her head and

Kate exhaled an involuntary sigh of relief. "Okay, thank you very much. I won't forget this."

"Don't worry boss," her employees assured her as they left the boardroom. "We can lie with the best of them!" they joked.

Tony pulled Alex aside. "Got a minute?"

"Sure," Alex grinned. "Your office or mine?"

"Mine," Tony replied with the same grin, and added a wink. "It's more private." Tony was about the same age as Alex, tall and handsome, the grey hair at his temples giving him a distinguished look. He was married and had two children the same age as Stephanie and Nicholas.

He closed the door and sat down in the chair facing Alex.

"What's up?" Alex was curious now.

"Talk about going out on a limb. I think this rates right up there in the 'above and beyond the call of duty' category." Alex shrugged, and his friend continued. "Sure this is wise?"

"No. In fact I think it's nuts, but…."

"But you can never say no to her, can you?"

"I guess not," Alex gave him a wry smile.

"You do realize this is only a temporary assignment."

Alex laughed. "Yes. Of course."

"I don't know…." Tony shook his head.

"Ton, I hear the wheels turning. What are you thinking?"

Tony leaned forward, his elbows on his knees. "Come on buddy … she can be cold and ruthless, but she's also a hell of a looker and you know you have the hots for her – major hots!"

"What?" Alex scoffed. Tony had started working at Wallace just after Alex. They'd become good friends over the last few years. They'd had similar discussions before.

"Alex, your face lights up when she enters a room. If she were to speak in an auditorium full of hundreds of naked women, you'd only have eyes for her."

"You're not going to start singing now, are you?" Alex said sarcastically.

"Hey, I was there four months ago when she announced that she was going to marry that mass of steroids. I saw your face. You looked as though you'd just—"

"—Tony, you're way off. I've told you before – she's my boss. Besides, you know perfectly well how my daughter reacts on the extremely rare occasion that I have a date. I can't even imagine anything long-term. And there is this little issue of her unavailability. She is engaged. That fact is not one easily forgotten, nor is her intended easily missed. Damned goof."

Tony chuckled. "Yeah I know."

The intercom buzzed. "Tony, it's your wife."

"Tell her I'll call her back in about five minutes Megan, I promise." Tony smiled and turned to Alex again. "It's her birthday today and I'm trying to pretend I forgot."

"Bugger! You'd better be taking her out."

"Yes *Dad!* The kids and I are taking her to her favourite restaurant and…. " Whirling his chair around the side of his desk, Tony reached over to a drawer and retrieved a small box, which he now held open for Alex to see. "Check this out."

"Whoa! I think she'll forgive you!"

Tony admired the simple diamond pendant. "Yeah, I might even get lucky!"

Alex laughed and Tony returned to the previous subject. "Speaking about getting lucky…. "

Alex covered his eyes as if embarrassed by Tony's remark. "Oh God!"

"I'm kidding, I'm kidding. But what I was saying before is that … the problem is that you'll be thrown together during this time. You honestly think you can stay passive, that you will remember that this is just part of your job – sort of?"

"I won't forget because a relationship involves two people. No matter how I – how you think I feel about her – that's just one person, and as they say it takes two to tango."

"Alex you've been her assistant for a year, her faithful employee, she's never had the opportunity to see you as anything else, but for the next few days you'll be her fiancé."

"In name only, Tony. She assured me that there wouldn't even be a need for hand-holding."

"Right! Don't you worry, the need will arise." Tony laughed suddenly and Alex couldn't help but join in.

"Besides, it sounds like you're implying that she may become carried away with her acting. She *is* engaged, Tony," Alex repeated. "To a nitwit no doubt, but nevertheless, engaged."

"Yeah, yeah," Tony nodded.

"Don't worry, nothing's going to happen. Are you done?" Alex smiled at Tony's skepticism. "I have work to do."

CHAPTER TEN

Alex seemed to be fighting with the mammoth sized butterflies that had invaded his stomach. Kate's grandmother arrived today. Today and for the next few days he would become Jerry Kent.

He was reminded of that fact the moment he entered the office the next morning. As he passed the executives' offices, those who were in would call out, "Good morning, Jerry!"

The secretaries, Connie and Angie, smiled mischievously as Alex drew near. "Hi Jer," they purred.

"Watch it," he warned, but the smile on his lips softened the tone and they snickered playfully.

"Morning, boss," he greeted as usual as he entered Kate's office.

Kate jumped. "You startled me."

Alex made his way inside and stopped at her desk. "Are you sure about this?"

Kate seemed to panic. She put down her pen and looked up at him, her hazel eyes round and questioning. "You didn't change your mind, did you?"

"I should have, but no, I didn't change my mind. I won't go back on my word, although my original opinion stands."

"And it's duly noted," she sighed. She should thank God for this man, she thought to herself. Her fiancé had refused to simply change his flight plan. Yet Alex had agreed to venture out on a limb for her, a perilously high one at that. Kate stood and started to pace, then she came to stand in front of him.

"I have a small request."

"Another one?"

"First of all I think … I think it would be a good idea if you didn't refer to me as 'boss', don't you?"

"Oh," he said realizing that it would seem rather odd to call his fiancée 'boss'. Alex had rarely used her given name, hoping to remind himself to keep their working relationship just that. "All right. You said 'first of all'. Is there something else?"

"Yes."

"What?" Alex was apprehensive.

"This is not a request…. How did we meet? Where did we meet?"

"Well, what did your mother tell her about Jerry?"

"Not too much, thank heavens. She mentioned that he has been starting to familiarize himself with my work here. Fortunately my mother didn't elaborate on any position Jerry might hold since his family has a business of their own. She told Gram that we're going to be married, but she assured me that she didn't tell her how we met. As for working here, you do already, so you don't have to pretend. In fact you're more involved, which can only please Gram more knowing that my husband will be sharing in the responsibilities of this company."

"And you think he will?"

"What – work here? Well, you've seen how interested he's been lately.... Besides, you know that's what I want."

Alex smiled. Yes, Jerry had seemed uncommonly interested, but Alex doubted that would last. She was wishing for the improbable if not impossible, but he didn't want to wake her from her dream world, especially not today. However he had to ask what had been brewing in his mind. "So should I be looking for another job?"

Kate looked puzzled and was therefore somewhat abrupt with her reply. "What are you talking about?"

"I was just wondering what position Jerry will hold once he's a permanent addition to the company. I mean ... I assume you'd want him to work closely with you—"

"—Alex, Jerry can never do what you do. Your job is secure, and I resent your questioning my loyalty towards you."

Alex grinned. "Okay, okay. So ... what do you want to say? How did we meet?"

"I don't know," she shrugged, partially sitting on the edge of her desk. "How about ... you came to me for the design of one of your buildings and ... and we ... well ... our relationship blossomed from there." Kate made a face. "No?"

"So ... we just fell in love while pondering a blueprint?"

"Something like that. What do you think?"

"Inconceivable," he said, drawing an indignant look from his boss. "Okay, I suppose it's possible," he smiled.

Kate exhaled. "Okay."

Alex dragged his eyes from the leg that she swung back and forth as it dangled from the desk. "Are we picking her up?"

"I'm sending a limo for her so she can be more comfortable. Her butler is accompanying her. Apparently," Kate managed a nervous little laugh, "she doesn't leave home without him! But I do want to meet her at the airport anyway."

"Did you want me to come along?"

"Definitely! The sooner we get the introduction over with, the sooner I can to start to calm down."

Alex chuckled. "Don't worry." This was abnormal behaviour for his boss. "If nothing else, your grandmother will be impressed with the success of the company."

"Yes well … I haven't been alone. You've been instrumental in this success."

"I've already agreed to your wacky plan," he joked. "You can cut the blarney!"

"It's not blarney. It's true … I just never told you before," she said as she twirled her fingers. The gesture reminded Alex of one of his children. "So … thanks."

Alex had to fight the strong urge to take her into his arms and tell her he would do anything for her, but he also had the feeling she knew that. She wouldn't have entrusted him with her future, even if just for the next few days, if she hadn't been certain she could count on him. "You're welcome," he said quietly.

Kate had been jittery all morning. This was definitely not like her, he thought as he glanced at his watch. It was time. He gathered all the scattered papers into their respective files and walked through to Kate's office.

"I think we should go."

"Oh!" she exclaimed, her mind obviously elsewhere. It would take them about 40 minutes to reach Victoria International Airport. The Vancouver Airport had informed her earlier that the flight from London was on schedule and so was the connecting flight from the mainland to Vancouver Island. No delays were foreseen.

Alex watched with an amused laziness as she searched frantically for her keys. "Boss?"

"What?"

"What are you looking for?"

Nervous, she snapped her answer. "My keys, what else?"

"Did you check your other hand?"

Kate looked down, discovering the lost keys dangling from the fingers of her left hand.

Realizing her less-than-attentive state of mind, she flipped the keys to her assistant. "You drive," she ordered, and Alex gestured for her to precede him out the door.

The Arrivals lounge was busy.

Alex and Kate made their way through the crowd as though poling for position at the Formula 1 racetrack.

"Ms. Wallace." A tall gentleman dressed in a chauffeur's uniform tapped her arm.

"Oh, hello Frank. I'm so glad you spotted me; it's unusually crowded today."

"Yes, it is. I just wanted to let you know that I'm here. The limo is parked just outside Arrivals. I have permission, but I'd better get back to it just in case."

Kate thanked the chauffeur who had worked for the Wallaces for years, and returned to stare at the large glass doors out of which passengers had just started to emerge.

Soon a slender elderly woman appeared. She was dressed impeccably in a navy blue suit. She carried a cane and walked slowly, but she refused the wheelchair that one of the attendants offered her.

Kate felt a lump in her throat. Her grandmother looked wonderful! Yes, she had aged since she'd seen her last, her hair having become completely white, and her cheeks had a few more lines, but she showed no sign of ill health. Kate knew her grandmother would hide that well.

"Darling Kate!" The surprisingly strong voice rang clear over the voices of the other passengers.

Kate pushed past the rude person who had just decided to block her view, and opened her arms to the woman who came towards her.

"Gram!" Kate's voice was tight with emotion. "I've missed you so much!"

"And I as well, lass!" her grandmother exclaimed, her Scottish accent surfacing.

Then the all-knowing pale blue eyes focussed on the handsome young man with the kind smile and bedroom eyes standing behind her granddaughter. "Ah … lo and behold! You must be the man who stole my Kate's heart!"

Kate's mouth dropped. How did she know that Alex was – Jerry?

"Am I mistaken?" her grandmother questioned herself suddenly, looking from one to the other.

"No, you're not," Kate laughed nervously. "Gram, this is A – Jerry!"

"I'm pleased to meet you Mrs. Wallace," Alex said graciously as he bent to kiss her cheek.

Kate watched with mixed emotions – in fact, two or three that she'd never experienced as her grandmother cupped Alex's face in her weathered hands. "No more pleased than I! I believe that if you were not my Kate's intended I would question her eyesight – and then marry you myself!" she laughed, as did Alex.

"I'm flattered," he told her in his gallant way.

Kate should have foreseen her grandmother's reaction to Alex. Gram had always had an eye for beauty – and handsome men! Her grandfather had been able to turn many a woman's eye right up to his sixties when he died. Although, she thought with a smile, her grandfather only had eyes for Gram. Wouldn't that be different!

A tall, thin young man pushing a cart with two suitcases moved a little closer to the group. He sported a goatee, which Kate gathered made up for the lack of hair on top of his head. He watched her grandmother with much attentiveness, assuring Kate of his kindness.

"Kate, Jerry, this is Reginald. Reginald calls himself my butler, but I call him my confidant, my helper, and my friend."

Reginald seemed to blush as he extended his hand in greeting.

"Welcome Reginald. I'm so happy to meet you."

"I as well, Miss. Sir," Reginald shook Alex's hand.

"Just Jerry, please," Alex corrected, and Reginald nodded in agreement.

"Reginald, I've hired a limo for you; it's waiting outside. You may keep the driver for the duration of your stay or drive yourself. It's up to you," Kate said looking at both.

"Reginald?" Mrs. Wallace questioned him.

"Well Ma'am, perhaps it would best if I don't drive here, what with the different side of the road and all," he gestured with his hands.

"Perhaps you're right!" Mrs. Wallace chuckled.

"Why don't you ride with your grandmother?" Alex suggested to Kate. "I'll meet you at the house."

Kate looked at him. She wanted to thank him for his thoughtfulness, for his willingness to help her, even for his good looks that seemed to have captivated her grandmother.

"Okay," she said simply. "I'll see you later."

"Mrs. Wallace," Alex nodded towards her.

"We'll be waiting for you, dear," Mrs. Wallace winked mischievously. "And please call me Gram."

The limo arrived home before Alex. Kate thought nothing of it at first, but after nearly half an hour had gone by, she started to glance at her watch. Had he decided to abandon ship? He wouldn't do that to her, would he? But the alternative explanation for his tardiness could only be a car accident and that was not something she wanted to even consider, in fact it filled her with an emotion she hadn't felt in a long time.

"He must have gotten tied up in traffic, darling," Abigail Wallace gave her granddaughter's hand a little squeeze.

"Oh yes, I'm sure...." Kate tried to sound glib, but knew full well that the highway was not too busy during this time of day. When the door opened and Alex walked in, she jumped to her feet, taking a few steps towards him. "Where were you?"

"Worried?" he whispered to her. "I was propositioned," he said as he neared her grandmother.

"Really?" Her pulse returned to normal and her tone was skeptical. "By a man or woman?"

"Kate, these days it's a compliment either way!" Gram chuckled.

"You don't believe me?" Alex asked his boss. "Look," he extended a card to her. The name Camille was written on the back and a number clearly printed underneath.

"Give me that!" Kate tried to take the card, an unexplainable jealousy creeping into her, but Alex refused, retrieving his hand. He laughed and played along the way he normally would have.

"No way! You never know when this might come in handy," he winked at the grandmother.

Abigail Wallace was absolutely delighted with the comical exchange. Alex was being himself and Kate realized her grandmother would never have taken to Jerry this quickly, perhaps even not at all.

They sat in the living room where the housekeeper, Mrs. Johnson, had prepared herbal tea and fresh scones.

"I was saying to Kate earlier, Jerry, the weather is just lovely!"

"Yes, we've actually had a remarkable spring," Alex replied.

"You mean we've actually had a spring!" Kate corrected, and Alex agreed.

"You're right. We have had better weather than the norm." Then he turned to Mrs. Wallace. "I've never been to Scotland. Does it rain there as much as it does in London?"

"Pretty much. As I'm sure you know I'm in Edinburgh, which has the added attraction of chillier weather, but it is a lovely city and my home. It's where George and I were born, where we had always intended to retire and I wouldn't want to live anywhere else."

"I know what you mean. I'm not too keen on our long rainy winters, but … I'm still here," Alex said with a crooked smile.

"Well at least it's dryer here in Victoria rather than Vancouver, by fifty per cent if I'm not mistaken," Abigail remembered, and Kate nodded in confirmation. "British Columbia is a beautiful province, but I remember the excess rain in Vancouver was part of the reason your father," she said towards her granddaughter, "decided to move his home to Victoria."

"Yes, I remember our old home. I liked it better," Kate said pensively. "But then I had Dad then, and you and Gramps lived nearby."

Alex watched her expression change, the tone of her voice suddenly forlorn.

"I know dear." Abigail lovingly patted Kate's hand, and drawing a breath, she changed the subject. "I'd really rather not bring up her name, but your mother told me that Jerry's been working with you. Is that right?"

Kate's stomach did a summersault. "Yes, he has been. He could be working with his father, but Jerry's decided to … to learn about our business, who knows, perhaps even join me."

"Truth is, I can't stay away from your granddaughter," Alex smiled at the elderly woman who was more than pleased to hear of his devotion to Kate and Kate was suddenly speechless, remaining quiet while Alex effectively changed the subject once again. He found it infinitely easier to ask questions about Mrs. Wallace's home in Scotland. "So where is Edinburgh, Mrs. Wallace?"

"Gram," she corrected and began to speak of her homeland, her love for it apparent in her voice. "Edinburgh is on the East Coast of Scotland. I'd love to have you come visit me. I'll take you to see Edinburgh Castle. It is perched high on a hill overlooking our city of winding medieval streets and splendid Georgian townhouses."

"I suppose you would live in one of those townhouses."

"You suppose correctly," Abigail smiled. "Do you golf?"

"Yes, a little."

"Well then you'd love St. Andrews. St. Andrews is called the home of golf. That's where golf was born, you know."

"That's not intimidating!" he laughed. "I'm not that good!"

It was not much later when a call came through from the office. Kate picked up the telephone. Connie informed her that a representative from one of their banks had shown up unexpectedly. The matter was not urgent, but she wanted to make certain that her boss knew he was there.

"Umm … Jerry…. " It was going to be difficult to keep from calling Alex – Alex. It's Connie. Brad Turnbull is there. Had you called him for anything?"

"No, but I think I'd better go. He never got back to us with those figures we wanted, remember?"

"All right, thanks." Then she turned to the receiver, "Connie, tell him to wait. A – Jerry will be there shortly. That is if he's not picked up by anyone along the way!"

"What?" Connie was confused.

"Never mind. You can ask *him*."

Alex rose to his feet and started to walk past the elderly lady that seemed to be saddened by his imminent departure.

"Will you be returning?" she asked, reaching for his hand.

"Yes. I will." Alex bent towards her and gave the soft wrinkled cheek a kiss.

A thought struck him. Was he supposed to kiss his fiancée good-bye? He turned towards her, lingering a bit. "I shouldn't be long," he said finally.

"I'll walk you out," Kate offered.

Kate followed Alex out onto the front stoop.

"I think she's smitten with you." Kate's voice held a musical lilt, and Alex smiled.

"She's sweet … but that was awkward, in there."

"She's very affectionate, do you mind?"

"I don't think we're on the same wavelength. Kissing your grandmother was not what I found to be awkward."

Kate tilted her head to a side, her eyes sparkling. "I suppose it would look odd if you kiss her and not me. A little peck on the cheek couldn't hurt, could it?"

Alex shook his head slowly, a smile dancing on his lips. "That extra vacation time you were so generous to allow me may soon grow!"

Kate raised her eyebrows in mock indignation. But that was quickly erased when Alex suddenly bent towards her and kissed her cheek. "Something like that?" he asked, his face lingering uncommonly close.

"Something like that," she replied, her voice a little quieter than normal.

"I think I can handle that. See you later," Alex called over his shoulder, and Kate watched him drive away.

Debra Farnicky-Wallace-Fondsworth-Boyd arrived just as Alex returned. She stopped him as he stepped out of her daughter's Jaguar.

"Was this an engagement gift?" Debra insinuated, obviously referring to the car.

"Hello Ms. Boyd – *is* it Boyd?" Alex didn't like Kate's mother, and couldn't pretend otherwise.

"Careful *Jerry*! We must behave ourselves, mustn't we?"

"So we must. After you..." he bowed as he opened the front door.

"Well, well, well, look what just flew in!" Debra couldn't pretend to like her ex-mother-in-law either.

"Hello Debra," the old woman greeted her, icily. "You haven't changed."

"You're looking well," Debra said as she flipped through the mail. "Did you have a good trip?"

"Yes, thank you, I—"

"I'm going to change. Is dinner almost ready?" Debra rudely interrupted the elderly woman and made her way upstairs.

Alex came to stand beside Kate who had stood when he and her mother had entered the room, as though ready to divert a possible attack. Kate raised her eyes to him, the annoyance of her mother clearly depicted.

"Don't let her bother you," he said quietly, leaning towards her.

"Come dear," Abigail gestured to Alex. "Come sit next to me." Alex did as he was asked, sitting next to her on the sofa. Kate sat on the large chair opposite them.

"Kate, during all our conversations about the merger

with the Kents, why did you never tell me about Jerry?" her grandmother questioned her.

"Umm, well Gram … I intended to come visit this summer … tell you in person, maybe even bring Jerry along and surprise you…. "

"How long has this been going on?"

"Fo – for a few months." Kate corrected herself, preferring not to specify the exact length of their courting.

"I see. So, tell me Jerry … how did you two become involved?"

Alex's eyes flew over to Kate who smiled nervously.

"I … was asked to procure an architectural firm for one of our buildings and through a business associate I was directed to Wallace. When I met your granddaughter … I found that I couldn't take my eyes off her." Alex watched his boss, whose eyes seemed to lock onto his. "I guess you might say we were given the blueprints for love. The business deal came later."

Kate's eyes rounded and Alex grinned, shrugging in response.

"How romantic! That's how it was with my George and me…" she said pensively. "We met in the library. We both reached for the same book. When our eyes met … that was it! I'm so happy that you found each other." Gram looked heavenward, sighing in contentment.

The housekeeper served dinner, and thankfully that deterred the topic from their love life!

"So Debra," Gram directed towards her ex-daughter-in-law as she cut her roast beef. "You're between husbands, I see." And Debra sneered. "What happened to the last one? Dalton Boyd, wasn't it?"

"Yes. Irreconcilable differences," she shrugged and drank a good portion of her wine.

"Net worth of zero, eh?" Abigail Wallace said knowingly and Debra fumed.

Kate thought it best to find another topic of conversation – fast. "Gram, remember that project I had told you about – the advertising firm of Gamble and Blaine?"

"Oh, yes. How is that going?"

"We've been awarded the contract," Kate said proudly.

"Congratulations! That's wonderful, dear."

"A – Jerry, I mean – he was influential in obtaining this contract. He … he brought them to us." Kate hated herself for lying, but she didn't know what to say about Jerry's credentials. Jerry had none to speak of.

"Kate, I'd love to come to the office tomorrow. Will you have a moment or two to show me around?"

Kate's eyes shot over to Alex. They had half expected her desire to see for herself the stability of the family business. At least they'd be ready for inspection.

"Yes of course Gram, but are you up to it?"

"I'm fit as a fiddle! You'll be there, won't you dear?" she asked Alex.

"Yes ma'am."

"Lovely."

Debra excused herself after dinner and soon disappeared out the door, for certain on her quest for husband number four.

Upon her second cup of tea Gram announced that she was ready to retire. "I've had a long trip my dears. I'm a little tired."

"Are you all right Gram?" Kate asked worriedly.

"Yes, I'm fine," she assured her. "It is called jetlag, Kate. Don't worry! But if I want to be coherent tomorrow, I'd better get some sleep!" Abigail reached up to Alex once again and he bent towards her allowing her to kiss his cheek. "I'm so happy to have met you Jerry. And I am so very glad that you will be marring my granddaughter."

Alex smiled. "So am I."

"I'll take you up, Gram. Excuse me," Kate said to Alex.

"*Blueprints for love?*" Kate repeated when she returned to the living room.

"I didn't hear you come to my rescue," he laughed as he leaned back against the plush pillow of the couch.

Kate plopped down beside him. "Humph! You're just lucky she believed you!"

"You realize you're only putting yourself down with that remark." Alex was smug.

"What?"

"Why do you think that what I said could be so farfetched?" Alex asked, and Kate turned questioning eyes towards his. "Is it so inconceivable that someone could fall in love with you so easily?"

Kate watched him for a moment and thought back to their conversation of that same morning in her office. "You're the one that said falling in love over blueprints was inconceivable."

"Touché." Alex got up and walked to the door, but he stopped and walked back. "I just remembered I drove your car. I'll call a cab."

"Don't be silly. Take my car. Just pick me up tomorrow."

"Are you sure you don't want to hang around a bit, have

breakfast with your grandmother – play referee between her and your mother?"

"Maybe you're right," she mused, biting her lip, as she walked towards the door. "If Gram still wants to come in tomorrow, I'll ride with her. I'm going to try and talk her out of it."

"Good luck," he called to her as he stepped into her vehicle. Alex started the powerful engine, but Kate's voice stopped him.

"Does she look ill to you?"

"No, actually she doesn't."

"No, she doesn't.... I'm so glad to see her like this. I don't know what I was expecting, but I'm afraid to ask her."

"Maybe she's just putting up a strong front, you know?"

"Yes, probably," she agreed. "Well, I'll see you tomorrow."

CHAPTER ELEVEN

Abigail Wallace was definitely not as ill as her ex-daughter-in-law had made her out to be. She stopped at nearly every office, wanting to be introduced to everyone. Kate was proud to say that her grandmother was so far impressed with the efficiency and dedication that was visibly apparent in every office, in every department.

"Hello, Mrs. Wallace," greeted the petite redhead who sat in the area just outside Kate's and Alex's offices. "I'm so glad to meet you. I've spoken to you on the telephone on a few occasions, but I wasn't working here yet when you visited last. I'm Connie."

"And I'm Angie," added the tall and slender girl of Afro-Asian descent. How do you do, Mrs. Wallace?"

"Fine, fine. I'm pleased to finally meet you both in person! You're so lovely!"

"Oh thank you, Mrs. Wallace." Connie and Angie smiled a little self-consciously.

Smiling mischievously, Abigail leaned towards the girls. "Is Jerry in?"

Angie giggled. "Yes he's in, Mrs. Wallace."

"Thank you." Abigail waved her hand and followed Kate through to Alex's office.

His jacket removed, the sleeves of his white shirt folded over exposing tanned forearms, Alex was busy at the drafting table when his boss and her grandmother entered.

"Good morning Jerry!" Abigail made her way towards him, and Alex met her halfway. He kissed her cheek again, and the elderly woman beamed.

Oh-oh, he thought. He'd have to greet his boss, and he couldn't just say 'morning boss'!

"Hi," Kate said, nearing him, and Alex held his breath as he bent towards her giving her too a little kiss on the cheek.

"I'm extremely pleased, Jerry. Kate was showing me around a little as we entered the offices. The accounting department is so efficient! And the art department – you've done well since I've been away," she said turning to Kate once again.

"Your granddaughter is quite capable, isn't she?"

"Yes, I know." Abigail looked around the office. "My, you're serious when you say you want to stay close to my granddaughter."

"Well Gram, if Jerry is to learn the business, what better way than to be placed right in the middle of it. His office close to mine … well, I like to be near him too," she smiled. "Jerry?" Kate wanted to deter the subject from herself. "Have the soil results come in on Andrews?"

"Yes, actually. Beach Sands, as expected. Tony's taking care of the site plans for that job."

"All right. Any developments on Gamble and Blaine?"

"Excavating as we speak."

"Good. So we're on track?"

"Yes ma'am." Then he smiled, rendering the remark a little more playful.

"I'd like to take a look at this project. May I, Kate?"

"Yes, of course, Gram." Kate retrieved all the files on Gamble and Blaine and proudly displayed the proposals on the large table in her office. The three sat for hours discussing the project.

"So Jerry," Abigail sighed, momentarily tiring of inspecting documents. "I read the proposal from your father's firm. I've given Kate my blessing at the union of the two companies, but I'd like to tell you personally, especially after meeting you, that I agree that it is not only the right move, but the only move."

"I'm ... glad you think so."

"I do. I know that your family has their own reasons for suggesting the merger, but since your heart belongs to my granddaughter, I have no doubt what the outcome will do for Wallace. Kate has done amazing work, and I'm confident she will continue to do so. Your help in achieving this is an added bonus, a seal if you will, that the firm can only prosper."

"I'll do my best to live up to your compliments, Mrs. Wallace."

"Oh, they're not mere compliments. I know what I'm talking about. And call me Gram! By the way, will we be meeting with your father?"

"Unfortunately, my father is away on business. Was there anything you needed to discuss with him?"

"No, no. I'm sure everything's in order."

Kate was ecstatic that her grandmother was impressed with

their current operations, their expertise. Gram hadn't yet mentioned turning over the reigns of Wallace itself, but Kate was in no hurry.

"Gram," Kate drew her grandmother's attention away from Jerry – Alex. "It's past noon. Shall we go out for a bite?"

"Oh darling, I'm really not that hungry. I think I'm still suffering the effects of jetlag. Could we not order in?"

Kate smiled. "Sure. What would you like?"

"Just a sandwich dear. Perhaps ham and cheese … on whole wheat."

"I'll go to the café downstairs. A – Jerry?"

"I'll go," offered Alex. "Turkey on white?" he asked Kate.

"Yes. Thanks."

Abigail turned to her granddaughter when Alex left the room. "Kate, do you still have the yacht?"

"No, I sold it. Do know how much it was costing me to keep that little toy for my mother and her friends?"

"I can imagine! Well then, how difficult would it be to get our hands on a yacht for the weekend?"

"Not *too* difficult, I suppose. Why?"

"Lovely. I'd like to take a cruise along the coast for a day or two. It's been so long since I've been back in Victoria. I wouldn't mind doing a little sightseeing. And it'll give us some time together away from work – not to mention your mother," she said, and Kate had to smile. "Besides, I'm sure my presence has in some way compromised your private time with Jerry. You can be together for the weekend. What do you think?"

Kate was at a loss. She did not expect her grandmother to want to sightsee. She expected her grandmother to be frail and ill. Abigail Wallace did not seem this way at all.

"But Gram. Are you sure you feel up to it? Wouldn't you rather take it easy?"

"Kate. I'm not on my deathbed yet! I want to spend some time with you – and your Jerry. I'll relax on the yacht."

"I … I just have to make sure it's all right with Jerry. I mean, he may have appointments or meetings that can't be rescheduled, not only here, but also with his family's business."

"Of course. We'll ask him. You go about securing a vessel just the same."

Abigail Wallace was not one to let things be. Once Kate was successful in locating the yacht of their choice, Gram was quick to pose the question to Alex when he returned with their lunches.

Alex grimaced. "A yacht?"

"Don't tell me you've never been on a cruise? My dear, you live on an island!"

"I've been in boats, Mrs. Wallace. I'm just not too comfortable with them or in them, for that matter."

"*Gram,*" she corrected again. "And what I have in mind is a little larger than what I think you have in mind, Jerry."

Alex was skeptical. "Oh, I don't know. I think the ferry that brings us to and from Vancouver is pretty large, and I'm not too keen on that either."

"The yacht will be very stable. As long as you can take the time, you'll be fine, you'll see."

This was an unexpected development, one that would require more lies and a whole lot more stamina on his part. "When did you want to do this?"

"How's tomorrow?" Abigail asked excitedly. "I figured

we'd start off nice and early – just after dawn in fact – cruise along the coast all day, we'll spend the night on board and return on Sunday."

Alex glanced at Kate who had remained quiet, looking from one to the other. "Spend the night?"

"Gram really wants to do this, will you check your calendar, Hon?" Kate smiled sweetly. "I have to let the marina know by tonight."

"I forgot my day timer at home. I'll pick it up and let you know when I come by the house."

Alex waited until he knew his children would be back from school and headed for his parents' home.

"The whole weekend, Daddy?" Leeza complained. "But we were going to see that new movie, remember?"

Alex shifted in his chair and raised her onto his knee. "I know, but the movie will be in theatres for weeks. This meeting can't be postponed for weeks. I'll have to take care of it now."

"But why does it take a whole weekend, Daddy?" Leeza continued.

"It's just that we'll be meeting with someone very important on … on this yacht and since we'll most likely be working till late we were … invited to stay on board for a couple of days. We just felt it would be more practical to accept the offer. Do you want me driving all the way home at one or two in the morning, just to drive back a few hours later?"

"No," Leeza shrugged.

Stephanie had remained as quiet as her other siblings as they all sat at their grandparents' kitchen table munching on milk and freshly baked cookies, but she was about to explode – she had to ask. "So, is *she* going too?"

And Alex knew it was coming. "*She?*"

"Your boss."

"As a matter of fact, yes." When Alex saw his daughter's eyes narrowing with suspicion, he added, "Her grandmother is visiting from Scotland. Mrs. Wallace and her butler Reginald will also be accompanying us." And Stephanie looked away.

"What about my soccer game, Dad?" asked Nicholas.

Mary Callahan put her hand to her forehead and turned to her husband. "We have that wedding this weekend, don't we?"

"Oh boy, that's right," confirmed Pat. "It's Donovan's daughter, we can't miss that. I'm so sorry Nick."

"That's all right, Grandpa," Nicholas hugged his grandfather.

"It's fine Dad. I've already spoken to my father-in-law. I remembered about your friend's wedding. So," Alex turned to his son again, "I've talked to Grampa Dan. He said he'd be happy to take you to your game. He hasn't seen you play in a while. Now, you have a choice to have Gramma Gloria and Grampa Dan come stay with you at our house, or you can go stay with them for the weekend. Which will it be?"

The four children looked at each other. Stephanie, Nicholas and Leeza all agreed to accept their maternal grandparents' invitation to stay with them for the weekend. Paul wanted to stay home.

"Sorry, buddy. Majority will have to rule this time. Bring your computer games."

"Oh yeah," Paul said, suddenly remembering that those games were mobile.

Alex called his boss and informed her that he would be able

to join their weekend excursion. He also told her that he wouldn't come to visit this evening. He felt he should stay home with the children. Kate understood.

CHAPTER TWELVE

Alex arrived at the Wallace home early Saturday morning dressed casually in khaki shorts, a white Polo shirt and sneakers. Kate and her grandmother were ready; overnight bags by the door.

Kate stifled a yawn while greeting her assistant as he entered. "Morning."

"Hi Hon," Alex grinned. Using the endearment Kate had used the day before was somehow easier than calling her by name.

"You're such a morning person!" he whispered.

"Oh hush! Even the worms are sleeping at this hour. I am awake."

"Right," he said knowingly and followed her into the living room to wait for Mrs. Wallace. Abigail was not yet present thus they were able to avoid physical contact, something that, Alex was certain, would not be as easily avoidable once they boarded the yacht.

Alex chose to take his own truck rather than ride in the limo. "I'd rather have my vehicle with me in case of emergencies," he explained when Abigail questioned his decision.

"That's fine, dear. I'll see you two at the marina!" she waved, assuming that Kate would ride with her fiancé.

"Thank you for this, Alex," Kate said when they were underway.

"It wasn't as difficult as I had thought – to get away – I mean."

"Why? What did you tell your kids?"

"I told them we had to meet with someone on their yacht and that we were asked to stay on board for the duration of the meeting. This is a meeting of sorts, I suppose."

"Yes," she smiled. "I suppose. But were they upset that you'd be away for the weekend?"

"Well … a little. Stephanie asked if you would be coming along."

Kate turned to look at him. "Really? Why?"

Alex shrugged. "She feels forbidden territory being threatened."

"You, I gather, are the territory, but threatened by what?"

"Whom. And that would be you?"

"Me?"

"You're female. That'll do it," he smiled ruefully. "I explained that your grandmother is visiting and that we'd all be together. I think that made it better."

"That's good. Who will be staying with them?"

"Actually, they'll be staying with my in-laws. I dropped them off last night. They have a pool. At least they'll have a little fun."

Alex followed the limo into the private parking area of the Cadboro Marina. Dozens of vessels were lined up on its shores: fishing boats, tour boats, small yachts, large yachts, and people, regardless of the early hour, were already bustling about….

Abigail Wallace emerged from the limo and made her way towards them and together they walked to the dock. Kate spoke to the captain and gave him the proper papers and identification, and he in turn welcomed the party on board the 100-foot yacht that Kate had rented for the weekend.

Alex made a face as he stepped onto the anchored vessel.

"Jerry," Abigail grinned. "You're not going to be ill, are you?"

"I'll let you know," he told her, holding his stomach.

"You wuss!" Kate pushed his arm playfully.

"Please! No unnecessary movement!"

Reginald brought their bags down to their rooms while Alex tried to become accustomed to the movement of the boat – yacht, and the captain raised the anchor and announced that they'd be starting the cruise along the southern coast of Vancouver Island.

"I'm going to go change," Kate said looking down at her black Capri pants. "I'm going to take advantage of this sunny day. Will you be all right?" she smiled again.

"I guess you'll know when you come back and find me hunched over the railing!"

"Oh, you'll be fine! Come dear, come sit with me." Abigail led him to the stern and motioned for him to sit on the upholstered benches along the rail as they headed out of Cadboro Bay. "Don't look out onto the water just yet. Get yourself used to the movement. You'll see it will get better, I promise."

Alex was still skeptical but he did as she suggested. After a short time Mrs. Wallace excused herself to go and speak to the captain and his mate, and Alex was left alone to contemplate his surroundings. He put a hand to his stomach. No, his surroundings were not something to contemplate just yet!

It was the sight of Kate in her hip-hugging denim shorts and matching halter-top that was just the medicine to make Alex forget about the water beneath him.

"What?" she said when she noticed his strange stare.

He replied with the same word, "What?"

"You're staring. Do I look that bad?" Kate was serious.

"No. Aren't you cold?"

"No. The sun's warm," she dismissed. "Are you going to come sit with me? Where's Gram?"

"She said she was going to speak to the captain."

"She's probably still with him then. I just saw Reginald heading that way. So, you coming?" she urged.

"Sure."

They sat on the lounge chairs situated on the large deck of the yacht. Kate chose the chair under direct sunlight, whereas Alex preferred the shade.

"Don't you like to sit in the sun?"

"As much as the next guy, but I don't want to add sunstroke to a queasy stomach," he said calmly and Kate laughed.

"It's not funny," he said joining in her laughter. The entire situation was not funny, actually. As his boss closed her eyes to the bright morning sun, Alex took the opportunity to scan her – in his opinion – perfectly proportioned body. A golden tan still lingered from her trip to the Bahamas the previous month. A tan line was visible on the soft mound of her breasts. His eyes followed the path to her flat stomach and firm thighs, to the legs that captured his attention every day, to her small perfect feet and unpainted toes. He'd better keep his mind on the possibility of motion sickness. It was much safer.

Abigail appeared beside them a short time later. "Well you two! We've certainly picked a wonderful day! How are you doing, Jerry?"

"Let's not talk about it, okay?"

Abigail grinned and waved her hand at his discomfort. "You land-lubber you!"

"And proud of it!"

Abigail had instructed the captain to maneuver the yacht to head north along the Sidney Channel around the small peninsula at the tip of Vancouver Island and then south along the Sannich Inlet. That would bring them just about twenty kilometers north of Victoria, if they had gone by car. By midday they docked at the Brentwood Bay Marina and a taxi brought them the short distance to Butchart Gardens.

"Ah, land!" Alex breathed with relief, and Abigail laughed again.

Given the choice to walk through the enormous park or stay on board, Reginald had decided on the latter. "No matter dear. You relax today," his employer had suggested.

Stepping out of the taxi, Abigail took Alex's arm on one side and Kate's on the other. Kate was concerned for her grandmother. This was going to be too long a distance for her to walk. "Gram, there's a wheelchair rental just inside—"

"Wheelchair? She turned to Alex, pretending to misunderstand her granddaughter. "Are you still feeling ill, dear?"

Alex grinned. "No. I think I'll be fine. But I'll lean on you if you don't mind."

Abigail winked. "You do that."

Butchart Gardens, which began as an abandoned limestone quarry in 1904, now holds possibly the most spectacular floral displays on the continent. The beauty of these gardens is breathtaking.

The three ambled along the paved pathways that lead through 20 hectares of exquisite arrangements of more than five thousand trees, shrubs and flowers. Although still spring, and many flowers not yet in season, the grounds were spectacular just the same. Kate was in awe of the incredible array of multi-coloured tulips displayed in masses and in patches within other plants and flowers. Stopping for occasional rest breaks, they walked along to see the sunken garden, rose garden, the Japanese and Italian gardens, the star pond, and the show greenhouse. Further along there was a concert lawn, fireworks basin, and a seed store, from which they purchased seeds for the birds. There was also a coffee bar and two restaurants. Choosing one with an outdoor patio, they stopped for a late lunch.

Alex seemed to be enjoying his food, sighing in contentment after finishing his shrimp cocktail. In fact, he waited anxiously for his main course.

"I suppose you're feeling better now?" asked his boss.

"Yes! Definitely. Although …" he added pensively, a frown creasing his brow. "If I think about it, I could still feel the motion of the water … let's change the subject!"

Kate and Abigail found his discomfort extremely amusing, but decided to do as he asked before he lost his appetite.

"Jerry, you've pointed out some of the different sights. I gather you've been here before – naturally by car?"

"Definitely by car! Yes, I visited a few times during the summer months. They have great concerts, and fireworks, not to mention fabulous puppet shows for the kids."

Abigail's eyes sparkled mischievously. "You've come for the puppet shows, have you?"

"Hey, they're pretty good, you know."

"Yes, yes. I know," she smiled. "We drove up a few times in the winter, as well. It's still beautiful even without the kaleidoscope of colourful blossoms."

Kate thought back. It had been years since her last visit. "I remember ... they decorate the entire place with ribbons of lights! Daddy used to bring me. We had so much fun.... "

Abigail hadn't intended for the conversation to become somber. She chose another topic as soon as the waitress placed their lunches before them. "Do you have any brothers and sisters Jerry?"

Alex's eyes looked up to his boss. They hadn't thought of that line of questioning. Alex had a sister, but Jerry had none. How was he supposed to answer?

"Jerry's an only child like me, Gram," Kate came to his rescue. "That's probably why we understand each other."

"I hope you won't stop at one child when you decide to start a family," Abigail commented.

"I didn't like growing up by myself, you know that Gram." Kate didn't exactly answer her question, but Abigail had been satisfied, proceeding to pose the same question to Alex.

"How about you, Jerry?"

Alex took a sip of his iced tea. "I'd like at least four," he said, hiding a smile. "You think you could handle that?" he asked his boss.

"At least," she returned, in an exaggerated tone.

"Have you set a wedding date?" her grandmother continued, bringing their eyes back to her.

"No. You would have known about it had we set a date, Gram."

"Well, what are you waiting for? If my opinion counts for anything, I give you my blessing! I approve wholeheartedly!" she said, patting Alex's hand.

The blue-green of Kate's eyes intensified in the sunlight as she turned towards her intended, and he was very much aware. "Maybe the beginning of next year. What do you think, Jerry?"

"I'll see if I could fit you into my busy schedule," he managed, tearing his eyes from her.

"I'll be so delighted to attend your wedding. Let me know as soon as you decide. I want to make certain there are no problems to hinder my return. But why wait so long, Kate? You know I'm not getting any younger."

"Well … we've been so busy at work, what with the merger and now this latest job…. You're thinking of coming to the wedding? That's – that's wonderful!" Kate had been told that her grandmother might not be well enough to return. It didn't seem that way at all. She was happy naturally, but she wondered if Gram wasn't pushing herself too much, just to put on an act for her granddaughter.

Much to Alex's chagrin, soon they were on the yacht making their way back along the Straight past Cadboro Bay, along southern tip of Victoria and up along the Victoria Harbour.

Later that evening Kate and Alex stood on deck. Alex was actually able to gaze out onto water without feeling too badly. In fact the scenery was absolutely beautiful, and surprisingly relaxing.

At night the grey stone of the stately Victoria Parliament Buildings are transformed by millions of white lights outlining its form, accenting in detail the archways, windows, and elaborate copper crowned rooftops. A few other buildings along the water's edge were similarly adorned or displayed large lantern shaped posts, their collective lights shimmering upon the still waters, illuminating further the otherwise darkened harbour.

There was a full moon, and the night skies were a blanket of stars. This would have been a perfect romantic evening.... "It's beautiful isn't it?" Kate sighed as she turned her back to the view, her hands on the railing behind her. Alex stood in front of her. Although not touching, he too placed his hands on the railing, one on either side of her. Mrs. Wallace had not yet turned in and therefore a need for closeness.

"Definitely... " he answered quietly. They stood in silence for a moment, before Alex decided to ask the question that had been on his mind since he'd gone below to change after their outing. "By the way, I have a question."

"What?"

"Our *bedroom* has only one bed. Are we sleeping together?" he asked with a mischievous glimmer in his eye.

"Gram was trying to be considerate in giving us the largest stateroom with the one bed. Will that be a problem? I promise to behave," she assured him, a smile playing on her lips.

"We'll see...." he said through narrowed eyes. "So, are you going to tell Jerry? Not that we're sharing a bed, but about this whole deal."

Kate shrugged, a frown now creasing her brow. "Oh, I don't know. If he'd stayed when I'd asked him to, there'd be nothing to tell. It would serve him right to tell him that he left me no choice but to beg my assistant to fill his shoes when I needed him most."

Alex's eyes shifted away for a moment. "I'd go with the latter if you want to bug him – I definitely think he'd be more offended with your choice of substitutes rather than keeping the secret from him."

Kate looked at him realizing that her remark had sounded like a putdown. "I didn't mean that the way it sounded. You know I see you as more of a friend than an employee."

Skepticism returned to his tone. "Really? I didn't know that."

"Well of course, why do you say that?"

"I'm a friend you knew nothing about."

Kate nodded. "I suppose you're right. You've been more of a friend to me than I to you. You're being a friend now – doing this for me. If I were a true friend, I wouldn't have put you in this position."

"I'm also your employee, and I am being compensated," he dismissed now.

Her grandmother appeared once again, ending their conversation. "There you are. I just wanted to tell you that I'm going to bed."

"Oh, all right. Goodnight Gram."

"Enjoy the evening," Abigail waved.

"What do you say we do the same?" Kate asked after a little while, and Alex agreed.

When they both entered their bedroom, she offered Alex first use of the bathroom. "That's all right. You go ahead. Just leave me some hot water. We do have hot water?" he added with a grimace.

"Yes, we have not water!"

At first sight of her, Alex thanked God that Kate did not return from the bathroom wearing sexy lingerie. Unfortunately, the little cotton knit pajama that clung to her every curve wasn't any less alluring.

Kate lay down on the bed while Alex took his turn. She turned a lazy eye to him when he reappeared in a pair of sweat shorts and a T-shirt, and she found herself wondering if that was what he normally wore for bed. "Do you have a preference as to which side of the bed?"

Alex glanced towards her, their sleeping arrangements seemingly having no effect on her sanity as it did to the man who had decided that cold water instead of hot would actually be the best choice of temperature given the circumstance.

"Left side I guess. That would be my left," he gestured. "But it doesn't matter."

"No that's fine. I normally sleep on the right."

"Mind you," Alex added as an afterthought as he climbed onto the bed. "I'm used to having the full bed to myself so don't be surprised if you find yourself on the floor."

"Same goes for you!"

Laying side by side, wearing decidedly less than their usual office attire, Kate suddenly found that she had to focus on something other than the man who would be sharing her bed. She returned to flipping through the satellite stations. Accidentally, however, she found herself in the adult section and she quickly fumbled with the remote to change the station.

"Whoa! Put it back!" Alex exclaimed.

"No way!"

"Give me that," he laughed as he snatched the remote from her and flipped back to the station that had caught his interests.

There, displayed on the screen was a woman with extremely large, deformed breasts and Alex seemed to find her amusing.

"Now aren't they something!" he declared.

"Sure, and they're real too," Kate agreed sarcastically. "I think she has to wear lead shoes to keep her from tipping over! They look like they're about to burst."

"You're jealous," he kidded her, and then he added in a serious voice, "do you realize that if she's ever thrown into a large body of water, she wouldn't drown; she has built in floatation devices."

They both laughed at the woman's ridiculous form, but Alex didn't yet change the channel.

"Have you finished?" Kate scolded now. "Give me that."

"No!" Suddenly Alex forgot about his intention to keep the relationship business only. The two began to fight over the remote, giggling like children. Kate shoved the remote into her clingy pajama top, holding it in place.

Alex loomed over her with a mischievous grin, his bare legs pinning hers beneath him. "You think I'm afraid to go in after that?"

"You wouldn't dare!" Kate tried to sound outraged, but she was laughing too hard. She managed to turn onto her stomach, only to be turned back with one strong hand.

Alex began to slide his hand under her pajama top, his eyes dancing with laughter. Suddenly he looked down. The remote was no longer there. "Hey! Where did it go?"

Momentarily forgetting the reason for the appearance of his hand on her bare midriff, Kate looked down as well. Realizing she'd lost her precious cargo, she once again began to laugh.

"Maybe you should invest in a set of those," he suggested.

"Eeew!" Kate broke away now and proceeded to punch him in the shoulder.

"That's just like you men. You prefer over-inflated life rafts rather than the real thing."

"No," he said matter-of-factly, starting to sober now. "Actually, I don't."

"Sure," Kate smiled knowingly, as she made herself comfortable on her side of the bed.

"I was just bugging you," he said, he too adjusting his pillows. "Personally, I'm not a boob man."

"Oh? And just what sort of man are you?" Kate smiled her question.

"I'm a leg man. I was never turned on by those things," he nodded towards the TV, which was now displaying an infomercial. "I mean if you're naturally big, you're big, and I, as a man, would not complain, but to do that to yourself – I mean, to that extent – is totally ridiculous and unnecessary."

"Jerry actually suggested I get myself ... enhanced," she said pensively. "Like my mother."

Alex turned his eyes towards her. "You're kidding."

"No."

"What's wrong with what you have?"

"Well, obviously to a male who *is* a boob man – not enough," she smiled ruefully.

"You're fine just the way you are."

"Yes, that's the word he used," she told him, keeping her eyes fixed on the program.

Alex stared at her in silence for several seconds causing Kate to finally raise her eyes to him.

"Well then, I'll use another. How about 'perfect'? Or perhaps two, 'just right'."

Suddenly Alex felt the need to draw the conversation away from the two of them. "You know, after my wife was done nursing Leeza, she was left with practically nothing at all and I still thought she was the most beautiful, sexiest woman in the world."

And suddenly Kate realized that she'd really never taken the time to allow herself to know this man who had made her feel better with a few gallant words, than Jerry had in months of gifts and attention.

"You still miss her," she stated, feeling sorry for his loss.

"I'll always miss her."

"You've never thought of remarrying?"

"I have to think of my kids, they come first."

"Don't you think it would be good for them to have a mother again?"

"Well … that's a difficult subject in our home."

"What do you mean?"

Alex sighed. "First of all, it's not easy to find a woman who would be willing to take on the very difficult job of mothering four children – especially not her own. Secondly, and almost as important as the first, I'm kept in line by my daughter. Did you happen to notice how Stephanie reacted when you came by the other night? And I told you on the way here, that she was concerned that we would be together this weekend." Kate didn't answer. "You're a threat, because you're young, and *she* thinks you're pretty," he chuckled, waiting for her reaction.

It took Kate a moment longer than usual to clue in. "Thanks a lot!" she retorted. "So you obviously don't!"

"How would I know? I just look at your legs," he said waiting for the expected pillow in the face, but it didn't come and Kate's stunned expression told Alex to return the subject of his daughter – quickly. "Steph's had a difficult time since the accident. She would never approve of me bringing someone home to – in her words – 'take her mother's place'."

"That's too bad. Have you thought about counseling?"

"Sure. We've all been at one time or another. Stephanie still sees a therapist periodically. That's why," he said hoping to conclude this subject, "I have to think of them first."

"That's very selfless."

"That's what a parent does."

"Not all parents. I never saw my mother when I was little. She'd either be out shopping or at the club, or the spa – she still is," she said ruefully. "That's why losing my father was so difficult. He was busy and he was not as attentive as you obviously are, but he did care. Aside from my grandparents, my father was the only one of my parents who showed affection." Kate sighed, remembering how she used to try to stay up late until her father returned from work so that she may recount to him the things she'd experienced that day in school, or perhaps cry on his shoulder about the crush on the boy that was not reciprocated…. "After he died, my grandmother took over as parent. I guess that's why I feel so indebted to her. My mother never put me before her and she never will. You must be a good father."

"I hope so." He lifted the covers and slid underneath onto the cool sheets. "I'm going to try to get some sleep. Maybe I won't notice the rocking so much," he smiled.

"Good night," was Kate's reply, and turned off the TV.

Mere moments later Alex partially turned on to his stomach and propping himself up on an elbow he turned his head towards his boss. "Does it ever stop moving?"

Kate laughed. "Try to keep your mind off it."

"And how do you propose I do that?"

"Think of something else."

Alex watched her through the darkness. "...Oh yeah, now *that's* going to help my insomnia." He punched his pillow and lay back down.

Kate didn't respond. She wasn't quite sure what he'd meant by that statement, but when he'd said it she'd felt an odd stirring within her. In fact, it seemed all of her senses had been placed on red alert....

CHAPTER THIRTEEN

Alex was sleeping when Kate awakened early the next morning. He hadn't tossed and turned, but just the same she knew he hadn't slept much. Then again, neither had she. She'd spent most of the night staring at his back, listening to the sound of his breathing and wondering if in fact their sleeping arrangements had been the cause of his insomnia or hers for that matter.

It had become quite chilly in the wee hours of the morning and finally succumbing to sleep, Kate had unknowingly snuggled herself against the warm body next to her. Naturally she didn't realize until now that the body belonged to Alex.

Turning slightly into his arms, she looked up at him as he slept, the quiet steady breath nearly lulling her back to sleep as well. Strands of shiny black hair fell over his wide forehead. Thick black lashes lay motionless against his cheeks, hiding the expressive brown eyes that she had only just recently begun to notice. Her eyes slid down to his mouth and had to suppress the urge to reach up and trail a finger against the full lips. He was so handsome. She felt comfortable in his arms. One of those arms lay possessively across her midriff, and she realized that his touch did not displease her. In fact … she should get up before he awakened, before things got far too complicated….

"Good morning dear." The elderly voice startled her as Kate stood staring out across the water.

Her thin wrap skirt fluttered open in the breeze and Kate held it closed. "Gram. What are you doing up so early?"

"I'm old. Old people don't sleep in. We don't have much time left to waste." Abigail smiled as she approached and Kate accepted her grandmother's embrace. "But I don't remember you to be an early riser."

"I've changed a bit. I actually get up when the alarm clock rings, but I'd still rather sleep in."

"So where's that handsome devil?"

Kate smiled at the glint in her grandmother's eye. "He's sleeping."

"And you left him?"

Kate had to laugh. "I wanted him to rest. He didn't sleep too well."

"Well, as long as you didn't have a spat."

"No, I promise you we didn't."

"Good. I like him."

"Yes … so do I."

Her grandmother chuckled knowingly as she led her granddaughter to the chairs at the stern. "Yes, I'm sure you do."

They sat down and soon afterwards Reginald appeared with a tray of coffee.

"Kate, I must tell you again how pleased I am with your beau. He's not only deliciously handsome, but he's courteous and intelligent. He's learned the business too. I was observing him yesterday. I cannot say it enough: Jerry will be an asset to the company, an asset to you. He seems reserved, however, when it comes to showing his affections towards you. Is he simply shy or is he not the demonstrative type?"

Kate took a sip of coffee from her cup. Oops. Her assurance to Alex that there would not be a need for closeness had already buckled, but now it seemed that they might have to look yet a little more believable. She wondered how to break the news and how he would take it. She, on the other hand, found herself anticipating the prospect with a little more interest than she should have.

"I wouldn't worry about … Jerry, Gram. Although he does seem to be a little shy around you, he's sufficiently demonstrative, as you say. I'm sure he simply doesn't want to offend you."

Her grandmother's eyes twinkled playfully. "Oh, I won't be offended, lass!"

"All right, I'll tell him that," Kate assured with a smile.

It was nearly an hour later when Alex finally joined the two ladies on deck. Reginald had just served the delicious breakfast consisting of croissants, scones, jams and jellies, fruits and yogurts, and now he scurried to provide Alex with a fresh cup of coffee.

"Good morning," Alex greeted as he neared them. "Sorry, I don't normally sleep in."

"Not to worry," Abigail said reaching for his hand. "Good

morning, dear. You certainly are a beautiful sight my boy – at any time."

"You're going to make me blush," Alex returned, kissing her cheek. He sat in the empty chair near his fiancée who had been watching him intently and bent towards her to kiss her cheek. "You were up early. Couldn't sleep?" he purred, and Kate remained silent.

"You know dear," Abigail interjected. "I know you're sleeping with my granddaughter, and I'm perfectly fine with that, seeing that you will be married," she added with a wicked smile, "so you may feel free to kiss her properly, I won't get my knickers in a knot, I promise."

Alex smiled at Mrs. Wallace's choice of phrases. Well, he'd have to do as she asked. He turned to his boss whom he had hoped would have been able to warn him of this turn of events. She didn't say a word.

"Kiss her properly? All right." Alex leaned over towards Kate, their eyes locking for several seconds. Finally his lips covered hers in a soft, gentle kiss that was much too short to accurately grade it, however it was long enough to cause her insides to stir, and that shouldn't have happened.

"Better?" he asked, seemingly unaffected by the kiss.

"Yes, much!" said Gram. Having been satisfied with their show of affection, she began to eat her breakfast. "I haven't known you long, Jerry, but I've grown quite fond of you in just these few short days. I can see that you are a good man and you definitely have a good eye for the business." Abigail reached for Kate's hand. "For this, I am confident that in giving my granddaughter and her new husband full control of our family business, you will both do all that is in your power to continue its success."

Kate hugged her grandmother. "Thank you, Gram. We'll do everything we can to continue to make you proud."

Alex was feeling guilty. He shouldn't be the one accepting her praises, although, he thought logically, he could only see Jerry hinder Kate's success, not help it. "Your granddaughter is the driving force. I can only promise to do my best to help in any way that I can."

"And I'm sure you will, lad. I only fear that you're just too perfect to actually be real."

"I'm far from perfect."

"Not too far." Kate spoke up, turning his surprised eyes in her direction.

"Sorry about that before." Kate offered later as they sat alone on the deck.

"About what?" Alex was being purposely evasive. He had an idea he knew what she was about to say.

"You know," Kate said, waving her hand, a habit she'd picked up from her grandmother. "The kissing thing."

"Oh. Well, my lips didn't fall off, so I suppose that means I'll live."

"Thank you so much!" she laughed, deeming it best to keep things light. "I thought I'd have time to warn you, but..." Kate shrugged, trailing off. "This morning Gram mentioned to me that she thought you were a little reserved. I guess she was just concerned that maybe you didn't love me or something."

"So.... " Alex's eyes sparkled with laughter, but his heartbeat was accelerating in anticipation. "Does this mean that I'm expected to be more demonstrative?"

Kate smiled as she turned her eyes to him. "That's the word she used, actually. I'm sorry. I thought we could get away with this without any physical contact, in fact I know I practically guaranteed it, but … I guess we'll have to look a little more real. Will that be okay?"

"How do you feel about it?"

Kate paused for a moment. "If you can do it, so can I," she answered bravely.

"Yeah, it's a horrible thought, but I'll see what I can do, all right?"

Kate smiled sheepishly. "Thanks."

As they cruised back towards Cadboro Bay, Abigail called to them to join her at the bow. Following her to the front of the yacht they noticed hundreds of boats; their white sails a stark contrast against the bright blue skies. Each May, competitors in the Swiftsure Yacht Classic race from Victoria to Cape Beale and back again. Unknowingly they had taken a front row seat to this exciting event.

The Captain made certain he maneuvered their yacht so that its presence would in no way interfere with the racing perimeter, and the three sat by the rails to enjoy the sights. Alex was actually able to watch without feeling too queasy. Perhaps he was becoming accustomed after all….

They returned home at dusk and after a short visit, Alex announced that he should be heading home. He said his good-byes to her grandmother, but Kate took hold of his hand and walked him outside.

They stopped at the door of his truck and faced each other

their fingers still entwined.

"Thanks again … for this weekend."

"You're welcome." After a pause, he added, "Do you think she's peeking from a window?"

Kate laughed, but her eyes suddenly became guarded. "It wouldn't surprise me, why?"

"Because I'll have to kiss you good-bye."

"Oh," was all she could manage.

Alex watched her for a moment, expecting her to say something more. "So?"

"So what?"

"Do I kiss you or what?"

"Oh. I guess it wouldn't hurt," she said quietly. "What do you think?"

Alex didn't answer. He brought her hand to his chest and let his own hands slide down to her waist, to the small of her back, drawing her closer.

Kate stood motionless, confused at the feelings that his touch was invoking within her. She accepted his descending lips willingly – for her grandmother's benefit, the voice in her head assured her. However, tangling her fingers in his thick black hair and responding with such intensity was for no one's benefit but her own.

She didn't stop him when one hand slid down over her hip to her bare thigh only to trail upwards again, raising the flimsy skirt with it, his fingers leaving a burning trail in the process.

Finally Alex pulled away leaving her somewhat dazed.

"Was that real enough?" he asked his voice husky.

Kate couldn't speak. She nodded her answer. The voices in

her head were arguing with each other. Her emotions were screaming *'Wow! What was that?'* Her logic and reasoning were telling her that she just missed Jerry and since she was upset with him before he left, it had been a while since she'd experienced a kiss like that. Logic won. Snap out of it, she told herself.

Alex headed straight for home, opting to take a cold shower before picking up the children from his in-laws'. Kissing Kate like that had been a mere fantasy for months. The reality had been far sweeter than that fantasy, but now that he'd had a taste of the forbidden fruit, how was he going to suppress his desire for a second helping?

CHAPTER FOURTEEN

Alex was at the office before her the next morning. He made sure to make himself extra busy when she walked in.

"Morning," she mumbled as she walked quickly through the office. Too many thoughts invaded her mind throughout the night. Two sleepless nights in a row did wonders for her moods! Morning revelations at home only added to her discomfort.

"Morning, boss. I didn't think you'd be coming in, today."

"Why wouldn't I?" she asked looking his way, pausing at the adjoining door. "And I asked you not to call me that."

"Sorry, and no particular reason – other than possibly wanting to spend time with your grandmother."

"Oh," she sighed, her eyes silently apologizing for her abruptness. Brought face to face with her assistant this morning, it was difficult to keep her mind from remembering the events of the previous evening, in fact the entire weekend. She should not have been affected and that fact unnerved her. She came to lean against the glass wall. "Well, I will – we both will. She's coming here again. I wonder how ill she really is, Alex. This trip and all this running around can't be good for her."

"Have you talked to her about it? I mean, have you asked about her health?"

"No, not specifically. I'm not supposed to know, remember? Besides, I don't know if I want to know, you know?"

Alex nodded. Tearing his eyes from her lips, he returned to work and so did she.

Kate and Alex were just about to enter the boardroom for their Monday meetings when Abigail arrived.

"Oh, may I sit in, Kate?"

"Yes, yes of course, Gram." Kate escorted her into the large boardroom and led her to the head of the table.

Tony Picaro, and the other senior structural engineers, Kevin and Bob, as well as Brian's assistant Carl Lee from the Electrical engineering department were present. Connie would be keeping minutes.

Abigail refused to sit in Kate's chair, but agreed to another chair being placed just beside that of Alex. Tony watched his friend, an eyebrow raised, and Alex simply shrugged in response.

Kate took a deep breath and hoping for smooth sailing, she began the meeting.

"The Hillside Avenue project is near completion, Kate," Tony answered his boss.

"The plans have been signed over?"

"Yes. Eldridge, the builder on that job, is satisfied. Everything's on track."

"Good." Kate turned to Kevin. "What about Mr. Wang's building on Bay Street? That should be ready for the concrete slabs, correct?"

"Yes," Kevin replied. "Brian's contacted the electrical contractor. He's having a problem with dates."

"Why? And where is Brian anyway?"

The usually quiet Carl answered for Kevin. "He's there actually, at the contractor's, trying to work out the glitches."

"If they can't do the job, we'll go elsewhere. Brian should be more assertive. I don't want to waste time. Have him call me the moment he returns," she instructed and Carl nodded. Kate flipped through pages in the thick files in front of her, her thoughts deeply immersed in her work. "Alex's taking care of footings, steel, et cetera for Andrews … and excavating for Gamble and Blaine…. How many more days do you estimate—" Kate stopped short, realizing that she had turned to Alex for an answer. Everyone looked up, but Kate quickly regained her composure. "Jerry, have you heard?"

"Should be done by midweek."

That was close, but her momentary mental lapse seemed to go unnoticed by her grandmother's sharp senses. The meeting over, the three retreated to her office and discussed yet another job.

During their discussions, Alex realized they were missing certain documents. He decided to ask Kate to retrieve them from the outer office hoping to show her grandmother that they were indeed a couple and he was not merely an employee. It was for this reason, he told himself, that Alex took it upon himself to be spontaneous with his fiancée, to be 'demonstrative'. He came to stand behind her, wrapping an arm around her waist, his face snuggling in her neck. "Kate…?" he whispered.

Alex had finally called her 'Kate' and Kate, feeling strangely giddy, answered in a soft, hushed voice…. "Alex…. "

Alex caught her error and rebounded quickly. "J e r r y," he said slowly, as if teaching her how to say the name.

Kate had felt as though she'd been in an animated state this morning. Her body was there, even her mind to a certain extent, but she'd been preoccupied, feeling oddly numb. She was alert now! "Oh my goodness, Jerry! I'm sorry!" Kate wanted to turn to him, but he wouldn't loosen his hold.

"Kate!" Gram laughed, "Did you know that given different circumstances, that could be cause for divorce!"

"She does that a lot," Alex smiled, making light of the mistake.

"Just who is this Alex, anyway?" Gram asked suspiciously. "You mentioned his name during the meeting."

"He's just an employee," Alex explained.

"Must be *quite* the employee!"

Kate, grateful that the error had turned into something humorous, joined in as well. Continuing her act was infinitely simpler than trying to analyze the situation, not to mention more pleasurable. "Oh yes," she elaborated, finally allowed to turn into his arms, arms that seemed to tighten their hold. Kate's hands slid slowly up the front of his shirt to wrap them around his neck. "Not only is he intelligent and witty, but he's a definite babe," she said in a seductive voice. "And sexy…. "

Alex listened and watched through guarded eyes. Calling him by his real name was a mistake, but one that he had expected Kate to make at a different time, like the little mistake during the meeting, not while he held her in his arms. Her description of her employee was just as unexpected.

Gram laughed, taking Kate's jabbering as a joke. "Jerry, dear, you'd better watch your back!"

"I don't think I have anything to worry about, do I?" he asked his intended. "I think you're pretty committed … right?"

Kate's answer was the lips she pressed against his, which left him nothing more to say as well as clearing all thought about the missing documents. Playfully pushing her away from him and telling her they had work to do was the only thing he could do. Taking his daily cold shower would have to wait.

A short while later, having forced all indecent thoughts to a side, Alex started to feel the pangs of hunger. Realizing it was nearly two in the afternoon he posed a question to Abigail.

"Mrs. Wallace – I mean, Gram … may I buy you lunch? But this time we'll go out."

"That would be lovely, dear! I suppose we'll have to take Kate along," she let out an exaggerated sigh.

"Gram! How could you?" Kate joked. "I'd better not leave the two of you alone!"

Abigail suggested that they all drive together in the limo. She called Reginald and Frank the chauffeur who were in the coffee shop in the lobby of the building and informed them that they would need the car.

The three sat down in the quaint restaurant and ordered their lunches. They sat in silence for a few moments, but Kate didn't mind. She was too busy watching her stand-in fiancé, remembering his kiss, his arms around her. She definitely wanted more. She reached across the small round table and reading her intentions he held her hand.

It was time for conversation; time to get his mind off of his boss. "So how are things back home?" Alex asked.

Abigail waved her hand in her usual way. "Oh we have our ups and downs … you know. The tabloids are having a field day with the Royals, but I'm sure you hear about that here."

"Yes, and how."

As lunch was served they spoke more about the Royal family and touched on the politics between Scotland and England, as well as the politics in the business world.

A short while later the maitre d' appeared at their table once again.

"Pardon me," he excused his interruption. "There is a call for Mr. Kent?" The man looked between Kate and Alex, displaying the portable telephone in his outstretched hand.

"Thank you," Alex said, taking the phone. "Yes?" Suddenly Alex's face paled and both Kate and her grandmother were immediately concerned, placing down their forks, waiting for Alex's reply to the person on the phone.

But Alex had momentarily forgotten where he was, whom he was with and who he was pretending to be. "What about my daughter?" Alex demanded anxiously.

"Daughter?" Gram exclaimed. "What daughter?"

Realizing his slip-up, Alex closed his eyes momentarily, only to open them again and apologize silently to Kate.

Gram looked at Kate who was busy biting her fingernails.

"All right," Alex was saying. "I'm leaving now. If she calls again, tell her I'm on my way."

"Jerry dear? Is everything all right?" Gram asked worriedly.

"What happened?" Kate wanted to know.

"Leeza fell at school. She needs stitches; I have to go." Alex rose to his feet and pushed in his chair and looking at Kate again, "I'm sorry."

Kate stood as well, her legs oddly shaking. "Would you like me to come with you?" she asked tentatively.

"You don't have to ask, Kate. He needs you. Go."

They both took a step to leave, but Alex turned suddenly, bumping into Kate. "We came in the limo."

"Oh bonkers!" Abigail declared as she rose from her chair. "I forgot. Well I'm finished my lunch anyway. Let's go. We'll drop you off to pick up your vehicle and then I'll have Frank drive me home."

"Are you sure Gram?" Kate asked.

"Yes, of course! Don't be silly. Come along, we're wasting time."

They rushed out of the restaurant and into the waiting limo. Once seated in the plush interior, Gram had to ask the question.

"Why didn't you tell me that you have a child?" she looked from one to the other.

"I was married before … my wife died in a car accident a little over four years ago. I'm sorry I didn't tell you," Alex apologized to her grandmother, as did Kate.

"Gram, I … I was going to tell you obviously … but I didn't know how you'd feel about my marrying someone who … I mean … you know, someone with a ready made family." Kate had no idea what she was saying and if indeed she made any sense.

"Good heavens lass! I thought you knew me better than that! I love children." Grandmother huffed. "I have a great-grandchild and I didn't even know it!"

Kate's eyes were fixed on Alex's. "Actually, in that case … you have four."

"Four!" Abigail exclaimed, her face breaking into a large grin, and Kate's heart suddenly seemed to overflow with joy and she didn't quite know why.

CHAPTER FIFTEEN

Alex and Kate hurried into the hospital emergency room. The nurse showed them into the room where Leeza and Gramma Mary and Grandpa Pat waited for the doctor.

"Daddy!" Leeza started to whimper.

Alex drew her into his arms, blood and all. "Hey! How's my little munchkin?"

Leeza tried hard to keep her tears in check, especially when she saw Kate standing by the door.

"Hi Kate," she managed.

"Hello sweetheart."

"Mom, Dad," Alex was reminded that Kate was there and that his parents had never met her. "This is … Kate Wallace … my boss."

"Pleased to meet you, I'm Mary."

"Pat Callahan. Very nice to meet you, Ms. Wallace."

"Likewise and – call me Kate, please. I wish we didn't have to meet under these circumstances."

"Yes, definitely," the Callahans agreed.

"Tell me what happened Leeza," her father urged trying to keep his daughter's mind off the pain in her head.

"I was playing and a big boy was running and he bumped into me and I fell and I hit my head on the step, but he didn't mean to push me; he didn't see me and he brought me to the office."

"Goodness, I got tired just listening to that!" Alex laughed and his little girl questioned her father's attempt at humour. "Nothing. That was very nice of the boy. Does it hurt a lot?"

Leeza nodded. "I cried just a little bit."

"Well, I think it's okay to cry, but I'm glad you weren't too frightened."

"You're very brave Leeza," Kate added.

"That's what Mrs. Byning said. She's the principal."

The doctor entered the room. "Wow! You must be a pretty important person to have all these visitors!"

Leeza nodded and gave her father a smile.

Dr. Leung introduced himself and shook Alex's hand. "Okay. Who's going to stay with you while I put you back together again?"

Leeza's eyes opened wide, a frightened expression taking over her china doll features. "Like Humpty Dumpty? They couldn't put him together again!"

The doctor waved his hand and gave a laugh. "They couldn't put him back together because they only called all the King's horses and all the King's men! Did anybody bother to call a doctor?"

Leeza laughed, nearly forgetting about her head. "Noooo!"

"So who will it be?" Dr. Leung asked again. "Mommy, Daddy, Gramma, Grandpa?"

Kate's eyes shot over to Alex who chose not to correct the

doctor. "I'll wait outside," she offered.

"You stay if you like, Kate," Mary Callahan suggested with a smile. "I don't think either of us can stand to watch!"

Kate looked at Alex once again.

"Up to you," he told her.

The doctor finished preparing all he needed for Leeza's stitches and came towards her. "Ready?" Leeza's eyes rounded again, but nodded in agreement.

After what seemed an eternity to Leeza's grandparents, Alex and Kate reappeared holding Leeza by the hand.

"How did it go, Leeza?" Gramma Mary crouched down to her granddaughter's level.

Leeza shrugged her little shoulders. "Okay."

"That's my girl!" exclaimed Pat.

"Actually Dr. Leung said he'd never seen a braver little girl," Alex boasted. "She didn't cry at all."

"I said ouch a lot," Leeza confessed.

"Well you're braver than your father was at your age. You should have heard him scream when he got his stitches!" Pat confided in his granddaughter and Leeza giggled.

Alex, Kate and Leeza drove home together. Pat and Mary went directly to the school to pick up the other children.

Once at home Leeza wanted to change out of her blood-stained clothes. "Will you help me Kate?" the little girl asked, taking hold of her hand. Again Kate eyes flew over to Alex who smiled his approval.

Changed into a clean outfit, Leeza sat on the couch, Kate next to her.

Suddenly the door burst open and Stephanie, Nicholas and

Paul stormed through the entrance, their grandparents close behind.

"Leeza, are you okay?" asked an anxious Stephanie.

"Cool!" exclaimed the boys, dropping their knapsacks on the floor. "Stitches!"

Kate moved away from Leeza, giving her siblings a chance to ask about all the details. She took the few steps to Alex. "I'm going to call a cab."

"You don't have to go. You can stay and have dinner with us."

"Oh, I don't think so.... " But Leeza's sharp ears overheard their conversation and quickly seconded the invitation.

Just as quickly however, Stephanie made her disapproval known. "Wouldn't you rather have dinner with your own family or your boyfriend?"

"Stephanie!" Alex reprimanded.

Kate felt Stephanie's coldness from across the room. The young girl's words stung a little – and that was unusual for Kate. "That's all right. I really ought to go. My grandmother probably has a million questions."

"You can call her," Alex said, his voice stern as he looked at his daughter. "You're staying."

Stephanie huffed and took her frustration out on the school bag that she bounced on every stair as she headed for her room.

In the meantime Leeza called her other set of grandparents and told them of her escapade. This was very important news, after all. Naturally, they were there within minutes, fussing over her, as did everyone else. Little Leeza loved all the attention.

It wasn't long, however, before Dan and Gloria noticed a stranger in their midst – a young beautiful, *female*, stranger.

"Oh, I'm sorry," exclaimed Gloria. "How rude of us, Alex.

We didn't even notice you had a guest."

"Mom, Dad, this is Kate Wallace, my boss."

They both shook hands with Kate and Kate gladly recounted how brave the little girl had been during her hospital visit.

"Oh my goodness!" Gloria exclaimed once again. "We'd stopped for ice cream – Dan! I forgot it in the car!

"Oh well, we'll have milkshakes for dessert," he shrugged as he headed towards the door.

Mary came over to Gloria. "Why don't we see if we can put on some supper?"

"Yes, we'd better get started. Kate, would you like to join us?"

Kate turned sharply towards them. She appreciated being included, although she doubted if she could be much help. "Thank you. I would love to help, but I have to warn you I don't think I've ever cooked anything," she said almost apologetically.

"Not to worry. We'll find something for you to do!" Gloria told her.

"Stick with us and before long you'll be cooking up a storm, you'll see," Mary promised.

Kate wondered if that could ever be possible, but in the meantime she accepted their invitation and followed them into the kitchen, all under the watchful eye of her assistant.

Gloria scanned the freezer. She pulled out a few packages of steaks and several sausages. She placed the vacuum-packed meats in water, and prayed for a quick thaw. From the refrigerator, Mary found peppers, zucchini, carrots and eggplants, and lettuce and tomatoes for salad.

"Okay Kate. We'll wash these veggies and slice them. The peppers in wide strips, the zucchini, carrots and eggplants about a quarter inch or so thick – we'll take care of the carrots, they're a little tricky," Gloria added. "We'll grill them on the barbecue. We won't bother the men with it," she called back as she opened the French doors leading to the patio and the large stainless steel barbecue.

Kate removed her jacket and washed her hands as well as the vegetables as Mary prepared a quick marinade for the meats. "Okay, I think these are clean." Ripping off a sheet of paper towel, she gently dried the vegetables.

Mary retrieved cutting boards from under the sink and knives from one of the drawers. "All right. What do you think?" Mary held a knife and board towards Kate.

"Sure, let me at them. I might lose a finger, but that'll just give us a wider variety of meat!" she joked and Mary laughed.

Gloria was back and washed the lettuce, while Mary helped with the slicing. "So I suppose you've always had a cook," Gloria started the conversation after a moment of silence.

"Yes. My mother was never one for the kitchen – or much else, so naturally she hired others to cook, clean, and do pretty much everything that needed any kind of manual labour! So I've had no exposure to the culinary arts."

"That's okay," offered Mary. "Take this meal, for instance. There's really no skill required, except of course to keep from cutting your fingers! The barbecue will do all the work."

"Sure," added Gloria. "I'm a pretty good cook, but in the summer months, I barbecue nearly everything. Dinner is ready within minutes and the rest of the time Dan and I can relax or go out with Mary and Pat. We don't always have to be tied to the stove for hours."

"I suppose I should learn to use a barbecue then," Kate suggested with a smile. "But what would I do during the winter months?"

Gloria and Mary answered almost simultaneously. "An indoor grill!"

"All kidding aside, I'm sure we were not all meant to be cooks," offered Mary. "You're a smart girl, why should you waste your intelligence or abilities in the areas other than where your talents lie? I think we all have a calling. Yours is to head a very prestigious architectural firm. For now at least. Are marriage and children somewhere in your future?"

This was a personal question, but for some unknown reason, Kate felt comfortable with these two ladies. They seemed kind and genuinely concerned. "Well, I do want children," she said with a sudden conviction. "I suppose I ought to get myself married first, though."

Gloria laughed. "I suppose that would be the right order."

Alex entered the kitchen, putting a stop to the conversation. "Hey, what's cooking?" Noticing Kate's expertise with the large knife, he raised his eyebrows and shot her a grin.

"What?" she said with mock indignation. "I'm not totally useless in the kitchen, right?" she asked turning towards the ladies for support.

"Not at all, and you're one to talk. It took you a while, didn't it?"

"Yeah, yeah," he laughed. "Don't you start with the stories. My kids have already revealed my lack of skills!"

Having drenched the meat in the marinade, Gloria placed it all in a container and brought it and the cut vegetables out to the grill. "Here, I'll do that." Alex insisted he take over and shooed his mother-in-law back into the kitchen.

Relieved of her duties, Gloria started to set the dining room table. Both Mary and Kate helped and they finished within moments. During the entire time, Stephanie's eyes did not leave Kate, and Kate was very much aware of that fact.

Dinner was delicious, and Kate felt proud that she'd had at least a tiny part in its preparation. Kate was told to sit where she had sat before; Stephanie had made certain to keep her from a certain chair.

There were ten people sitting at that dinner table, and at least eight were speaking at one time. Kate sat watching everyone in amazement. It was wonderful. It was noisy and homey and she loved it.

A question was finally posed to her, bringing Kate out of her thoughts. "So Kate," Pat Callahan asked. "I hear you're doing work for Hubert Andrews."

"Yes, do you know him?"

"Yes, I met him a while back. Is he still indecisive?"

Kate laughed. "Yes. Yes, he is."

"Ah, he's getting better," offered Alex, coming to Hubert's defense.

They talked a while about a few of the different jobs they currently had on the go. The Callahans and the Barkers found it interesting. Alex wasn't secretive with his family, although he rarely talked about work, but when he did he'd always described his boss to be extremely capable and intelligent. He hadn't overstated. Pat and Dan were impressed and so were the ladies. Stephanie, choosing not to join in the children's conversation, simply festered.

Dinner over, Kate helped once again, this time with the clean up. It had been a lovely evening and she found herself feeling somewhat sad at the prospect of its end. It seemed that the feeling was mutual amongst the Callahan crowd, except for Stephanie of course. She sighed in relief when her father announced he would be taking Kate home.

"Oh, I though she was going to sleep here too!" Stephanie said under her breath, but she'd made certain it was loud enough for Kate to hear. Unfortunately, so did her father.

"Stephanie! What's the matter with you?"

Stephanie's eyes did the usual spin around their sockets and she huffed noisily. "Sorry!"

"We'll talk later," her father promised, and allowing Kate to say another good-bye, he led his boss to the truck.

Alone, en route to Kate's home, Alex found it necessary to break the silence. "I'm sorry about Stephanie's outspokenness." He tried to excuse his daughter's behaviour.

"Wow. You weren't kidding about her." Kate smiled suddenly and shook her head. "I thought she was going to throw her dinner knife at me at one point."

"I know, I was watching her," he admitted.

"Well, I guess I can understand what she's feeling," she sighed. "Tonight was incredible. Your parents and in-laws don't even know me, yet they made me feel welcome."

"Unlike my daughter. God, I can't believe her sometimes. I'm really sorry."

"That's all right. Besides I have to apologize too, Alex. My grandmother knows about your kids now and she's happy about it! What are we going to do?"

"What do you want to do?"

Kate looked over to him. "Maybe I should just tell her the truth."

"That's up to you."

"Stephanie doesn't like me."

Alex smiled cynically. "Stephanie doesn't like anyone who might be a contender for my affections."

"So, how would we pull it off?"

"I don't know. I didn't think I'd have to involve them, remember?"

"I know. That's why I'm thinking to just come clean and—"

"I don't want to lie to them."

"I know. That's why I—"

Alex seemed not to hear her. "If I tell them what's going on, I'm not sure if the little ones won't get mixed up and say something, especially Leeza ... I don't want them to think it's alright to lie, either."

Alex pulled up into the drive. He turned in his seat and watched her, wanting so much to pull her into his arms....

Kate too watched him in the darkness. She had been enjoying this little game of pretence, perhaps too much; perhaps that was why that little voice in her head was telling her to put a stop to it – now! "It's your call, Alex. I've involved your kids when I promised that wouldn't happen. You decide. Let me know what you want to do."

Alex nodded, but didn't step out of the truck. He wanted to rush home. He knew he wanted to pursue this regardless of the peril of the unknown outcome. Thus this decision would involve at least four more people, besides his kids.

The children were in the living room watching TV when he arrived home. Alex tried to greet them, but they were so entranced by their program that they barely waved hello. Stephanie was trying hard not to make eye contact. She was not in the mood for a lecture. Asked where the grownups were, they pointed towards the kitchen where his parents and in-laws were gathered.

"Coffee dear?" his mother asked pouring her son a cup. Alex accepted the coffee and sat down.

"You've mentioned your boss before, but you never told us she was so young," Pat started.

"I think she's twenty-eight, twenty-nine."

"Smart cookie," he commented, and Alex nodded.

Dan held out his cup for a refill. "Yes, she is. She certainly knows her craft."

"She's not married," his mother-in-law said suddenly.

"No, she's engaged."

Gloria and Mary exchanged looks. "Yes … pity," Gloria said quietly.

Alex took that in. "Actually … it's good you're all here together. I have to tell you something."

This time everyone exchanged glances. "Oh my goodness!" exclaimed his mother-in-law excitedly. "Don't tell me *you're* the one she's engaged to!"

Alex nearly choked on his coffee. Then he laughed at his mother-in-law's knack for jumping to conclusions. "Of course not! Don't you think I'd tell you?"

"Sure hope so!" Dan chuckled.

Alex took a deep breath. "But, it's funny you should

say that.... "

"You're engaged to someone else," his father tried his hand at guessing.

"Will you stop," he laughed. Sobering, he got up and walked over to the kitchen door. "Hey guys. Guys!" he called in a louder voice. "Come in here for just a minute please." Alex sat again and waited for his kids to come into the kitchen. Leeza sat on his lap; the other three hung around their grandparents.

"My boss has run into a little problem and I've agreed to help her out of a bind," he began and everyone listened attentively. Stephanie stiffened instantly. "As you know," he said towards the children, "her grandmother is here visiting from Scotland," he continued. "Mrs. Wallace came to meet Kate's fiancé, but he ran off to Africa on some insignificant safari. Apparently the grandmother is ill, and hoping to grant her that wish, Kate asked me to pose as Jerry – that's the boyfriend, for the duration of the grandmother's stay – which is just a few short days." Alex stopped and looked around the table. There were no comments from the adults.

"And?" said Stephanie skeptically.

"And ... I agreed to help her. I didn't think I'd have to involve you kids or anybody else for that matter, but with Leeza getting hurt ... well, the call came in while we were having lunch with the grandmother and unfortunately she now thinks that her granddaughter's fiancé has four children.

"Oh great!" exclaimed a sarcastic Stephanie.

The adults all exchanged glances. "So now what?" asked his father.

"Well, I don't know what to do. I'd like to help her out. Kate offered to just tell her grandmother the truth, but if she does that, then Mrs. Wallace might be heartbroken and since she's old and ill, she might never meet the real fiancé. She really wanted to see her granddaughter settled...."

"Wow, what a tangled web. What happens when the fiancé returns?" asked his father-in-law.

"Dad, she's apparently very ill." And Dan nodded in understanding.

"You think she'll want to meet the kids," his mother stated.

"I'd bet on it," he confirmed. "How would you guys feel about that?" Alex asked his children.

"You want us to pretend that you are engaged to your boss," Stephanie said in an incredulous tone. "Wouldn't that be lying? You want us to lie, Dad? Haven't you always told us it's wrong to lie? I mean, what happened to that? We're supposed to forget all about that just because of her—"

"—Okay! I got the point Stephanie." Alex sighed. Had he expected any other reaction from his eldest daughter?

"It wouldn't really be a lie, honey," Mary intervened and at Stephanie's raised eyebrow, she added: "Well maybe just a little white lie. How long will she be staying, Alex?"

"She leaves Sunday."

Gloria decided to try to reason with her granddaughter. "Well, Steph, this request is a little strange, but your father is only trying to help Miss Wallace, who you know very well is his boss, to help make her old grandmother happy before she goes back to Scotland. I honestly don't think she'd be asking for your dad's help if she didn't feel absolutely compelled to do so. If you were in a similar situation I think you would go out of your way just to make one of us happy," she gestured around the room, and

Stephanie was momentarily shut down.

"It's okay with me, Dad," said Nicholas.

"Me too," shrugged Paul. "But do we have to kiss her and everything?"

"Kiss who?"

"The old grandmother."

"Oh, well maybe you can just shake her hand when you meet her."

Stephanie found her voice again. "*When* we meet her? So this is already a done deal?"

Alex shot her a look, but his youngest daughter posed another question and he preferred to answer her.

"I don't understand, Daddy?" Leeza was confused and he hated putting her in this predicament most of all.

Alex smiled down at his little girl, his fingers gently touching the area around the ugly stitches on her forehead. "It'll be like playing a game, Leeza – a pretend game, you play that all the time, don't you?" Alex asked and Leeza nodded. "Well, in this game, we are going to pretend that Daddy and Miss Wallace are engaged."

"What's engaged?"

"That's like boyfriend and girlfriend, only they've decided to be married."

"Oh."

"So if we have to meet Miss Wallace's grandmother, do you think you can just pretend that Miss Wallace and I are … engaged?"

"Why can't you really be engaged? I like Kate."

"Yes I know you do, but … well that's nice." Alex decided not to try to explain the improbability of this temporary situation to become permanent. "It's great that you've all agreed to help her – and me."

"I didn't agree," said Stephanie defiantly.

Alex's temper suddenly got the best of him. "Well, Steph, remember the other day when we were talking about majority ruling in decision making? Guess what? Majority wins. There's nothing for you to worry about, Stephanie. You really have to stop being so suspicious all the time. Kate is my boss; I work for her. She signs the cheques that I bring home so that I can pay the bills and all the activities you like to do and the clothes you like to wear. But you know something Stephanie, I might just want to have a real girlfriend one day and I don't think that's such a horrible thing for me to do. I loved your mom, I always will, but sometimes I get lonely. You have your brothers and sisters to play with or to fight with. I'm alone. I'd like to spend time with another adult."

"Am I the only one that's noticed he's calling her 'Kate' now? You never called her Kate!"

"Stephanie, I can't exactly call her Miss Wallace, if I'm supposed to be engaged to her! And isn't it just like you to change the subject and disregard the point I was trying to make."

"I didn't disregard anything, I made an observation. What's wrong with that? As for your 'point', you have adults you can talk to. You have a sister and parents and a mother-in-law and a father-in-law, and you have friends, lots of friends."

Alex put up his hands and shook his head in defeat. There was no winning with his daughter.

"Stephanie honey," interjected Gloria. "That's not the same thing. I know that if and when your daddy finds someone he'd like to be with it wouldn't mean that he's forgotten about your mom, that he doesn't love her anymore. But I think we're getting a little ahead of ourselves," she smiled. "Your dad is just helping out a friend, that's all, okay?"

Stephanie eyes turned towards her father and then looked away. "Fine," she said simply.

CHAPTER SIXTEEN

It was Alex who was late for work the next day. In a strange, pensive mood, he was surprised to see Kate and her grandmother both there so early.

"Good morning dear," Abigail came over to kiss him hello.

"Good morning." Alex had no choice now but to meet Kate halfway and accept the lips she offered.

Kate tried to convey through her eyes that she didn't know Gram would decide to accompany her to the office this morning, but Alex kept his eyes averted.

"Jerry dear, I was concerned about your daughter, Leeza, is it?"

"Yes, Leeza. She's better thanks." Alex gave her a strained smile.

"Kate tells me she's a real trooper."

"That she is, but today I let her stay home from school. She had a headache."

"That's understandable – four stitches on such a little forehead, after all!"

"A – Jerry, Gram was saying that she'd like to meet the children before she returns home," Kate relayed the news in a tentative voice, as if awaiting Alex's denial.

Alex looked tired, as though sleep had not come to him until the early hours of the morning, and Kate felt guilty. "When are you leaving?" he asked the grandmother.

"I'm booked for Sunday afternoon. Will it be a problem dear?"

He raked his fingers through his hair, his hand remaining at the base of his neck. "School nights are usually a little difficult, especially with all their activities," he said quietly. "How about Friday, tomorrow evening?"

Kate's head nearly became unhinged, and Alex looked up at her now.

"Are you sure?" she asked. "I mean, is … is Leeza up to it?"

"She's fine."

"That's wonderful," added Abigail.

"Why don't you come for dinner?" Alex invited in the same quiet tone, and Kate's eyebrows shot upward.

"No, no, dear. That's too much trouble." Abigail put up her hand, stopping Alex from insisting. "Jerry, we'll come for coffee tomorrow night, but what would you say about bringing your children to the house to spend the day with us on Saturday?"

Oh boy … thought Kate. This was going too far.

"Besides, I hear *Drucilla* will be out, so we need not worry about her frightening the children."

Alex had to smile at the old woman's description of Debra. "All right," agreed Alex, shocking Kate with his answer. "But the boys have a soccer game in the morning. We won't be free until about two o'clock."

"That's all right. At that time the children can still enjoy the pool in the sunshine, and they can eat when they want, whether it be lunch or dinner. I'll have Reginald man the outdoor grill. How's that?"

"Fine." Alex smiled his response.

"Wonderful! I look forward to that and to meeting the children tomorrow night!" Mrs. Wallace picked up her purse and made her way to the door. "Have a good day you two! Reginald is taking me shopping!"

Kate waited for the door to close behind her grandmother before turning to her assistant once again. "Alex … are you all right?"

"Yes, why?"

"You look so serious this morning."

"No, I'm fine."

"Alex, are you sure you want to do this? I know this must be very difficult for you. I mean … what about Stephanie?"

"What about her?" he asked off-handedly.

"Well…" Kate sighed. "Will she be okay with this – I mean, meeting my grandmother and all?"

"I had a talk with her last night – actually with everybody."

"And they think I should be committed."

"No. I told them the truth. You're my boss. You needed my help and that's what I'm doing. Besides, Stephanie can definitely handle the truth better than the lie."

"You mean lying that we're really together?" Kate asked and Alex nodded. "This is much more than either of us had planned for. Why are you doing it?"

"Because you asked."

"You think I'm awful, don't you?"

"I didn't say that."

"You didn't, because you're too kind. Alex, I'm using you and now your family, for my personal gain. Doesn't that bother you?"

"I'm helping out a friend," he shrugged. "And you're not really doing it for personal gain. I do know you – at least to some extent – remember?"

Kate watched him for a moment. "Thanks," she said simply.

"Finished?" he grinned and finally he transformed to the Alex she knew and – cared for so much.... "I have that proposal for you to look at.... "

Problems cleared with the electrical contractors, every job seemed to be running smoothly and on time. Business was on track. Their personal life was another story. The same thoughts invaded both their minds throughout the day.

Alex threw his pencil onto his desk and turned to stare outside the large window. People outside hurried to and fro, tourists snapped photos, boats sailed by in the distant harbour, but he saw nothing. Kate had enjoyed herself last night. She had helped the ladies prepare dinner; she had conversed with his parents and in-laws as though she'd known them for years. His touch too, she seemed to enjoy. She wasn't supposed to, but she did. He could tell. Did he dare hope for something more permanent?

Kate paced the carpeted floor of her office. Things were not supposed to have become so complicated. Alex was supposed to pretend to be Jerry for just a few days. Her grandmother would have left and everything would go back to normal. That's what she had expected. She hadn't planned for Gram to meet his children; then neither had *she.* Her grandmother had been beguiled by those children, but then hadn't *she*? Her grandmother had already fallen in love with Alex, but then—

The telephone rang. Saved by the bell, she thought to herself.

Kate was a bundle of nerves by the time Alex arrived that evening. Her mother had decided to have dinner at home, much to her daughter's displeasure. Debra's animosity towards Alex was blatant and Kate was certain that she wouldn't hide it tonight.

When the doorbell rang she was quick to answer it. "My mother is staying for dinner," she whispered, leaning close to her assistant.

Alex handed her the bottles of red and white wine. "This should be fun," he replied with a smile, as Abigail walked towards them.

Oddly, his appearance calmed Kate, at least until her mother made her grand entrance into the dining room. She wore a lime green dress. Short and snug, it revealed her assets well. Orange nails matched her lipstick, as well as her hair. "Good evening … Jerry," she drawled as she made her way to the far end of the table. She raised an eyebrow towards the rest who had remained standing. "Well? What are you waiting for? Cook said dinner was ready. I have an appointment."

Within moments, a delicious dinner of roast pork, baked potatoes, steamed vegetables and rice was being served. Kate didn't taste it. She awaited her mother's scorn to manifest into words at any time. It did.

"So tell me Kate," Debra blurted suddenly, interrupting the conversation between Alex and Abigail. "What do you intend to do with Alex once you and Jerry are married?"

Kate choked on her third glass of wine. "What?"

Abigail looked from one to the other, and Kate tried to regain her composure and reply in a calm and steady voice. "Alex will retain his position. There's no reason for anyone to be transferred from their current post."

"What is Alex's position Kate?" Abigail asked innocently.

Kate's eyes flew to Alex. "Gram, Alex is an architect and a structural engineer and in fact he often—"

"—And he often forgets he's *just* an employee, paid to do a job, and nothing more."

Alex took a sip of his wine, glaring at her atop the rim of his crystal goblet. His boss wasn't so quiet.

"How dare you? You have no right to judge Alex or any of my employees for that matter! You have nothing to do with the business, thank God!"

But Debra continued her accusations. "I don't have to be there to see what's going on!"

"Really?" Kate raised her eyes heavenward. "My mother, the all-knowing, all-seeing!"

"Yes, I am – just that! *You* on the other hand, have lost all sense of perception – in fact all of your senses! You stop this Kate, before it's too late! You stand to lose everything and I won't have it!" Debra dropped her fork noisily and stormed out of the house.

The sigh of relief was common and audible amongst all three.

"What was that all about?" Abigail wanted to know. "Why does she dislike this Alex lad so intensely?"

Kate was too angry to answer immediately. Alex responded instead.

"I don't think you have anything to worry about. I believe that Debra ..." her name stuck in his throat, "only wants what's best for Kate."

"Oh yes! She's just trying to resemble a caring mother, and we know how plausible that is!"

"Dear ... you know I don't think very highly of your mother, but for some reason she believes that you should be wary of this man."

"Wary? I would trust Alex with my life!" Kate spoke with conviction and Abigail seemed to be taken aback with that claim. Realizing that her supposed fiancé was still sitting across from her, she poured herself another glass and drank it down. "Can we change the subject please? She's gone; I'd like to pretend she won't be returning."

Abigail looked at Alex who in turn gave her a sheepish smile and a shrug, hoping to make light of the entire strange conversation.

Thankfully, Abigail did not pursue it further, and instead reverted the conversation to a simpler one. "Jerry, come. Let us have tea in the living room."

Alex looked over to Kate who seemed to be immersed – *literally* – in her wine, and then helped Abigail to the couch.

Pouring the last drops into her glass, Kate looked down into the bottle. It was gone, all gone, she thought sadly, but so was her mother. She knew what her mother had meant. Perhaps her mother *was* all knowing.... It didn't matter. She sighed. Nothing mattered ... nothing except love and happiness....

Feeling inexplicably claustrophobic, Kate left the table to walk quite unsteadily to the living room. She watched her grandmother as she listened with a smile to whatever Alex was saying. She watched Alex intently. Then abruptly she pushed away from the wall on which she leaned for support and came to stand behind him, bending towards him.

"I have one question," she said, her voice taking on a suggestive tone. "Isn't this tie choking you yet?"

Alex looked up at her as she reached around his shoulders to undo his tie. He chuckled at her obvious tipsy state, all the while his vital signs skyrocketing at her closeness. "It wasn't."

Dispensing with the tie, Kate's arms continued their journey over his chest, snuggling her face in his neck. Alex caressed her hands as they slid across the front of his shirt, hoping to nonchalantly stop their movement.

Abigail smiled at her granddaughter. "Well, I think this is my cue to call it a night!"

And stopping Alex from protesting, she stood and waved her hand. "Goodnight, lovebirds!"

Left alone, Kate walked the short distance around the couch and draped herself onto his lap.

Alex watched her, his eyes sparkling, but the feelings she was stirring in him bordered on erotic. "What are you doing?"

Kate started to unbutton his shirt, reveling in the touch of his skin under her fingers.

"What does it look like?" Her lips replaced her fingers, scattering kisses.

Okay, this wasn't funny anymore. Alex took hold of her shoulders, lifting her from him. "Kate...."

"I love it when you say my name," she breathed, unsuccessfully trying to kiss him.

"That's your name."

"You never call me 'Kate'. You call me 'boss'.

"Because you are my boss, remember?"

"I'm not your boss right now..." she purred, undoing her own buttons, revealing the lacey white bra underneath.

Alex watched her, unable to avert his gaze and this time when Kate cupped his face in the palms of her hands and pressed her lips to his ... this time she succeeded, she had succeeded in bringing down his defenses.

Alex returned her kiss with the same ardor, the same passion. He knew it was wrong, but he wasn't in the mood to listen to his brain at that moment.

He lay her down against the plush pillows of the couch, his hands sliding along her hip to rest against her bare ribcage, stopping for a moment as if willing himself from going further.

"Alex.... " Kate whispered his name, her invitation obvious.

However, it was not going to be accepted. Reason finally surfacing, Alex slid his arm under her legs and lifted her to sit away from him.

"Alex?"

"I think you need to get to bed," he said standing.

Kate stood as well, and took hold of his arm, again trying to reach for him. "All right, let's go."

"No. I mean, you need to get to bed – to sleep – alone."

Kate giggled. "That's no fun. Come on, I promise to be gentle."

Alex shook his head. He wondered just how much of this she would remember tomorrow. "Good night."

"Good night? Where are you going?"

"Home."

"Home?" she repeated, following him, oblivious to the fact that her blouse hung open, as did his shirt. "Why?"

"Because I have to pick up the kids from my parents."

"Oh. Well, can't they stay there tonight?"

"No. They have school tomorrow."

Kate whined. "Bummer!"

Alex tried to pry her from him, unable to hide his amusement at this point. "I think you had a little too much to drink tonight don't you?"

"Maybe ... but it feels good, you feel good. Again she spread her hands on his bare chest. Again she pressed herself against him, offering her lips to him and at least once more he accepted, crushing her against him for one more moment before pushing her away from him.

"Kate," he said, holding at arm's length. "Go to sleep. I'll see you tomorrow."

Alex listened outside the door to make certain Kate had locked the door behind him, and satisfied, he climbed into his vehicle and headed for home – or his parents' home. He'd better put himself together before his daughter saw him. He didn't feel like being scrutinized tonight. Not tonight.

He realized Kate had one too many glasses of wine and that he shouldn't have taken advantage of the situation, but how could he deny her invitation? There was nothing he wanted more. How could he deny himself the touch of her hands, the taste of her lips....

Dark sunglasses hid Kate's bloodshot eyes the next morning. That earned her a chuckle from her assistant/fiancé.

"What's so funny?" she snapped.

"Nothing. Headache?"

"No," she denied defensively, albeit untruthfully. "Why?"

"Just a hunch," he smiled and returned his attention to his paperwork.

Kate glared at him overtop the sunglasses and entered her office. She stayed there for hours before she finally resurfaced for a cup of coffee.

Alex was at the photocopier. "Feeling better?" He couldn't resist.

Kate looked at him, suspicion creeping into her eyes. "What happened last night?"

"What do you mean?" he asked innocently.

"You know what? You're not going to goad me. I obviously made a fool of myself, but hey, I don't remember, so...."

Alex flashed her a grin. "You didn't make a fool of yourself, you just had a bit too much to drink, but okay, I'll drop it. Morty Schefield called," he informed her, and Kate followed him to his office. "The groundbreaking ceremony is today. He asked if we're going to be there. It begins in an hour."

Kate rubbed her temple, unknowingly admitting to the headache. "Sure, I guess so."

So an hour later, her eyes closing behind her sunglasses, Kate stood alongside her assistant at the groundbreaking ceremony. The owners of the building, the city councillors and other officials, as well as Kate and Alex, the representatives of the architectural firm, were there to commemorate the event. Photographers were there to immortalize it. But through it all, Kate racked her brain trying to remember to events of the previous evening.

Stifling a yawn upon returning to the office, Alex's suggestion that she go home and go to bed caused her memory to come rushing back. Kate swung around to face him, removing her sunglasses in the process. "Alex! My God, I tried to – why didn't you stop me?" she asked quietly and he realized she had remembered.

"I should have, I'm sorry."

"No. I have to apologize. You wanted this to remain simple. What must you think of me? I shouldn't have behaved like that."

"Hey, you just said ... I didn't stop you, well ... not completely anyway. I ... you didn't exactly overpower me."

Kate tried desperately to understand what that meant. "No?"

"No." Alex smiled and a warm giddy feeling spread all over her. "Did you see your mother this morning?"

"Are you kidding? She doesn't like sunlight unless a beach is involved, which disproves the theory that she's a vampire."

Alex chuckled. "So your grandmother didn't mention anything about last night's events?"

Kate felt her temperature rising again. "Events?" She hoped he didn't mean her behavior!

"What your mother said...."

"Oh! What was that again?"

"She was saying, more or less, that I am a threat to you...."

"Right. I'm sorry about that. But no, thank God, Gram didn't mention anything about that. I think she realized that my mother is simply a lunatic."

"Good. Now I'm going to leave, so I can prepare for my fiancée's visit tonight."

Kate put a hand to her mouth. "Oh my! That's tonight! I'd better get home too, cake on a tube of make-up under my eyes; make myself presentable!"

CHAPTER SEVENTEEN

Alex put away the last of the dishes that Stephanie and Nicholas had dried.

"So Dad … what's she like?" asked Nicholas, and his sister turned watchful eyes towards him.

"Who?"

"Your boss's grandmother. I mean, is she really sick?"

"She doesn't look sick, if that's what you're worried about."

"Oh. I was just wondering if she was going to start coughing all over the place.

"Nicholas!" Alex reprimanded and Stephanie rolled her eyes in disgust.

"Well? I was just wondering, that's all." Then, "What about your boss?"

Alex glanced over to Stephanie, before answering his son. "What about her?"

"What happens when her real boyfriend gets back? I mean,

what's she going to say to her grandmother then?"

Alex had wondered how that was going to unravel, but at that point it would be out of his hands and none of his business. "I don't know Nick, obviously she thinks that need won't arise. She thinks her grandmother may never meet Jerry, but if something changes ... well that's something she'll have to deal with at that time." The doorbell rang and that put an end to their conversation, and a start to Stephanie's uneasiness.

Abigail Wallace arrived with gifts for the four children, and Kate brought dessert for all to share. This was a generous gesture, a kind gesture, one that Alex had not expected, but the children seemed very willing to accept. Even Stephanie had been in awe when she opened her gift to reveal a beautiful manicure set. Well, Alex thought, at least that kept her eyes on something other than his boss – if only for a short while!

Stephanie still remained quieter than the rest, speaking only when a question was posed to her, but the other children warmed quickly to Abigail. She seemed to love being with children. Leeza informed her of her daily events, the recent stitches at the forefront of the conversation. The boys too, told her about the various activities and sports they enjoyed, and Abigail recounted stories of Scotland and visiting the Queen when she was just a girl Stephanie's age.... And Stephanie was actually intrigued.

Alex glanced over to Kate and found her watching him. She gave him a little smile, shrugging her shoulders. He understood. They were getting along wonderfully, and soon it would all come to an end.

Before long it was bedtime, and the children said their good-nights and scurried off. Leeza held back.

"I'll come tuck you in, Leeza," her dad offered.

"Daddy? Can Gram tuck me in tonight?" Leeza asked shyly. "Maybe she can tell me another story?"

"Oh, Leeza, I don't know–"

"What a dear! I'd love to, Leeza!" The elderly woman took the little girl by the hand and walked slowly up the stairs to her bedroom.

Left alone, Kate helped clear the dessert dishes and wrapping paper that had been crumpled and left on the floor. That done, Kate came to sit next to Alex, and he had to find something to talk about.

"She's amazing with the kids."

"Yes, she is. You see what I meant before? That's what I remember about her. That's why I couldn't disappoint her."

"I doubt that you could," Alex said quietly.

"I doubt that *you* could either. She loves you." Kate's hand was suddenly on his thigh. It had been an innocent gesture this time, it hadn't been a pass, but the effect was the same nevertheless.

"Hey," he said, trying desperately to make light of it. "Watch where you put your hands, I'm only human."

Kate decided to play along. "Why, Alex Callahan, do I turn you on?"

"Naturally, without the aid of a bottle of wine, you'd remain indifferent if I had my hand two inches.... " Alex stopped short as his hand slid up her bare inner thigh. Her breath caught in her throat, her heartbeat accelerated to dangerous speeds.

"You didn't take advantage of my less-than-sober state last night," she stated quietly. "Why was that? Was it because you didn't want to or because you were being ... nice?"

"I'd say the latter."

"Maybe you should stop being so nice." Her eyes held his as her words rushed through Alex's brain. She hadn't had anything to drink tonight. Not unless she spiked her coffee while he wasn't looking!

Perhaps it was wishful thinking, but Alex thought he'd heard Abigail start her descent from the second floor. He had to take advantage of the opportunity given to him; he had to stop being so nice, after all. "She's back.... "

Her hand covered his, silently revealing her pleasure in his advances, encouraging him to continue. Still, Alex's hand made a slow retreat from her thigh, although it didn't leave her body altogether. This time his hand was more discrete, choosing to slide over her short cotton skirt to rest at the curve of her hip. The fingers of his other hand pulled playfully at the stands of her hair, continuing their path to the base of her neck, drawing her towards him as he covered her willing lips with his in a soft, wet kiss that seemed to last forever.

"All tucked in! Shall we go, Kate?" Abigail announced as she entered the living room. "Oops, I'm so sorry!"

Alex reluctantly lifted his lips from Kate's. Her eyes were dazed with passion, her fingers brushing across his mouth.

Kate didn't want to leave, but she had no choice. She mustered the strength to pull herself from that couch and stand on her wobbling legs. And with a possessive hand on her hip, Alex suggested to walk them out to their car.

He helped Abigail into the passenger seat and then went around to Kate's side, leaning on her open window. "I'll see you tomorrow."

Kate nodded in response and put a hand to his cheek, drawing his face close so that she may again feel his lips on hers. " 'Night.... "

During their ride home, Kate contemplated telling her grandmother the truth. She probably would have if not for her continuous praises of this new extended family. Abigail gave her blessings once again, and told her granddaughter that she could not have made an old woman any happier. Kate bit her tongue.

The Callahan clan arrived at Kate's home Saturday afternoon with towels and swimsuits tucked away in five separate totes.

"Welcome, children!" Abigail exclaimed as she greeted each one and led them outside where Kate and Reginald prepared chairs and umbrellas.

Kate too said her hellos and introduced the children to Reginald. Reginald, it seemed, had a soft spot for children as well as the elderly. Immediately he led them all to the cabana where they changed into their suits. This left Kate to finally greet her fiancé – properly.

She took the few steps to Alex while he stood speaking to Abigail. "Hi," she whispered and raised her lips to his.

Alex responded willingly – and – hurriedly. All contact had to be kept in check today, and that was something that did not sit very well with him. An arm around her back, he gazed down into her upturned face as if trying to read her thoughts. Her longing, he thought, was too well displayed and that was too confusing. He detached himself as the first of the children appeared from across the yard.

"So ... your mother's not going to be here?" he asked, trying to start conversation that involved someone or some*thing* other than the two of them.

Abigail was quick to answer. "No, thank goodness!" And they all laughed.

"Yes, that would have been interesting!" Alex said sarcastically, picking up his tote bag. "I'm going to go change."

"Need any help?" Kate asked mischievously.

Alex glanced back towards her, and knowing full well the impossibility of that occurrence, he called back, "Sure!"

Kate shuddered. If the children were not there… "You tease!"

They all played in the pool for hours. Marco Polo, volleyball, and even tag were games that were sure to include everyone. The children were enjoying themselves – even Stephanie seemed to have forgotten to see Kate as a potential threat. The adults as well, were content. Gram, in her walking shorts, laughed from her seat under the protective shade of the umbrella as she watched Reginald repeatedly being hit in the head with the soft sponge volleyball. Their games also gave Kate and Alex the opportunity to touch without suspicions surfacing, and that alone made the day worthwhile.

They stopped for dinner, only to return to the pool after a short game of Cricket. Reginald was the instructor and his comical antics delighted the children and adults the same.

As the bright orange sun descended into the western horizon, Alex decided it was time to vacate the pool and change. The day had been successful. Dare he wish for a continuance?

Without much fuss the boys headed for the cabana, and Kate made a suggestion.

"Girls, how 'bout leaving the cabana to the boys? Want to go upstairs? You can each have your own bathroom and then we'll all change in my room. It'll be fun. What do you think?

Leeza was naturally the first to agree, but Stephanie surprisingly did not refuse. In fact, she found herself wanting to go inside with Kate, seeing her room....

After their showers the girls gathered in Kate's room as she had suggested. She handed Stephanie perfumed body cream and helped Leeza with hers. "The chlorine will dry out our skin, but I'm sure you know that," she said and the girls nodded.

"Yes," Stephanie agreed. "We always use a moisturizer after swimming, but I like this one."

"You may keep the tube – both of you."

"No, no. That's okay," Stephanie protested, but Kate insisted and Stephanie thanked her, actually smiling. She watched with interest as Kate slipped on a red floral sundress. Her brain wrestled with the idea to issue a compliment. Oh well, what the heck? "I like your dress," she said almost shyly.

Kate felt extreme joy suddenly. Stephanie was not merely acknowledging her presence – she was actually making conversation. This was a good sign, a wonderful sign.... "Really? Thanks. You know I'd be happy to take you to the store where I bought it."

"Oh well forget that!" Stephanie waved disappointedly. "It wouldn't fit me. I'm still wearing kids' clothes."

"They have smaller sizes, Steph, but either way don't feel bad. You're just a late bloomer, that's all."

"Sure," Stephanie was skeptical.

"Honest. We're all different Stephanie, but our bodies don't make us who we are. Someone may have all it takes as far as physical appearance, they may not necessarily have anything here," she pointed to her head. "And what would you rather have?"

Stephanie managed a smile and Leeza giggled.

"You're petite like your mom," Kate told her.

"How do you know?" Stephanie's expression became somber once again and Kate thought she that may have overstepped.

"Your dad told me one day. He also said," adding quickly, "that he thought your mom was the most beautiful woman in the world."

Stephanie's heart swelled. "He did?"

"Yes, he did."

Stephanie's eyes rounded. "I have a picture of her."

Kate was pleased. It looked like she'd finally broken the ice. "I'd love to see it."

Stephanie dug into the little purse that she had tucked away in her bag and retrieved a small wallet and from there she extracted a picture. She looked at it for a moment and then extended it to Kate.

Kate felt something constricting her throat. It was a family photo taken soon after Leeza was born, she imagined. Julie Callahan was pictured holding the baby. Alex and the other children gathered all around. Her long brown hair was gathered away from her delicate face. Warm eyes and a welcoming smile told Kate that she was a wonderful person.

"Your mom was *very* beautiful. This is a beautiful picture, too." Guilt suddenly jabbed her and Stephanie felt like a heel. It could very well be that Kate had no interest in her father, that she had no hidden agenda other than truly trying to make her grandmother happy. She was being so nice, and in return, Stephanie was being deceitful. The conversation she'd overheard in Kate's office affected not only her father, but his boss as well. Perhaps she should come clean and tell her what she'd learned, but her father would naturally have to be told as well, and then what? What would he think of her, having kept such a secret? Telling could make matters worse! No … she couldn't….

"We have a larger one in our rooms," Stephanie informed her, returning the picture to her wallet and guilty thoughts to the back of her mind.

"I'm sorry about your mom, Steph."

Stephanie never knew what to say when people said that. She was actually grateful for her sister's interjection.

"My nail polish came off in the pool," Leeza announced.

"Let's fix it. Come on, we'll give each other a manicure."

When the girls finally made their way downstairs, Alex gave a questioning look towards Kate. "Everything all right?" he asked. "I was about to send a search party."

Leeza giggled. "Daddy, we were doing *manicures*!"

Later, after an array of desserts ranging from layered cake to butter tarts, the children sat scattered on the living room carpet playing board games with Reginald. It had been an absolutely wonderful day.

Abigail had been brought back in time to a much happier era, a time when her own son was just a tot. Hers had been a well-behaved child with only minor temper tantrums, she thought with a smile. Raising four small children was a task not easily achieved, and she felt compelled to tell Alex so. But raising four small children not your own could be impossible in some cases.

She turned to her granddaughter who sat next to her and

took hold of her hand. "I'm so proud of you as well, Kate."

Kate was a little taken aback. "Why me?"

"Because it takes a special kind of woman to be able to handle a ready-made family, no matter how perfect it may be."

Stephanie choked on her juice.

"However, I'm also proud of you children. I also know that it is not easy to accept someone new into your home. I am so happy that you have. I think you and your father are just what my Kate needed to make her life worthwhile, to make her life complete. I've never seen her happier or more at ease and I thank you for that."

Kate was ready to burst, but then so was Stephanie. Unfortunately Stephanie didn't have the experience to suppress her emotions; she asked to be excused and left the room.

"Did I say something wrong?"

"No, not at all." Alex tried to dismiss his daughter's abrupt retreat. "You're very kind. It's just that Stephanie's a little overwhelmed by the whole situation. It's been a little more difficult for her to be all that you said."

"Oh! I hope I didn't upset her too much …" she said pensively.

"I'm sure she's fine. I'll just go speak to her." Alex forced himself to remain calm as strode off in search of his daughter, although his stomach was in knots. Kate, her heart in her throat, watched in silence.

Stephanie had gone outside to sit on one of the cushioned patio chairs.

"Steph? Are you okay?"

"This isn't right, Dad," she said quietly, and Alex understood.

"Mrs. Wallace is a nice lady."

"You're right. It isn't right. It wasn't supposed to go this far. You children were not supposed to be involved."

"So you keep saying, but we are and now we've been forced to lie to her too. If she wants to lie to her grandmother ... well that's up to her, but we shouldn't have to."

Alex bowed his head. So, it seemed he'd taught his children well.... Unfortunately he'd learned this because he'd placed them in this awkward situation. His determination to help Kate – to please Kate whatever the cost blinded him from determining right from wrong by involving his children. He shouldn't have done that.

"I'm sorry about this Stephanie. I'll talk to Kate. I'm going to suggest we tell Mrs. Wallace the truth, but ultimately the decision must be hers."

Stephanie shrugged. "I don't think Mrs. Wallace will be too happy with her. What if she never wants to see her again?"

This was a first, Alex thought to himself. Was his daughter showing concern for Kate? "She won't be happy, I'm certain of that, but the rest ... I don't know," he told her quietly and he motioned to return inside.

"There you are!" Abigail said unnecessarily. "Mrs. Johnson has just served some delicious triple fudge ice cream. Come Stephanie," she patted the empty cushion on her left – Leeza sat on her right. "Sit, have your ice cream before it melts."

Alex scanned the room for the missing Kate, and noticing, Abigail informed him of her whereabouts. "Kate asked me to tell you, dear, that she'd remembered she'd forgotten to do something at the office. Apparently it was quite important – something about Mr. Andrews, I believe. She said to tell you that if she's not back before you leave, she'd call you later."

"Oh." Alex knew this had been a fabricated excuse to leave the house. Her grandmother's words had intensified Kate's guilt much like that of his daughter. She was upset and as usual she'd escaped to the comfort of her office – and he had to go to her.

"I think I know what she's referring to, but I was working on that file today. I'd better go and give her a hand."

Stephanie looked up at him, suspicion resurfacing. "You're going?"

"Would you mind very much? I won't be long I promise, but I think I may have the information Kate's looking for. I should go help her or she might be there all night."

"I guess. So do we wait here?"

"If it's all right with Mrs. Wallace – I mean Gram."

"Definitely dear. You go on. We'll be fine, won't we," she asked, tightening her arm around Leeza, and Leeza giggled.

"Reginald!" Gram called her trusted friend who had gone to retrieve another board game.

"Come help me keep these children amused, will you dear?"

Alex promised his children he'd be back soon and hurried to Kate.

She was in her office, as he had expected. Alex didn't bother to turn on the light. The full moon was shedding a strange blue-grey hue into the room, illuminating her slender form as she sat slouched in the leather armchair, her head in her hands. Startled by the sound of footsteps entering her office, Kate looked up, her tear-stained face shimmering in the moonlight. "What are you doing here?"

"I know you didn't forget anything. Are you all right?"

"No, I'm not all right! Did you hear all that? She's making me sound like Joan of Arc's sister or something! I feel horrible!" Kate bowed her head once again. "I'm a horrible person. I've lied to my grandmother and as if that wasn't enough, I've involved you in my lie and now your kids have had to lie as well – just to keep my original lie!" Kate stood now and paced. "I put so much emphasis on things that in the end are really not so important after all."

Alex took the few steps to stand in front of her. "Look on the bright side. It's over. She'll be leaving tomorrow. You've accomplished what you set out to do, didn't you? She's handed you the business and most of all you've made her happy. That's the important thing, isn't it?"

Kate watched him in silence.

And Alex had to voice the fact that tore him apart. "When Jerry comes back, you'll be married as planned and you'll have everything you wanted."

"Will I?"

Alex wasn't sure what he'd missed.

"I won't have you," she said quietly.

Alex's heart skipped a beat. He shook his head slowly. "Kate."

"I thought you were married. That blinded me to the obvious—"

"Kate—"

"Why did you have to be so damned perfect?"

"I'm not perfect," he stated, still reeling from her declaration.

"No? Should I use another word?" Kate slowly closed the gap between them. "How about 'wonderful'? How about 'amazing', 'remarkable', 'extraordinary'?"

The fingers that she placed on his chest trailed upward to tangle themselves in the thick black hair that covered the collar of his polo shirt. "Perfect," she whispered.

Alex's mind was racing just about as fast as his heart. He wasn't sure what was happening, but all he was certain of at the moment was the fact that her body was pressed against his and the lips that she offered couldn't be kept waiting any longer.

His hands circled her back, drawing her closer still as he surrendered to her requests, fueling his own desires at the same time. "Kate..." he breathed against her mouth. "We can't...."

"Shh.... " Kate tugged on his shirt, lifting it over his head, dropping it somewhere behind him. She buried her face in his neck, her lips following the hands that slid over the smooth skin of his shoulders, over the silky hairs on his broad chest to the waistband of his jeans, pushing them away.

Alex surrendered to her demands. Lifting her to him, his hands too pulled on the thin straps of her dress, slipping it down over her shoulders, over her hips and onto the floor. His eyes drank in the sight before him. "You're so beautiful," he whispered, as he trailed his lips over her soft skin. His hands slid down over her hips, disposing of the last stitch of clothing, as his mouth covered the pulsating vein in the curve of her neck.

Alex lay her down onto the plush carpet beneath them. Lowering himself onto her, they made love as if it had been the first time for both. They savoured every moment, every inch of their bodies until finally they lay spent in each other's arms, completely satisfied, completely content.

"Alex?" Kate whispered.

"Umm?"

"I—" The telephone rang and both sat up, startled by the sound. "Do you think it's the kids?" she asked.

"Stephanie," he returned with a wry smile. Alex stood and walked to the desk to answer the call. "Yes?"

"Hi, Dad," Stephanie replied. "Are you almost finished?"

"Just about," he answered as Kate came to stand behind him, wrapping her arms possessively around his chest.

"Are you leaving soon?"

"Yes, Steph, we'll be leaving shortly. Is everyone behaving?" he asked, stopping Kate's hands from wandering.

"Yes. Just hurry up, okay?"

"Okay, see you in a few minutes." Alex hung up the receiver and turned into Kate's arms. "You're naughty. I was speaking to my daughter."

"Sorry," she smiled mischievously. "I guess we have to go."

"I guess," he agreed watching her, admiring how the moonlight seemed to somehow enhance her beauty, shedding a soft – almost angelic glow around her features. Unable to refrain himself he lowered his lips to hers once more, as if branding her his – tonight, tomorrow, forever….

Preferring to drive back with Alex, Kate left her car at the office. She held his hand for the duration of the ride, kissing hungrily at every traffic light.

When Kate and Alex entered the living room, both laughed at the sight of Reginald contorting his tall body, stretching his limbs to reach the round coloured circles on the mat of the Twister game. The children were enjoying themselves and Alex couldn't have been happier. Stephanie's eyes, however, were quick to scan her father's employer. Kate's eye makeup was a little smudged, but she looked – normal and she returned her attention to the game.

"Did you do what you had to do?" asked Gram.

"Yes," replied Kate, squeezing Alex's hand behind her.

"Coffee?" Gram offered, and both accepted, sitting down on the opposite couch.

They stayed a little while longer, enjoying the children's laughter and Reginald's antics. Occasionally their eyes would lock, speaking their unspeakable thoughts, plainly reliving the events of mere moments ago.

Finally Leeza had had enough. "Daddy, I'm tired," she announced rubbing her eyes.

"You've had quite a day. Why don't you go and thank Mrs. Wallace and Reginald and Kate of course, and we'll get you home to bed, okay?"

"Okay," Leeza nodded.

"Same goes for the rest of you," he called to the others. Paul and Nicholas complained, but they did as they were told. Stephanie didn't need coaxing.

Their hearts pounding in their chests at prospect of being separated and without being able to properly say goodnight, Alex and Kate stood close together, their fingers again entwined behind them as the children said their good-byes at the door. They gazed into each other's eyes, both feeling what the other felt, silently expressing their thoughts and desires.

"I'll see you tomorrow," Alex said finally.

"Early," Kate urged and he smiled as he stepped into his truck.

Alex couldn't have been happier. Something he had thought could only be a fantasy had become a reality. He had wanted to make love to her. He had never denied that, but Kate had wanted it too. He had no reason to feel awkward or out of line. In fact it was Kate who had initiated the intimacy during this charade. It was Kate who had initiated what had happened tonight. Neither had actually spoken about their feelings for each other, but their actions, what they'd shared, spoke volumes.

The difficult task was to tell Stephanie how he felt about Kate; how he was convinced that she would become a good mother to his children. This task was something that he was dreading. "Guys," Alex called, stopping them from going up to their rooms. "Come sit with me for a minute. I'd like to run something by you."

Stephanie's eyes immediately narrowed with suspicion as she joined her brothers and sister on the couch next to her father.

"What's the matter Daddy?" asked Leeza.

"Nothing's the matter. I'd just like to ask you something."

"What?" they asked.

"How was your day today; did you have a nice time?"

They all nodded their heads enthusiastically. "Yeah, it was fun," they agreed.

"Well … I was just wondering … how would you feel if I told you that I might like to … go out with Kate – for real?"

Nicholas and Paul shrugged their shoulders finding no problem in the possibility. Leeza's eyes rounded as she grinned with her reply. "Oh yes, Daddy! I like Kate!"

Alex returned her smile, having expected that response. Then he looked at Stephanie, who as he'd also expected, had remained quiet, although he knew far too well that this state of calm was only temporary. The storm would hit – and with fury!

"Steph?"

Stephanie gave a cynical laugh. "How did I know this would happen? How did I know?"

"Well Steph, I don't know how you knew, because I sure didn't."

"No? You think I'm stupid?"

"No, I don't think you're stupid. How can you say that?"

"You did so know! As soon as I saw her when she first came here, I knew you liked her! This was just a lie. You said you had to pretend to be her boyfriend for her grandmother's benefit, but that wasn't true, was it? It was just so you could break the news to us!"

"No, Steph. You're wrong. What I told you was the truth. I didn't lie to you. You're right about one thing and that is that I did like her before," he admitted, and Stephanie huffed indignantly. "I have for while now, but she was not only my boss, she was also engaged."

"And what? Now she's not? You said she still is, isn't she?" she said smugly.

"Yes … but while we've been pretending to be engaged to each other we – I've realized that I'd like to be with her for real."

Stephanie huffed again. "Oh, so all of a sudden it doesn't matter that she's your boss and that she's engaged to someone else?"

"It matters … but I think that she feels the same way – that … that makes it different."

"You kill me! When you do something wrong, it's okay because you're an adult, right?"

"Stephanie, I know how you feel about me becoming

involved with someone else—"

"—Well then, why are you?"

"Because Steph … I'm lonely. I love you – all of you; you're my life, but you're not going to stay little forever. As you become older you'll find your own way with your friends and relationships; you won't have time for me anymore. I don't think it would be so wrong for me to want to share my life with another woman. I'd like it to be Kate."

"Looks like you've made up your mind. Why are you bothering to ask for our opinion?"

"Because we're a family and I've always asked your opinion on things. We've always discussed everything. Your brothers and sister lost their mother too, Stephanie. They're willing to accept the fact that I'd like to move on, why can't you?"

"You don't have to worry about what I think, Dad. Majority rules, right?" she spat.

Alex could only stare after her as she strode determinedly up the stairs to her room.

"She'll get over it, Dad," Nicholas assured him. "She just misses Mom."

"I know. So do I and I'm sure you do too."

Nicholas and Paul bowed their head and nodded. "We do Dad," Nicholas said quietly, "but Mom's gone. It's not right that Steph wants you to be alone forever."

Alex rustled his son's hair and drew him into his arms. "Thanks," he told him quietly. Paul and Leeza joined the circle and Alex kissed the tops of their heads, as his eyes became misty with tears.

CHAPTER EIGHTEEN

Stephanie was the last to arrive at the breakfast table the next morning.

"Good morning," Alex greeted her, but Stephanie didn't answer and kept her eyes averted as she poured herself a glass of milk.

"Pancakes?" Alex asked.

"No thank you," she mumbled.

Nicholas, Paul and Leeza all looked at her and then their father. Alex shrugged and made a funny face drawing laughter from the three. Stephanie didn't even look up.

"Steph," Alex said, "I was just telling your brothers and sister that Gramma Mary will be taking you to church this morning."

Stephanie's eyes did the usual inspection of the ceiling, annoyed at the realization that nothing had changed since last night. "Oh gee, I wonder where you're going."

"Kate's grandmother leaves today. Kate and I will be taking

her to the airport," he answered curtly, and Stephanie shrugged her indifference. "And Stephanie, maybe we need to make another appointment with Dr. Weisberg." Uncommonly clueless that morning, she turned narrowed eyes towards her father. "Yes, maybe he can give you something to stop this continuous eye rotation."

There was a burst of laughter from the other children, which only infuriated Stephanie more. "Very funny!"

The doorbell rang and that put an end to further discussions, although the laughter continued. After receiving a quick explanation for this morning's merriment, Mary and Pat gathered the children into their car.

"Should I make lunch for the kids, Alex?" Mary asked her son.

"Sure Mom. That'd be great. I'm not sure what time I'll be back."

"Okay. Gloria and Dan are coming for lunch too. Come by later."

"Bring Kate," winked his father, sticking his head out of the opened window.

Alex smiled at his parents. "I will. Thanks," he called after them as they pulled out of the driveway.

Alex took a deep breath. His parents approved of Kate; he knew his in-laws would approve and his children approved – well three of his children did. Stephanie, he sighed, would need a little longer to get used to the presence of another woman in their home, but she would come around eventually – at least he hoped so.

However, as he drove up the long drive to Kate's door, Alex's brows drew together in consternation. Kate's car was there. Unfortunately, the reappearance of her car was not the cause of his panic. Reginald and Frank had obviously gone to the office the fetch it. His eyes had focused on another familiar car in the drive, and his heart sank. He paused a moment, his finger suspended a few inches from the doorbell. "Don't be stupid," he told himself, and proceeded to push the button. Debra had probably borrowed that car.... No, he knew that was wishful thinking, but either way, he couldn't desert her now.

Kate bounced down the stairs to open the door. Her heart leapt with joy at the sight of Alex standing on her stoop, looking as handsome as he did. She threw herself into his arms, apparently oblivious to the fact that there had already been a previous visitor.

"Kate—" Alex tried to stop her, to tell her, but couldn't help but return her hungry kiss.

"I missed you," she breathed, kissing him again.

"Kate.... " Alex tried again, but Abigail Wallace's voice was more successful in claiming her granddaughter's attention.

"Good morning," Abigail greeted as she walked towards them.

Alex searched her face, knowing that all had gone wrong. He tried to pull away, but Kate hung on.

"It's such a pity, really," Abigail said sadly.

"What is, Gram?" Kate asked smiling happily.

"You two make such a wonderful couple...."

Kate looked at Alex and laughed. "Why is that a pity?"

"Oh ... because Jerry just returned from his safari. He's out on the terrace with your mother," Gram stated calmly waiting for her granddaughter's reaction.

Kate wanted the floor to open up and swallow her whole, she wanted to bolt through that opened door, she wanted ... she wanted Jerry to go back to his safari!

"I can explain, Gram," she said slowly, finally pulling herself from Alex.

"I'm sure you're going to try dear." Abigail tapped her cane on the floor.

Alex exhaled the breath he'd been holding. "I'm sorry for the deception."

"He was only helping me, Gram." Kate was quick to relieve Alex from blame.

"I know. I'm sorry too, Alex. That is your name, is it not?" she said perceptively.

"Yes," he admitted.

Abigail nodded, and started to turn away.

"Gram," Kate took hold of her arm. The dismay she saw in her grandmother's face broke her heart. She had done all this for her, and in the end her good intentions had disappointed her just the same. "I'm sorry. Let me explain, please.... "

"I should go," Alex said quietly.

"No!" Kate turned back to him. Her awakening towards Alex was the only positive element that survived this now defunct scheme. She was not about to lose him as well.

"It's over ... boss. Jerry's back. Time for me to leave, before my truck turns into a pumpkin," he said cynically.

"No," Kate repeated. "It's not over," she said almost desperately.

Alex had to be rational; he didn't think Kate was thinking logically yet. "I think you owe Jerry an explanation and he'll probably be a lot more sympathetic if the guy who's been impersonating him is not here."

"Yes, you're right," Abigail agreed.

"I take full blame in my part in this, and I'm ready to accept whatever punishment is due," he said to her grandmother, then turning to Kate, "I'll see you."

"Alex, wait!" Kate called after him.

Abigail had had enough. "Kate! Let him go. You have a great deal of explaining to do."

Kate continued to watch Alex as he drove down the driveway. She wanted to be with him. She didn't care about explanations; she didn't care about Jerry being outside. She just wanted Alex.

"Well, good morning sweets," Jerry said sarcastically as he walked towards her.

Kate closed the door and turned to her fiancé – her real fiancé. She sighed, mustering the strength to deal with him and everyone else for that matter.

"Hello Jerry."

"Hello Jerry? That's it?"

"What did you expect?" Kate questioned coldly, catching sight of her mother sauntering towards the group.

"A little more affection for one," he smiled cynically. "You do remember who I am, don't you?"

"Just barely."

"Kate!" Debra snapped. "How dare you speak to Jerry this way. He cut short his trip for you and that's the thanks he gets!"

Kate glared at her mother, shaking her head in disbelief. "You'd think he was your child, mother! He didn't seem to care about my feelings when he left did he? Yet you defend him!"

"Looks to me that you've actually forgotten who I am, Kate," Jerry continued calmly, ignoring her outburst. "I'm the one who put that ring on your finger, remember?"

"Oh, how could I ever forget! You remind me continuously!" Kate suddenly pulled off the large diamond from her finger and flung it across to her fiancé. "Why don't you take it back?" She picked up her keys from the entrance table and stormed out the door.

Kate hadn't forgotten who Jerry was. In fact, the memory of his attitude, his behavior and his selfishness came rushing back with just a few sardonic words. This was the confirmation she needed to run out of that door and out of his life for good. Kate knew exactly what she wanted and she knew exactly where to find him.

Kate was at Alex's door within minutes. Mary's car was in the drive, but Kate didn't mind. What she had to say involved his parents; it involved everyone.

Stephanie had forgotten a textbook at home and she had asked her grandmother to drive her back to retrieve it before church. They had plenty of time and Mary took this opportunity to sort through the laundry and put in a load of whites. It was Stephanie who came to the door.

Kate greeted her with a smile. "Hi Stephanie."

"Who is it, Steph?" Mary called from inside.

This visit could not be a good thing, but then again.... Immediately she was in damage control mode. "It's for me, Gramma," Stephanie replied as she closed the door behind her. Kate was a little taken aback. Why would Stephanie say that? Why would she not tell her grandmother that Kate was there? Why did she not invite her in?

"Is ... is your dad home?" Kate asked suddenly nervous.

"No, he's not. Wasn't he supposed to take your grandmother to the airport?"

"Well yes, but he ... I thought he'd come home."

"Nope."

"Okay. May I wait for him?"

What did she want? Why would she come looking for him? Had her father already expressed to her his feelings? Stephanie gave Kate a little smile, but her voice bordered on sarcastic. "Sorry, but I don't know how long he'll be – especially since he wasn't supposed to be home in the first place."

Kate felt a sudden chill, but she remained calm. She knew it would take time, but Kate was positive that eventually she'd be able to win the girl's affection – or at least her tolerance. "You're right, I'm sorry. Well, I'd like to speak to you for a moment … may I come in?"

"We can talk out here." Stephanie stepped away from the door and walked over to the far side of the veranda. She turned towards Kate, her arms folded across her chest waiting for her to speak, as if trying to ward off what she knew was bad news.

Kate watched curiously. "Are you okay Stephanie?"

"I'm fine. You wanted to say something?"

"Yes, I did." Kate drew in a deep breath. "Stephanie … I know your dad told you that this whole thing between him and me started out as a big hoax for my grandmother's sake."

"Wasn't it?" Stephanie asked cynically, her heart pounding painfully.

"Yes, yes it was … but somewhere along the line … I don't know how it happened, and I certainly didn't mean for it to happen, but all I know is that … Stephanie … I fell in love with your dad – and you and Nicholas and Paul and Leeza!" Kate said laughingly, reveling in the simple admission of this fact.

And there it was … the news she had dreaded…. Stephanie's

only saving grace was realizing that for some unknown reason her father had obviously not yet spoken to Kate. "Really?" she drawled. "What about your real boyfriend – Jerry right?"

"Yes, Jerry. Steph, I knew a long time ago that I didn't love Jerry, but I didn't know how to end it because of our two companies … it's complicated. Anyway, it was a comfortable situation all around, and since I knew no other I thought it would be all right, but it's not, it would never be…. " Kate looked up to the sky and sighed. "Your father's made me see what real love is. He's made me realize that no amounts of material things are important, not money, not even family businesses. I don't care about any of it. All I want is to be accepted into this family. I am prepared to give you all the time you need in order for that to happen. There's nothing in the world I want more."

Stephanie shook her head slowly from side to side. Her father knew full well how she felt about Kate – about any woman trying to infiltrate their family, and yet last night he'd told her and her brothers and sister that he wanted to pursue a relationship with his boss. That had been a blow, but the fact that these feelings were reciprocated made it infinitely worse. The realization that her fears, her suspicions, were justified from the beginning was almost too much for her to bear. She felt betrayed, but unfortunately anger outweighed all other emotions. The guilt she'd felt for keeping the conspirators' information hidden was all in vain. She needn't have wasted precious thoughts on Ms. Wallace! But all was not lost – not yet!

"Well it's not going to happen," Stephanie blurted rudely, her slender body trembling with anger, fear … betrayal….

Stephanie's words were as forceful as a prizefighter's punch having made direct contact with Kate's chest. "What?" she asked quietly, finding it painful to speak.

"There's not enough time in the world for it to happen. We'll never accept you. I knew this was going to happen. I saw the way you looked at my dad. But my dad was just helping you with your lie. Why would you think he would want you? Did he tell you?" she asked, her voice low, but unusually shrill, and Kate shook her head. "He's lonely, that's all. He told us so. He doesn't love you. He's just lonely," she repeated. "He misses my mom. And even if my dad and my brothers and my sister would be stupid enough to fall for you, or to accept you, I would never! I would move out! There's no way I'd ever live with you! I'd never let you take my mom's place, never!" Tears stung her eyes, but she was determined to keep them in check.

"Stephanie," Kate said quietly. "I would never expect to take your mother's place. I just—"

"—My father promised me that this was temporary. He told us that you are just his boss and he was just helping you out because you sign his cheques. Maybe he didn't mind pretending with you because … well, he's alone and you're young and pretty. But really he had no choice, understand?"

Kate was destroyed. The pain in her chest threatened to constrict the life right out of her. "Yes. I understand." Her voice was strained, but she forced a smile. "Well then, I'll ask you a small favour – from one girl to another."

Stephanie's expression remained cold and unyielding. "What."

"I just feel a little foolish … about all this, I mean. Maybe I saw more to this than there really was. I suppose I was lonely too. Don't tell your dad I was here … okay? Don't tell him what I said."

"Sure," Stephanie shrugged. This she could do.

When Kate arrived home, she realized she had no idea how she'd gotten there. The entire drive was gone from her memory. Only Stephanie's declaration replayed in her mind over and over until she actually questioned herself if it had really happened or if she had just simply imagined it. Her head ached, but the day wasn't over yet. Jerry was still there.

"You're back," her mother stated unnecessarily. "You were very rude to Jerry. He has every right to be upset after you substituted him – and with your assistant, no less!"

Kate remained quiet. She couldn't speak just yet. She knew that if she'd open her mouth, she wouldn't be *able* to speak; she would just cry and she didn't want that.

"Do you realize," Debra continued, "that Jerry came back for you? He left the safari and came back. He realized that he should have stayed when you'd asked. But you didn't give him a chance, did you? Like I said before, you could have told your grandmother that he was away. But no, you couldn't wait. Your grandmother wasn't going to drop dead, Kate! Looks to me as though she'll outlive us all!"

The words were out before Debra could stop herself. She'd told her daughter just the opposite – that Abigail was going to do just that – drop dead – and soon! She could only pray, if she remembered how, that Kate didn't catch her little slip.

"What are you talking about? You said Gram was sick!"

"Shh! Lower your voice! You don't want her to overhear you, do you? Of course she's sick … I … just meant … in case she's eavesdropping, you know she does that…. "

No, she didn't do that, but … perhaps her mother was right. Kate had not given Jerry the benefit of the doubt. She had behaved impulsively. She had begged her assistant to perform a job that was, as he had called it, not at all in his job description. But Alex had done the job well, so well in fact that she fell head over heels in love with him. Kate had been certain that Alex felt the same way, but after speaking to Stephanie…. In any event, even if it were true, if he did in fact love her, she would never wedge herself between Alex and his daughter. Therefore in the end, what had her impulsiveness gained her? Nothing. She'd gained nothing but a broken heart, a guilty conscience and the disappointment of her grandmother.

Thankful that Kate had believed her newest lie, she continued with her 'motherly' advice. She nodded towards the patio. "Jerry's in the garden. I think you owe him an apology."

"Where's Gram?" Kate's voice came in a whisper.

"She's in her room."

"I have to speak to her."

"Yes well, Jerry first," her mother insisted.

Kate glared angrily at her mother, and ignoring her demands, she walked up the stairs to her grandmother's room.

"Gram," Kate called tentatively from behind the door.

"Come in."

Kate closed the door behind her and walked over to the elderly woman who was strangely unpacking her suitcase.

"What are you doing?"

"I'm unpacking, what does it look like?" Abigail answered crisply.

"I'm sorry," Kate closed her eyes in realization. "You've missed your flight haven't you?"

"Yes I have. There was a later flight; I just decided not to take it. I'll be staying a while longer."

"Oh Gram," Kate rushed to her side. "I'm so glad."

Abigail did not return her Kate's embrace. "Yes, well, I had to at least stay long enough to make certain you get yourself out of this mess."

"I'm so sorry, Gram."

Abigail threw down the sweater she had just folded and turned to face her granddaughter. "Whatever possessed you, Kate? What were you thinking?"

"I … I just wanted to make you happy…. "

"By lying to me? By pretending to be engaged to your assistant? By letting me become completely captivated by him and his family?"

Kate swallowed back the lump in her throat. "I'm sorry."

"So you've said, Kate. I've yet to hear the reason."

Kate looked up her grandmother. She had refrained from telling her grandmother that she was aware of her state of ill health. She wasn't altogether sure if she should tell her now either.

"Gram, I … when I learned you were coming, Jerry had already booked this safari of his and when I asked him to postpone it, he wouldn't. He wouldn't!" Kate's tone was resentful. "I begged him. I wanted so much for you to meet him, because I knew that's what you wanted."

"Kate? You hadn't told me about him yet. What was the hurry now?"

Kate shook her head in confusion. "I don't understand."

Abigail threw up her hands. "*You* don't understand!"

"Gram, I wanted you to meet him to make you happy. I

thought that's what you wanted. I wanted to make you happy in case—"

"In case what?"

"I … I know you haven't been feeling well, and I—"

"I haven't been feeling well? Who told you this? My arthritis acts up once in a while, but that comes with age; it's expected Kate. Besides that I'm perfectly healthy. Why would you think otherwise?"

Again Kate shook her head, but this time in disbelief, disbelief that she could be so naïve to believe her mother to tell her anything but whatever would suit her in the end.

Abigail noticed her granddaughter's irritation. "Kate?"

"It was my mother," she hissed. "She told me that you'd called and told her that you were not well – in fact very ill. She said you wanted to come see me and meet my fiancé before you, before you … died!"

"Oh Kate," Abigail said disappointedly. "I didn't call your mother. I've never called her before, why would I do so now – and to tell her about my impending death, no less? Why would I want to give her that satisfaction; that pleasure? Your mother called *me*. She called me, so she said – to inform me of your engagement, and we both know why, don't we? That woman can't wait to squander the rest of your inheritance!"

"That horrid woman," she said quietly. If she hadn't been so heartbroken, she would've been furious. "I'm sorry, Gram. She told me that you didn't want me to know. That's why I didn't call you myself. That's why I believed her; that's why I was so upset when Jerry wouldn't postpone his trip and that's why I asked Alex to pretend to be him. I didn't want to disappoint you. I wanted you to see that I was settled or was going to be; I wanted you to be happy." Kate shook her head disappointedly. "You know … just now, downstairs, she confirmed her part in this and I … I didn't even see through her fumbling to cover it up."

It was Gram's turn to shake her head. "Kate, this was all your mother at her finest. But dear, even if I were at death's door, it would have sufficed me to know how well you've handled the business on your own and how you've managed your life on your own. That would have been enough to satisfy my thoughts for your future. The fact that you were engaged would only have been an added bonus. You didn't have to do this."

"I wasn't really thinking. I was just so upset over what my mother had said about you being ill and then with Jerry … I wasn't thinking straight."

Abigail sat down on the bed and pulled her granddaughter down to join her. She inspected her pale face, the stress lines around her mouth, the creases on her brow. "Well, perhaps you were after all."

"What do you mean?"

"Alex is wonderful, Kate."

Kate looked away and Abigail was quick to arrive at the conclusion that the trip Kate had obviously taken to his home that morning had not turned out as well as her granddaughter had hoped.

"Kate?"

"Yes he is Gram, but he's my employee."

"So, he really is your assistant. He is the one who works with you?"

"Yes. Jerry was starting to become more involved, but he

could never be compared with Alex. He could never replace him."

"I have a feeling you're right. Well, he's quite the employee to put himself and his family in that position – just for the benefit of his boss's grandmother."

"He's very loyal."

"Yes, I'll bet." Abigail studied her granddaughter's strained face. "You're in love with him," she stated.

"What? No. No, I'm not, Gram," Kate denied.

"And I'd be surprised if he didn't feel the same way," Abigail continued.

"No, Gram. We were just playing a part," Kate shrugged.

"That's some acting!" she chucked and Kate shuddered at the memory of Alex's touch. "You went to see him before, didn't you?"

Kate shrugged again. "He wasn't home."

"Why didn't you wait for him?"

"I can talk to him tomorrow at the office. I only went to see him to apologize for all this mess."

"That's all?"

"Yes Gram, that's all." But Abigail arched an eyebrow and Kate tried to be logical. "Gram … you have to understand that regardless of any possible feelings that may have developed … we can never become involved."

"And why not?"

"Because … he works for me."

"Oh balderdash! What kind of a reason is that?"

Kate sprang to her feet and took a few steps forward. "All right, what about the fact that Stephanie doesn't want me anywhere near her father?" she blurted painfully.

"Ah! Stephanie, the eldest! Well … I suppose that would

make things a little more difficult, but she just needs time—"

"—No. It's best that we just stop this charade while it's still just that, before things get more complicated." Things had already become complicated, she thought to herself. Last night had been wrong. She couldn't help but wonder what Alex was thinking at the moment, but regardless, this had to end now.

She turned to her grandmother, and took her hand. "What do you think of Jerry, Gram?" It was best to return to reality.

"I don't know. I haven't had much time to form an opinion. Although … I liked Alex straight away…. "

"Gram…." Kate sighed. "I'm going to go speak to him – Jerry I mean. I guess I owe him an apology as well."

Jerry was still sitting outside under the covered patio. He stood when he saw Kate walking towards him. "Kate … I'm sorry," he told her surprisingly, and suddenly Kate found herself bursting into tears, allowing him to gather her into his arms.

But it wasn't just guilt that had unleashed her tears. There was anger for her part in this whole ordeal, sadness in the disappointment of her grandmother and perhaps … a sizable portion had to do with the fact that her true feelings had to be forbidden….

CHAPTER NINETEEN

That extraordinary moonlit night he'd shared with Kate in her office had been all Alex had dreamed. But it was morning – in fact the second morning – after and with yet another brand new day came the realization that Kate had to have made a decision. However he'd received no phone call, no visit. At the back of his mind, the knowledge brewed that nothing would come of their evening together.

Alex was forcing himself to see the blueprints that lay unraveled on the drafting table in front of him when Kate entered the office. She didn't wear the same look she had sported the previous morning when he had arrived at her door. His heart began to pound painfully in his chest. He knew what was coming.

"Morning boss," Alex said, immediately reverting to his usual greeting. "Everything straightened out?"

Kate paused and took his cue. "Yes," she sighed, feigning relief. "We talked and we fought and we talked, and … and we made up." Her tone was flip; her insides mush.

That's good." Did his pulse just stop, he thought to himself.

"Yes, it is. I mean Jerry *is* the man I'm engaged to after all." Kate forced herself to look straight into Alex's eyes, hoping that her eyes wouldn't wander down to his lips, the lips that had kissed her so passionately.... She shivered. "I think I was so angry with his leaving that I ... I just wanted to get back at him, you know? He cut his trip short so that he could come and meet Gram."

"That's big of him. I wouldn't have expected that."

"Yes, well neither did I, which makes me feel extremely guilty. I mean I misjudged him and flew off the handle before really giving him a chance," she raised her hands to make her point.

Alex's voice was steady and calm. "That happens sometimes."

"Gram is going to stay a while longer," she deterred the subject slightly.

"Really?"

"Yes.... "

Alex's eyes were guarded, but he didn't lower his gaze. "That'll be great ... having her here. Is she all right with everything? I mean, was she very upset?"

Kate shrugged. "She was disappointed. That's understandable I suppose, but I think she understands why I did what I did. I'm ... I'm sorry for putting you and your family through all this ... and you have to know that Gram doesn't bear any ill feelings towards you. She knows it was all my idea." Kate's eyes wandered momentarily, finding it increasingly difficult to remain impassive to his attraction or to the feeling of despair in her heart. "She's fine, you know," she said looking up at him once again. "Gram's not ill. My mother made it all up just so I wouldn't call her myself and learn that it was she who called Gram so that she might to try to expedite the matter of my inheritance."

"That doesn't surprise you does it?"

"No."

"Well, I'm glad she's all right."

"Yes, so am I." She paused, trying to muster the courage to continue. "Alex … about the other night … I don't know what to say." Kate tucked her hair behind her eyes. "I don't know what came over me. I shouldn't have—"

"—Don't give it another thought," he dismissed. Alex lowered his eyes momentarily, as if searching for inner strength. That was the confirmation he was waiting for. "We were placed in an awkward situation," he continued. "I think what happened was inevitable given the circumstances. I mean there's a certain element of attraction and well, we're only human, right? It happened, but now it's over," he shrugged, relieving her of any further embarrassment. Alex felt as though he wasn't even there. His body was there, he knew that, but his mind, his soul; his heart … was back in her office….

Kate nodded, averting her gaze. "I hope that things won't change … here I mean."

"There is no reason for anything to change, is there? Unless you're uncomfortable—"

"—No. No of course not…. "

"Okay…. Did you tell Jerry?"

Kate eyes shot quickly to his. "Tell Jerry?"

"About the other night."

"Oh! No, I didn't. I thought it would best not to, don't you?"

"Whatever you think."

Kate nodded again. "Thanks."

"For?"

"For everything. For being so understanding; for being a gentleman."

"No problem," he said with a strained smile.

Kate returned the same smile, and walking through the adjoining door to her office she disappeared into her private bathroom. Closing the door behind her, Kate leaned against it, taking a few calming breaths. Things would never be the same; she was deluding herself if she thought otherwise.

In his office Alex smiled cynically. "What did you expect?" he asked himself out loud. He had forged ahead giving no heed to the inevitable eventual disaster once he accepted to play the part of fiancé. He had been selfish, allowing his physical attraction to blind him into believing that nothing would go wrong. He had put his feelings above his job, his family, and he had compromised both. This turn of events was an expected probability; this conclusion should not have surprised him.

What he didn't expect was for Jerry to stride into his office later that afternoon.

"Alex," Jerry stated his name in an uncustomary acknowledgement of existence.

"Jerry," Alex returned.

He walked directly towards Alex and leaned a hand against the glass partition. "I'd like to speak to you."

"Sure." *I'd like to beat you to a pulp,* Alex said in his mind.

Jerry glanced towards the opened door between the two offices. "Can we step outside?"

"Sure," Alex said again and followed him out of the office and down past the cubicles and into the small kitchenette at the far end of the large room. "Okay, what did you want to talk about," he asked lazily.

"Well, I suppose I ought to thank you for stepping in for me, but I don't feel too generous today," Jerry declared defiantly.

Alex shoved his hands in the pockets of his slacks as though deeming it safer for Jerry to do so. "Pardon me?"

"You could have said no."

"And why should I have? I was merely helping out a friend."

"Were you?" Jerry was suspicious.

"Yes. I did what *you* should have done."

Jerry was indignant. "Look, don't you get self-righteous with me. I know you don't like me, so I also know how much you'd like to get rid of me, but lookie here, it didn't work."

"What didn't work?"

"Deb was right not to trust you. She told me that the two of you were ... shall we say ... enjoying your acting abilities."

Alex shrugged. "We were merely playing a part."

"Yeah right. Well, I'm back and she came back to me."

"So?"

"So, back off. Remember your place."

"I know exactly who I am and what I'm doing here – which is my job and nothing more. I was asked to help and I did. That's over. You may as well *can* your insecurities; you have nothing to worry about where I'm concerned."

Jerry watched him for a moment as though trying to determine if Alex's declaration was indeed fact. "Well good. Like I said, just remember your place."

Alex glared after him. This was not going to be easy.

"Hey Alex!" Tony greeted as he entered the kitchenette.

"What!" Alex snapped.

"Whoa! Who bit you?"

"Ahh," Alex dismissed, "that jackass."

"Yeah, that he is. So it's Alex again; I got your memo this morning."

"Yes, thank God." Alex continued to stare towards the opened doorway.

"So … how did it go?" Tony was very perceptive.

"It went. I did what I was asked to do and now he's back."

"And that's it?"

Alex sighed. "He came back early."

"I gathered that. What happened?"

"Jerk can't do anything right," Alex huffed. "We were caught."

"Caught? Caught doing what?" Tony smiled mischievously.

"Get your mind out of the gutter, Ton," he reprimanded.

"Sorry."

"Her grandmother caught us in the lie, naturally. He came back Sunday morning just as I arrived to take her to the airport."

"I see. Was she upset?"

"I think *so*," Alex said sarcastically. "She didn't really say much to me, but I can't see her being overly content with the situation."

"I guess. What did Kate say?"

"When?" Alex was evasive.

"I don't know when. Yesterday, today…. "

Alex shrugged indifferently. "She thanked me for my help and hopes that everything will go on as usual."

"And will it?"

"Why wouldn't it?"

"Alex," Tony placed a hand on his friend's shoulder. "You look like hell. You can fool her, you can fool the grandmother, even Jerry, but you can't fool me. You're in love with her."

"No I'm not and I really hope you won't say that again."

"Okay. I'm sorry," Tony bowed his head. "If you feel like talking; if you want to go out for a beer or something, just call me, okay?"

Alex regretted snapping at his friend. Tony was only concerned for his well-being – his sanity. "Sure, just stop worrying about me. I'm fine."

The door between his and Kate's office was closed. It remained that way until Jerry reappeared hours later.

"Kate needs the drawings for the Andrews strip plaza."

"What's wrong with the intercom?"

"I came to get them. Do you have a problem with that?"

"Not at all." Alex retrieved the prints and handed them to Jerry and then watched him close the door behind him once again.

It was starting, Alex thought miserably. Jerry was taking over.

When Kate finally resurfaced, her expression was not somber, but puzzled as well as somewhat perturbed. "I thought you told me that the soil results came back as Beach Sands," her voice was uncommonly accusing.

Alex looked up from the paperwork on his desk. "Which job are we discussing?"

"Andrews."

"Okay. I did. Why?"

"Apparently the report you sent them shows the soil as Native Clay."

"That's impossible."

"They've halted the job again. They're hitting water. The improper footings have been delivered … we need caisson footings, not conventional. How do you explain that?"

"I read the reports."

"Yes, so did I." Kate extended the several sheets just faxed from Claude Sorenson.

"I just got off the phone with him. He's fuming!"

Confused, Alex reached for them and skimmed through the sheets. Instructions displaying his signature showed the soil to be Native Clay: stable. "What?" Alex shook his head in denial as he retrieved the file in question. Quickly locating the reports received from ESI, he flipped through the pages and found what he knew to be correct. "Look.… " The results were clearly marked as Beach Sands. "That's the report I sent Sorenson. I know it."

Hubert Andrew was tall and lanky. He was soft-spoken, and usually indecisive, unlike Liam on both points. Today, however, his normally fair complexion seemed to bear a little more colour, and his demeanor and unannounced arrival were unusual as well as unnerving.

"I'm very disappointed, Ms. Wallace. Disappointed, indeed."

As if the situation wasn't bad enough as it was, Abigail Wallace appeared just behind Hubert. Kate's face had lost all colour at this point. This was not a good time for a visit, although Abigail was not in the mood to socialize.

"What's happened? What's the problem?" she demanded to know.

"Gram, please." Kate motioned for the tall elderly gentleman to enter her office. Abigail followed. "Alex, join us please, bring all the files."

Abigail was becoming impatient. "Will someone care to explain? Oh, hello Jerry," she added, spotting him sitting at the large round table.

Alex sighed. He wished Jerry didn't have to be there – not now. Not when he was unable to explain how he could have transposed incorrect information. Even if the report itself bore the wrong result, Alex's signature would only prove that he misread the fallacious report. Kate's voice brought him back from his thoughts.

"Please, let us sit down." Kate introduced her grandmother and her fiancé to Hubert, but he didn't want to socialize either, nor did he want to sit. He wanted answers. "Mr. Andrews. This was an error on the part of the geo-technical firm, I'm sure."

"Ms. Wallace, a geo-technical firm would not release two sets of results!"

"Not unless they don't know what the devil they're doing!" Abigail intervened. "Who did the testing?"

Kate answered without a second thought. "Foresters."

"Kate.... " Alex spoke her name, somehow wanting to rewind time, stopping her from speaking.

Hubert's face became red with anger. "Foresters? By God, I think I know who is truly to blame here. You don't even know which firm you used!"

Kate was indignant. "I beg your pardon?"

"Kate ... we used ESI—"

"—Who?"

"ESI. That's the firm Jerry suggested."

Kate's memory came rushing back and she tried to correct her blunder. "Yes, yes that's right – ESI. All right, so as I said before, they are at fault. Obviously, they're incompetent. We will call in another company. The soil will be retested just to be safe, and proper footings will be delivered, if not by the end of the workday, by tomorrow morning at the latest, and at no expense to you, of course. Mr. Andrews, there will be no further delays, I assure you."

Hubert glanced at his watch. "I don't have time to waste, Ms. Wallace. I have already been delayed for an important meeting. I will hold you to that assurance. In the end all that matters is that my complex is built. If there are any other problems, I assure *you*, Ms. Wallace, that you will be off the job. Claude will be awaiting your call. Good day."

Kate stared after Hubert. Alex stared into space. Jerry stared at Alex, and Abigail watched them all, a look of dismay on her weathered face. "How could this happen?" she asked finally.

Alex was the first to speak. "Mrs. Wallace, I don't know."

"Why did you use this unknown firm?"

Kate answered quickly. "Gram, I told him—"

But Alex couldn't allow Kate to be blamed. "Mrs. Wallace, Kate had suggested I use Foresters—"

"—Alex, no. Jerry suggested ESI, and I—"

"Jerry!" This information did not pacify Abigail; it only intensified her displeasure. "From what I've learned, Jerry knows nothing of the business. Why would you, in God's name, choose a firm based on his suggestions!"

Jerry was quick to defend himself. He turned wide eyes towards Abigail. "Mrs. Wallace, I was only trying to help. The firm was suggested to me by one of my father's associates. Either way, this is clearly not the fault of ESI, but that of the person responsible for sending the false results to the site in question."

It had been Jerry's suggestion, and Kate had agreed, but ultimately the fault lay with Alex. He made an error – either that, or someone was playing an extremely absurd game.

"He's right, Mrs. Wallace." That fact stuck in his throat. "The fault lies purely with me." Alex gathered scattered papers and returned them to the file. "I will reimburse the company for whatever costs this predicament has accrued and accept whatever actions you wish to take."

"I'll have Tony tally the costs—" Jerry began, feeling suddenly significant.

Kate shot him a look and Jerry stopped in mid sentence. "That won't be necessary. This was an honest mistake. It could have happened to anyone. The error is being rectified. There are no actions to be taken." Kate was adamant. "Let's just get back to work."

Alex was about to speak, but Kate raised her hand to silence him. The meeting was over.

When Alex picked up the children from his parents' that evening, the expression on his face matched his mood. Hadn't it been enough to be rejected so calmly after having shared a night as they had done? Did his competence in his work have to come under such scrutiny? ESI must have erred in printing the results, but Alex signed their receipt and sent them along. Alex was indeed to blame.

"Alex honey, are you all right?" Mary asked her son.

"I'm fine, Mom. Are they ready?"

Mary knew better than to press her son. "Yes, yes. Come on kids, Dad's here!" she called.

The children came running with knapsacks in tow. "Hi Dad! Hi Dad! Hi Daddy!" Stephanie was the last to join the group. "Hi Dad!" she greeted him with an extra spark in her voice.

"Hi. Ready? Let's go," he said simply and soon they were on their way.

Nicholas recounted the way his class had beaten another during their Phys. Ed. soccer game. Paul relayed the fact that he received a much deserved A on his Egypt project and Leeza wanted to display her latest finger painting masterpiece. Stephanie remained quiet until they arrived home.

"Dad," she said tentatively when they entered the house. "We have a class trip next Tuesday. Mr. Glenn said two parents are allowed to accompany us, can you come?"

"Sure," Alex answered off-handedly.

"Sure?" Stephanie repeated. "Next Tuesday?"

"I said yes, Stephanie."

"Okay. Thanks Dad." Stephanie watched her father roll up his shirtsleeves and season the chicken he had placed in the refrigerator that morning and put it in the oven. He looked upset, but she didn't dare ask him why. She had a feeling she knew exactly what was bothering her father.

Alex was quiet during dinner as well. After a few more quipped answers the kids realized that their dad was just not up to talking that evening.

"Daddy, what's wrong?" Leeza asked innocently, and Stephanie's stomach started to flutter nervously.

"Nothing, honey." Alex tried to smile his response.

"You look sad. Did you ask Kate to be your girlfriend yet?"

Alex looked up at her and then scanned the faces of his other children. "No, I didn't."

"Are you going to?" pressed Leeza.

"No."

"What happened Dad?" asked Nicholas.

"Well, Jerry came back, so Kate decided to give that relationship another try. It's best that we keep *our* relationship on a purely business level." Alex smiled at Leeza's puzzled face. "She's still my boss, I still work for her, but that's all."

"Oh," was Leeza's reply.

Alex glanced towards his eldest daughter. "What, no comment from you, Steph? Aren't you happy?"

"Yes, I guess so … but I don't want you to be sad, either."

"Well, I guess you can't have everything," he retorted icily, and Stephanie lowered her eyes.

CHAPTER TWENTY

Not another word was spoken about the problem with the Andrews plaza, but nevertheless the tension at the office was almost unbearable. Alex greeted his boss as such and Kate barely spoke to him. When Jerry wasn't there to act as go-between, she'd have no choice but to call him for information and on the increasingly rare occasion that she used the door between the two offices, she would ask him if he wanted a cup of coffee while she poured one for herself. However, things were strained to say the least.

Alex had barely put down his briefcase one morning later that week when Kate appeared in front of the drafting table where Alex stood. "Have you spoken to Emilio, the site-super for Gamble and Blaine?" Kate asked.

"I thought you spoke to him yesterday."

Kate mused. "Two days ago. You haven't spoken to him since?"

"No, why?" he returned.

Kate was becoming increasingly agitated. "That was him just now. He was questioning the elevations."

Alex shook his head in confusion. "Why?"

"I think we have a problem. Liam was yelling so much in the background that I could barely hear Emilio, but I know there's something wrong."

"I'll go down there," Alex told her, reaching for the files. He had a feeling this just wasn't going to be his week!

"I'll come with you," she offered, surprising him.

Alex's large truck drove easily over the mounds of dirt and rubble on the massive construction site. Both had been silent during the hours on the ferry to Vancouver and the drive to their ultimate destination on Georgia Street. Now his attentive eyes, squinting against the noon sun, scanned the site. Several excavators were sitting idle along the perimeter. Kate seemed to be in a daze, but Alex had a sinking feeling he knew the cause of Liam's anger.

Both changed into the required construction boots, and donning hard hats, made their way towards the trailer. They could hear the heated voice of Liam Gamble from outside.

When Alex and Kate entered the makeshift office, Liam nearly lunged towards them.

"Just the two I wanted to see! What kind of incompetents do you have working for you?"

Kate looked at the strained faces of Emilio and the foremen gathered around the small desk. Todd stood quietly against the wall.

"What happened?" Kate asked.

"What happened? What happened? You call yourselves engineers? You can't even prepare a simple site plan. Damn it all to the devil, the elevations are wrong! Do you have any idea what this is costing us? There's no way in hell we're paying for this foul up! That's what happens when we let a woman do a man's job! I'm going to sue, so help me I'll—"

"—Mr. Gamble," Alex's stern voice put an end to Liam's angry threats. "If you'll just calm down for a second.... "

Kate preferred to speak to the more rational of the two partners. "Todd, can someone please explain – I mean anyone can make a mistake, a mere slip of the pen.... "

"Kate, the entire plan is off eight feet. There's no slip of pen here. It's a matter of miscalculations. They've dug eight feet deeper than they should have, in all areas."

Kate was incredulous. "What? Well they misread the plan obviously."

Todd continued to speak in his usual calm tone. "No, Kate. The blueprints are wrong. The numbers are wrong. The excavators were only following your site plan. We will have to back-fill. The dirt's been carried away. Think about it. You realize how long it will take to reverse this fiasco and how much it will cost, don't you? This is a major problem, Kate – a major setback."

It was Alex's turn to be in a daze. He had been responsible for plotting the elevations. His voice was quiet when he spoke. "Emilio, are these the plans?" he asked, walking towards the desk.

Emilio scratched his head and shrugged. "I should take some of the blame, Alex. I was away the last couple of days, but still I should have realized earlier that this was wrong."

The unraveled prints weighed down at the corners with bricks and rocks were laid out on the desk. Both Kate and Alex inspected the drawings. Alex was dumbfounded. This couldn't be....

Kate looked at Alex in horror. "Alex? These are not the elevations we discussed. I don't understand.... "

"That's the problem," Liam nearly spat. "You don't understand! You don't know what you're doing! Go home little girl! You're fired! You're fired and what's more you're paying for all the delays and the extra work and time required to adjust your incompetence. If I have my way I'll see to it that Wallace is never awarded another contract."

Alex shook his head, bewildered. He could have sworn he had marked down the correct elevations. How could he have made such an elementary, yet costly mistake? But now was not the time to determine 'how'. Liam wanted answers; he didn't want excuses. "Liam, there's no need to take your anger out on

Kate or the entire firm. I don't know how I could have miscalculated ... but this is my fault."

Kate's head swung around to stare pointedly at her assistant. "Alex!" Hoping to deflect blame from him, she turned to Liam once again. "There must be a perfectly logical explanation for this, and we'll get to the bottom of it, but ultimately it is my responsibility—"

"—Kate!" Alex stopped her short. "They are *my* site plans."

Liam glared in disgust from one to the other. "You two are going to make me cry! Either that or drive me into a murderous rampage! You, Kate, are correct only in your admittance of fault. *You* are the boss; *you* hire incompetents. Hence, *you* are to blame!" he concluded. "Like I said, you're fired! Go home! Everybody go home! The day's shot, the week's shot, everything's shot!" Liam burst out of the trailer and strode away towards his vehicle.

Todd Blaine spoke now. "I'm sorry Kate, but he's right. A lot of money has been lost and there are more expenses pending to correct this problem. This will have to be discussed. You'll be hearing from us – well, most likely me," he smiled ruefully.

Once in the quiet confines of Alex's truck, Kate turned to Alex again. "How could this happen?"

Alex didn't start the engine. They just sat there staring out the front windshield as if in shock. "I don't know."

"Those were not the elevations we discussed," she repeated.

"I know."

Kate sighed. Something wasn't right – aside from the obvious. Alex wasn't capable of such errors. "Why were you so quick to accept blame?"

"Because this is my second mistake! Because I am obviously to blame!" Alex raked unsteady fingers through his hair. He sighed heavily. "I don't know how, but I must have made some type of miscalculation at the beginning … naturally everything afterwards would be incorrect." Alex shrugged, an incredulous laugh escaping his throat. "The only other explanation is that someone changed those numbers and those plans didn't leave my sight until they were delivered…" his voice trailed off. Jerry had been extremely interested in Alex's job before he left for his trip, and he did deliver the drawings….

"Alex, don't even go there. Jerry doesn't even know what a site plan is. He wouldn't know what changes to make. I would understand one incorrect number, but not the whole dammed thing! Besides, why would he do that? What would he gain by it?"

"I suppose you're right," he told her. "Which only leads us back to me. In any case, what's the point of bringing the entire firm down over this? Liam is thoroughly peeved, or hadn't you noticed? And he has a right, but there is no reason to cause undue havoc to the company and/or its employees." Alex shook his head again. "Look, I know what the elevations were supposed to be, but I also know what I read on those plans today. I can *see* it," he extended his hands towards the enormous hole in front of them, "in fact I saw it the moment we arrived. I … don't know how I could make such an incredible error, but obviously I did. You can't take the blame; you're the boss. *I'm* expendable." Alex started the engine now, and put the truck in gear. "Let's get back to the office. We'll talk to Tony and Kevin and it wouldn't hurt to talk to David in legal. Liam wants blood."

"You're not going to take the fall for this," Kate stated matter-of-factly. "I won't let you."

Upon their arrival, Kate stopped the elevator on the seventh floor so that she may call on David Ingram. Alex was right. David's legal services would indeed be required for this. Alex went straight to his desk in search of his original plans, work sheets, anything that would shed some light on this confusing turn of events.

When Kate entered the office a short while later, Alex was up to his elbows in paper, but the look on his face was one of puzzlement, not victory or even clarity.

"What?" she asked tentatively.

Alex held out several sheets of paper. "It's all here in black and white. My work sheets show I had the correct elevations. Somewhere between there and the finished product … I goofed." Kate took the reports from his outstretched hand. She shook her head in confusion. "But Alex, how?"

"I must be losing it. I can't explain this, I'm sorry."

Kate looked heavenward as she leaned against the glass wall. "What are we going to do?"

"What did David say?"

"He says he'll start securing the fort, he thinks we should brace ourselves for an attack."

Alex nodded. "An imminent one."

"What's this about an attack?" Abigail's voice jump-started both their hearts.

This had turned out just wonderfully, Kate thought sarcastically, and she thought things couldn't possibly get any worse!

"Gram! What are you doing here?" Again she had shown up unannounced and at a most inopportune moment.

Abigail ignored her granddaughter. "Everyone's scurrying about like plump turkeys during Thanksgiving! What's happened? Who's going to attack?"

Kate glanced at Alex who gathered the damning evidence and handed the pile to his boss.

"Gamble and Blaine, Mrs. Wallace."

"Whatever for?"

"Because I screwed up."

"Alex!" Kate tried to silence him, but the grandmother's interest had been piqued.

"Would you care to explain – either of you?"

"Yes Gram. Let's go sit in my office." Kate glanced once again to her assistant, who, understanding her unspoken thoughts, joined the two in her office for the first battle.

Abigail had been very disappointed. It was evident in the

way she lowered her eyes while Alex spoke. It was evident when she kept quiet until they'd both finished explaining the events that led to this disaster, or at least the events that they were aware of.

"I see. Well, this is not good for our reputation. Not at all. They'll want damages naturally, that is to be expected. We were wrong, after all. Obviously we will be hearing from them soon. Frankly, off the top of my head, I don't know how we could win any type of lawsuit." Abigail rose to her feet now, her chin raised, her tone as stern as the look in her eyes. "I want to be informed the moment they call. I will attend the meetings. Does Jerry know?"

"No. Gram, we just found out."

"Well, I just hope that this embarrassing situation does not hinder our agreement for the merger." She turned and walked out the door to join the waiting Reginald just outside.

As everyone had expected, lawyers for Gamble and Blaine contacted Wallace Architectural within two days. The meeting was set for that Friday morning in the boardroom, and Abigail Wallace was there. Also present, to Alex's displeasure, was Jerry.

Abigail had sat quietly throughout the better part of the meeting, while lawyers from both sides spoke their lawyer gibberish, but now it was time for her to speak. The company could stand to lose all hope of survival. Its future was at risk.

"Mr. Gamble," Abigail's cool voice turned all eyes to her. "I can empathize with your outrage in this dreadful circumstance. However, an offer is on the table. You will be compensated. The matter is being corrected. What more do you want?"

"Mrs. Wallace, I apologize in advance for my language, but this is horseshit! Yes I expect compensation, and I appreciate the fact that Kate is willing to accept responsibility, but this entire 'circumstance', as you so eloquently put it, smells of incompetence. This is an extraordinarily large project, Mrs. Wallace. I cannot trust that this is the last problem we would encounter. Frankly, I've lost all confidence."

Alex too had remained relatively quiet, but this meeting was going nowhere. Compensation would not pacify Liam Gamble. There was only one thing to do. "Liam. The incompetence lies with one person, not the entire company. Would you be content with the resignation of the culprit?" Alex's voice was steady, his determination unwavering; turning Kate's shocked eyes to him.

"Alex, I know Kate's in charge. Ultimately the fault is hers, and naturally, the entire company."

"No. I made the calculations for the excavating; I plotted the site plan. The fault is mine. No one else's."

"Alex!" Kate nearly jumped from her chair, but his glare and her grandmother's angry voice silenced her if only for a moment.

"Kate! That's enough! I understand your loyalties with Mr. Callahan, but this is a monumental blunder! It cannot be excused!"

Kate was outraged. "Gram, this is wrong. You don't know–"

"I know that this is best." Abigail Wallace was forceful. "Alex Callahan's record is impeccable; this was a baffling error, but an error notwithstanding and an unforgivable one at that. Mr. Gamble and Mr. Blaine have a right to be angry. We have the ability and the know-how to rectify the matter. It will be best rectified with the proper employees doing the job," she concluded and Liam nodded in agreement.

"Look, stop the lynch mob, all right. I cannot believe you people. Granted, an error has been made, but it was unintentional to say the least. We are willing to rectify and compensate, why must you draw blood? Are you all so perfect? My God, I'll bet you'd have us believe you've never even told a white lie for the good of the whole!"

"Oh, we've all lied at one time or another, haven't we dear?" Abigail looked pointedly at her granddaughter. "But although this is not a trial, as it stands it appears that only one person is indeed at fault and this person has accepted blame. Therefore it ends here," and that left Kate staring back in disbelief and in utter dismay. "Alex," Abigail continued, "you are to be commended. Another employee would have been quick to pass the blame onto another. You have rare qualities, lad. You have scruples; you have morals. It is with sadness that I accept your resignation—"

Kate was indignant. "—*You* accept?" But her grandmother continued.

"But, I will accept it nonetheless. You can be certain to receive an excellent letter of reference from me personally, as I'm certain from the firm."

"I appreciate your generosity, Mrs. Wallace." Alex stood to leave and as Kate motioned to do the same, Abigail took hold of her hand, keeping her in place, forcing her to sit down.

When Alex was out of the room, Todd turned to the elderly matriarch. "We've had little dealings with this firm, but our resources depicted Alex Callahan as an extremely competent individual. You were quite correct in saying that he is to be commended for accepting blame and readily offering to resign. I also appreciate the fact that you've accepted his resignation, regardless of your loyalties and feelings towards him. This was an unfortunate turn of events. I don't begin to understand what happened here or how it happened—"

"—But it did!" interrupted Liam. "And that's something that gnaws at me. My partner here may be inclined to let things go, praising Alex for his admission to guilt, but that's of little consolation to me!"

Kate glared at her grandmother. It seemed Alex's resignation had gone to no avail, after all.

Then, maybe not.... Jerry cleared his throat suddenly, sitting forward in his chair. "Mr. Gamble, Mr. Blaine, if I could just intervene for a moment.... "

Both Kate and Abigail turned surprised eyes to Jerry.

"And you are?"

Jerry expected an introduction from his fiancé, but when none came he introduced himself. "I am Jerry Kent of Kent Developments. I realize we've never officially met, but I'm sure you know my father."

"Yes, yes, of course. Formidable individual. We've done business several times."

"Yes, well ... it hasn't been made public yet, but it might interest you to know that Kent Properties and Wallace Architectural intend to merge as soon as Kate and I are married."

"Ah, I thought I heard rumors to that effect," Liam nodded his approval. "Congratulations."

"Thank you. So as you see, as well as Kate's expertise, you will have the prestigious name of Kent alongside that of Wallace. Its reputation is untarnished, and its existence renowned across the country." As Jerry spoke, Kate's face distorted in disbelief. Since when did Jerry praise his father or his company? "Kent Developments back Kate one hundred per cent. You won't have another problem, I guarantee it."

Liam and Todd exchanged looks. Kate looked at Jerry, who bore a satisfied grin when he in turn looked at Abigail.

"Mr. Gamble, there you have it. Our agreement with the Kent family is based on the reputation you mentioned. I believe this development, which had not been announced for purely personal reasons, should put your mind at ease."

It seemed Jerry had pacified Liam. "Well, I feel decidedly more confident now." Liam stood, followed by Todd. "With you and the Kents at the helm I foresee blue skies ahead. We will accept your settlement, Mrs. Wallace, and I'm certain I speak for the both of us when I say that we look forward to completing this job without further problems."

Abigail Wallace stood also, accepting his and Todd's handshake. "Mr. Gamble, I don't want you to misunderstand, my granddaughter is still in charge of this firm and I am sure you are familiar with her abilities to carry out the job, otherwise you would not have awarded her the contract in the first place. I will be here for a while longer to lend her my support if need be, but I must stress that Kate will be in charge as always." Abigail stated the fact as she glanced at her granddaughter, who had been sitting in a state of shock for the last few moments. "I trust that this setback will not hinder relations during the completion of this project or in fact any further endeavours."

"This was an unfortunate gaffe, for everyone concerned, Mrs. Wallace, but I believe it's best to venture forward now." Todd took a few steps towards Kate, who finally found the strength to stand as well. "I look forward to hearing from you so that we may go over the structural designs once more, Kate."

Kate nodded and reluctantly shook his hand. She accepted Liam's handshake as well, although she would rather have strangled him. The two thanked Jerry for his input and finally it was over.

Jerry's face only inches from her ear startled her. "You can thank me later, sweets. I have to run." Kate could only stare after him.

The moment Liam and Todd and their entourage were out of the boardroom she ran to her office in search of Alex. Abigail was close behind.

Alex wasn't there, he was gone and Kate turned angrily towards her grandmother.

"How dare you?" she accused.

"To what are you referring, Kate?"

"Let's start from the minors and work our way to the majors, shall we? You effectively cut me out of that meeting!"

"I did no such thing. I only spoke up when I realized negotiations were going nowhere. Did you want to lose that contract?"

"You made me look like a child who'd gone to work with her mother – or *grand*mother on parent day!"

"They know you're in charge. I made certain of that, in any case."

"Yes, *you* made certain of that! You know something? I've done a hell of a job without ever having to ask for your help in any way. I would have been able to correct this problem myself, without your input, but you obviously didn't trust me!"

"Kate, I've trusted you with this business since you graduated, but your judgment has been somewhat clouded of late, don't you agree? You have to admit your behaviour during this meeting was less than professional."

"Thank you. This brings me to the major issue. How dare you agree with Alex's decision to resign? You just told them I run the show, yet you sat there and played God, graciously accepting his resignation!"

Abigail shook a finger at her granddaughter. "Kate, be grateful I didn't mention the Andrews job."

The Andrews job.... Kate had almost forgotten about that, but it didn't make a difference. "Regardless, you had no right!" she yelled, tears stinging her eyes.

"Yes she did," said the voice behind her.

Kate swung around to face Alex, her loyal assistant, her trusted friend, and her heart and soul. "Alex," she whispered, swaying towards him. "Thank God ... I thought you'd left—"

Alex moved from her obvious advance. "I had to check on a job first. I'll send for my things."

"Alex, you're not leaving. I don't care about Liam or Todd; Gram has no right to accept your resignation," Kate said in a strained voice. "You work for *me* and I don't accept it."

"Boss ... there's no other way to fix this. This is a huge contract. Think about the man-hours we've put into it. You've already had to compensate them, which takes care of a good portion of your profit. If they walk, it would be a substantial blow to the firm. Jobs are at stake. Be logical. My resignation has already pacified them somewhat. Chances are they'll award you the next building like you'd hoped. They just want to be sure that the person responsible is no longer in a position to make another mistake. We can't condemn them for that."

Kate shook her head vigorously. "No one is infallible! Mistakes are inevitable; we're human!"

"Yes, well, I've made two – one after the other," Alex simply stated the fact.

"You don't have to go to such lengths! What's with you people?" she looked from one to the other as though they'd conspired against her to make her go mad.

"Kate! It's the right thing to do." Alex was being logical. It was just as well. He knew that he would never be able to work with Jerry. This was his way out, the perfect opportunity to leave. Unwillingly, he was going out somewhat of a martyr.

"Alex, don't do this," she begged, her voice strained. "We can find some other way to pacify Liam."

"It's done. You can't stop me. Truth is … I'm honestly starting to question my abilities. I'd rather leave. It's time to move on."

Kate grasped the lapels of his jacket, tears now welling up in her eyes. "No. You can't just leave. You can't."

Alex's voice was stern as he pried her fingers from him. "Sometimes we have to do what is best rather than what we want. You've made your choices, allow me to make mine. *You* have no right to tell me what to do." Having said that, he turned and walked out the door, leaving Kate crying behind the door like a child, perhaps the child who had sat in the meeting, unable to stand her ground….

Abigail gave her a few moments to unleash her obvious anguish. She returned after a few moments to Alex's former office to find Kate sitting against the door, her arms wrapped around her knees.

"Kate … I can understand how you feel, but it was the most logical solution." But her granddaughter continued to stare into space as she tried unsuccessfully to control the painful sobs from tearing at her chest. "You know, this doesn't necessarily have to be permanent," Abigail's words finally brought Kate's eyes to hers. "When this job is over … you might make Alex an offer to return…. "

Kate rose to her feet. "You don't understand," she said accusingly. "He won't come back. I screwed up everything. I could not have asked for a more qualified, loyal assistant – no, *partner* in this business, a better friend! And now I've lost him…." Kate's voice trailed off as she walked towards the glass partition and leaned against it, as if wishing it were Alex instead. "I almost tore his family apart, you know. At least I was able to stop myself from accomplishing that. It should be consolation, but it isn't."

"Kate, if things changed between you … whatever happened or didn't happen has really no bearing on what has taken place here." Abigail paused and then nodded knowingly. "Perhaps it does. But Kate dear, after what you told me about his daughter … you decided not to pursue the relationship, correct? Was he of the same opinion?"

Kate bowed her head, as the sobs continued. "I let him believe that I overreacted and got carried away with our acting."

"Well then Kate, did you honestly expect him to stay – even if this hadn't happened?"

"Yes!" Kate blurted, although in her heart she knew that her grandmother was right. She had half expected Alex to resign; she just hoped it wouldn't happen. Kate walked past her grandmother and strode into her private bathroom.

She glared into the mirror in disgust. It was her fault; everything was her fault. A relationship with Alex was out of the question, but at least working by her side, she could see him, touch him … call him 'friend'. Now that was taken from her as well. Kate splashed water on her face and inhaled a deep breath.

She had something to prove to her grandmother now. She could do the job and she'd do it well. Her job was all she had left – actually that's all she ever had.

Returning to her office, she buzzed her secretary.

"Connie, call a meeting for the engineering staff on the Gamble and Blaine project."

"Right away," Connie replied.

Abigail looked up at her granddaughter from her seat on the couch. *That's my girl,* she said to herself.

The meeting was set within minutes. Everyone quieted down when Kate entered the room. The men rose from their chairs when they noticed Mrs. Wallace accompanied her.

"Sit, sit, please," Abigail instructed as she sat as well in a chair next to Kate who glared at her grandmother one last time before proceeding with the meeting.

"All right. As you know we've had to do some fancy footwork to get back on track with Gamble and Blaine. It's cost us substantially…. " Kate swallowed that lump that returned to her throat. "They've agreed to allow us to continue. So … I'll need the revised site plans, costs for backfill and so forth. Tony, can you please help me to oversee the various departments? I'd like—"

"Excuse me, Kate, but where's Alex?" Tony finally asked the question on everyone's mind.

Kate raised her eyes from the papers in front of her. She looked at no one in particular. "Alex is no longer with the firm." There, she said it and yet the pain in her heart only worsened.

There was a unified gasp from everyone in that room. They all looked from one to the other. Tony was the only one to voice his thoughts. "How did I know this would happen?" he said quietly.

"It was his decision, Tony," Kate snapped. "Are you going to help me or not?"

Tony only now noticed her red puffy eyes, the strained lines around her mouth. This had not been her choice. "Yes. Yes, of course."

"Fine. You can forget about going home for dinner tonight people, I need this yesterday."

No one moaned or groaned or complained. They had seen their boss angry and upset, but this was different. She was distraught.

CHAPTER TWENTY-ONE

Needless to say, Alex was home uncommonly early that day. He would be able to pick up the kids himself. He gave a cynical laugh. He'd be able to do that every day, until he found another job!

Alex changed out of his suit and drove over to his parents' home. Pat was in the garage rebuilding his old hot rod. He hit his head on the raised hood when his son walked up behind him.

"Hey! What are you doing here?" his father asked. "Come to give me a hand?"

"I might just do that. I seem to have a little extra time on my hands," Alex said wryly.

Pat Callahan looked at him, a curious expression crossing his face. "What's wrong?"

Alex stood in a lazy stance, his hands in the pockets of his jeans. He shrugged indifferently. "I came by to tell you I'd be picking up the kids today."

"Okay," his father said slowly. "And?"

"And … I quit my job."

"You quit? Why?" Pat was stunned.

"Time to move on."

"But you were so happy there. Does this … by any chance … have anything to do with Kate?" he asked tentatively.

"Yeah."

Pat shook his head sadly. "That's too bad. I was kinda hoping that the two of you – you know…. "

"Yeah, so did I. But," he forced a smile. "It didn't work out. As far as my job … it was best for me to leave. I'll find something else."

"I'm sure you will." Pat watched his son intently. "I'm sorry, son."

"I'm fine Dad," he assured his father. "I'm going to go pick up the kids. I'll see you."

"Sure. If you need anything…. "

"Thanks Dad," he waved, and drove away.

Every mother waiting for their kindergarten children noticed the new arrival at the parents' waiting area. Alex's good looks would not go unnoticed, but Alex saw no one.

Stephanie, Nicholas and Paul exited from their door at the side of the building and walked around as usual to wait outside the enclosed kindergarten area.

"Dad!" the boys exclaimed when they spotted their father.

"Hi guys." Alex lovingly accepted their hugs and looked over to Stephanie who as always looked at him with suspicion.

"What are you doing here, Dad?" she asked curiously.

"Well, that's a nice greeting."

Stephanie came to give her father a kiss hello, but drew back as she waited for her answer. Just then the kindergarten children started to appear. Leeza's teacher spotted Alex and with a surprised wave, she sent the little girl running to her father.

"Daddy, Daddy!" Leeza exclaimed.

"Leeza, Leeza," Alex copied, swooping her up into the air. "How's my munchkin?"

"Happy! You picked us up, Daddy!"

"Yes, I know! Let's go home!" he continued in the same tone.

Dozens of eyes followed them to their truck. Several women waved towards them, saying their hellos to the new schoolyard attraction. Alex returned their greetings with a quick nod or wave, but was glad to leave the parking lot.

"Wow," he commented, feeling strangely as though he was the last male on earth.

Nicholas laughed. "Boy Dad! If you want a girlfriend, all you have to do is pick us up every day."

"Aren't these women married?"

"I don't think they care," Stephanie said under her breath.

"Probably not.... " Alex returned.

After dinner, Alex relayed the news of his resignation to his children. This was something that affected them and either way, something that he could not and would not keep hidden.

Stephanie felt a pang of guilt. "Did you quit or did they fire you?" she asked softly, holding her breath until her father answered.

Alex watched his daughter's face grow pale. "I just told you I resigned, I quit. Why would you think they'd fire me?"

"I don't know. I'm just saying ... well they better not have fired you…." She didn't know what to say.

"Well they didn't, and you don't have to worry, I'll get another job real soon."

"But Daddy," Leeza spoke up after remaining silent during Alex's speech, "you won't see Kate anymore."

"No. I won't."

"And Kate won't come over here anymore."

"Probably not."

"But I like Kate."

"I know you do, but she's a busy lady. We can't expect her to come visit us, now can we?"

Leeza raised her little shoulders and bowed her head is disappointment.

"It'll be all right Leeza," Alex assured his daughter as he gathered her to his arms. "I promise." He only wished he felt as confident as he sounded.

It looked like he was to repeat his story several times before the end of the weekend. Sunday afternoon, Tony Picaro dropped by to say hello. Alex was throwing a baseball with Nicholas and Paul when he arrived.

"Hey! How's it going, guys?" Tony called out to the boys. Nicholas and Paul waved hello.

"Nick, you and Paul play for a bit." Alex walked towards his friend. "Hi. I guess I was expecting you," he smiled.

"I was going to wait till you called, but I couldn't take it any longer. What happened?" Tony asked pointblank.

"I quit."

"Sure," he said skeptically.

Alex repeatedly punched his baseball mitt. "I did."

"Why?"

"Hasn't Kate asked you to redo the site plans?"

"Yes she did. She didn't give me much of explanation as to why."

"Why do you think, Tony? They were incorrect and I'm to blame. I'm to blame for Liam flipping his lid and threatening to pull the contract – everything."

Tony's eyes narrowed. "Yeah, right!"

"I worked on those plans. I botched them, I have no other explanation."

"So they canned you?" Tony exclaimed, flabbergasted at the mere thought.

"No, I told you I quit."

"And how does that help?"

"Tony … Liam wanted blood. Better the blood of one than that of hundreds…. Besides, I could never work for that jerk," Alex told him, preferring not to elaborate on the other reasons.

Tony knew whom he meant. "You didn't work for Jerry."

"I would. He's been in her office more than I have. When she needs something, she asks him. The two companies are going to merge, how long do you think it would be before he moves into my office?"

"That wouldn't happen. You're sounding paranoid and that's not like you. Since when do you worry about that idiot? As far as what happened … did they force you to accept fault Alex? You have four kids; you wouldn't just up and leave a job like yours."

"I told you this was entirely my decision. I'm human; what can I say? I just plain screwed up! And Tony, this wasn't the first time either."

"What do you mean?"

"I misread or transposed incorrectly the soil investigation results on Hubert Andrews' plaza." Tony's eyes narrowed, wanting to question his friend, but Alex continued, stopping him. "Don't even ask, 'cause I don't know how. But this last one was a doozy, and I've accepted responsibility for it, that's all. As for my kids, I think I'll be able to find another job before they're forced to use food stamps, Tony."

"You know what I mean. I know you won't have a problem landing another job, but it's just that you loved that job. Damn it, you loved—"

"Don't say it Tony."

"It's the truth."

Alex stared out into the distance. "I don't know about that Tony, but … you were right about that entire impersonating Jerry thing. Things *did* become very complicated."

"No kidding. But," Tony said putting up his hand, "I'm not asking. I'm … I'm just sorry to see you go, Alex. I've enjoyed working with you."

"So have I – with you I mean," Alex laughed, hoping to brighten the somber mood. "Hey, doesn't mean we can't still get together for a beer."

"Well I'm counting on it."

"So am I."

CHAPTER TWENTY-TWO

Abigail Wallace watched from the French doors as her granddaughter ambled slowly along the ample garden snipping roses and lilies and placing them in the white wicker basket. Kate had been extremely quiet during the last few days. Abigail was aware that Kate was upset with her. Her disappointment, in fact, her anger, was blatantly obvious. Her grandmother had agreed with Alex's choice to leave; she had accepted his resignation. She believed that this was best for the firm and for Kate. Working so closely with him, unable to show or act on her feelings … that would not be healthy for anyone concerned.

Kate, however, did not see Alex's resignation as a positive course of action and could not forgive her grandmother. There was more to this than what was obvious to her grandmother and she simply would not let it rest. She couldn't shake the feeling that something was amiss. The next morning she stopped to speak to Tony before continuing to her office.

The secretaries were aware of her foul mood of late, but they politely greeted their boss just the same as she passed their desks.

"Hmm? Oh, yes, good morning," she replied off-handedly.

Kate knocked on Tony's open door. "Tony, do you have a moment?"

Tony quickly rose from his chair. He noticed immediately her frown of consternation, the dark circles under her eyes. "Yes, of course." Realizing she wanted to speak to him here in his office, he gestured towards a chair. "Please…. "

"Tony … all of Alex's working copies … they're all correct. Yet the actual finished product was wrong. How could that be?"

Tony shook his head. This was baffling him as well. "I don't know, Kate. It sounds fishy to me."

"Yes … but what happened?"

"I've gone over those plans with a fine toothed comb – well actually, I've used a magnifying glass. Excavation depths were changed. The imprints of the correct numbers are just barely visible, but indeed visible."

"Look Tony, I tend to believe there's been foul play, but this doesn't prove anything though. He could have erased the correct numbers in error."

"You think?"

"No. But we're unable to explain why else they were changed."

Tony tilted his head. "Or by whom? Why do I feel as though I just crossed into the twilight zone?"

"Okay. Who else had access to those plans?" Kate stood and paced the floor.

"Access? Most of us up here could have gotten to them if we wanted to. Although they were kept in Alex's office," he added.

"And we don't habitually promenade through there."

"Alex said that aside from taking them home, the only time he was unaware of their whereabouts was when they were sent to the contractors."

Tony seemed skeptical. "Are you thinking they had something to do with this – wouldn't they be digging their own grave?" Kate looked up at him, narrowing her eyes at his choice of words, and Tony shrugged. "Well? Wouldn't they?"

"You're right. But, it's no secret how greedy people can be. Who knows what someone will do when his palms are greased. You know … if someone wanted someone else set up…. "

"Kate, we've used those guys for most of our jobs. I sincerely doubt they'd be involved in something like this, but if you want, I'll do some checking. Who knows?"

"Would you?"

"For Alex, anything."

Tony Picaro made an appointment with the excavating firm of Galibon and Sons. Matthew Galibon, owner and president of the firm, was a middle-aged man with a receding hairline and full grey beard. He was happy to meet with Tony.

"What can I do for you Tony? You said you wanted to discuss the job over at Georgia Street?"

"Yes, the Gamble and Blaine building. Matthew, you know Alex couldn't have possibly made those errors."

"It did seem incredible, but is there another explanation?"

His secretary buzzed in. "Mr. Galibon, sorry for the interruption. Herman Ganz is on line one. You said you wanted to speak to him."

"I did, but I can't take the call just now. Tell him I'll get back to him in just a few minutes, and Marsha, hold all calls for now." Matthew walked over to the door of his office and shut it. "So, what are you thinking, Tony?"

"Those numbers were changed. We're probably grasping at straws, but do you know of anyone here that had some sort of run-in with Alex?"

"No, of course not. We've always had a wonderful working relationship."

"What about ... have you hired anyone new? I'm thinking perhaps someone was planted to make the changes.... "

"Boy, you really are grasping at straws. No Tony, I haven't hired anyone in the past year or so. The work's been steady, no significant growths unfortunately, and thus no need to hire more people. Besides, I received those plans myself. I looked at them first. The elevations plotted were the ones we dug." Matthew Galibon lifted his right hand. "I swear on everything I hold sacred that I did not change them."

Tony nodded. Dead end. "I appreciate your time, Matthew."

Matthew rose from his chair, as did Tony. "Well Tony, if there's anything else I could do. I have to tell you, I'm glad the plans went through me. I'd hate to be wondering if I might be employing someone who would go to such lengths."

"I know what you mean." Tony left the office and sat in his car for a few minutes. Who else could it have been? Could the culprit be working for Wallace?

Tony relayed his findings, or lack of, to Kate.

"Then it was someone from here, but who?"

"Kate, Alex is well-liked. No one is jealous of him—" Tony stopped short. Except perhaps for Jerry, but then Tony shook his head. Jerry was an idiot; he wouldn't have had the skills or the intelligence.

Kate noticed his hesitation. "What? What are you thinking?"

"Nothing, Kate."

"You're thinking of Jerry," Kate said knowingly, and Tony couldn't deny it. "Tony, I didn't even want to consider the possibility, but I did ask pointblank and he swore he had nothing to do with those plans. And logically, why would he? I mean this could have been disastrous; we almost lost the contract, and the merger with his father would have been at stake … it would serve no purpose Tony."

Only the purpose of removing an excellent, capable employee to make way for himself.… "You're right, Kate. It would serve no purpose. At this point, I don't know where else to turn. I'll continue to make inquiries around here, maybe someone knows something."

"Okay." Kate sighed. "Thanks for your help."

The fact remained that those numbers had been tampered with. Tony was certain of this. He was skeptical that Alex could be responsible for not one but both situations. However, after discovering that the telephone number on file for ESI was disconnected, Tony's suspicions increased. He immediately made an appointment to see the president of ESI. He wouldn't tell Kate until there was something to say.

The meeting was both enlightening and confusing. Geoffrey Fine, president of ESI, was a tall robust young man with curly red hair. He welcomed Tony into his office and offered him a cup of tea.

"Let me just say that we were grateful for the opportunity you've given us. Working on one of your jobs … well, it can put us on the map, so to speak. What can I do for you, Mr. Picaro?"

"Yes ... well, unfortunately there might be a problem and all I ask at the moment is for clarification."

"I don't understand."

Tony was just as confused. "First of all ... has this always been your telephone number?"

Geoffrey Fine glanced at the number Tony had written on the inside cover of the file. "Yes, of course; since our beginning, which would be six years ago. Why?"

Tony's blood pressure was rising. "Because our contact number was this," he pointed to another number, to which Geoffrey shook his head in ignorance. "Is Malcolm Fish in today? Perhaps he should join us."

"Malcolm Fish? He worked here several months ago. He was only temporary, filling in.... Why?" Geoffrey asked again.

Tony handed him the soil investigation results faxed to Alex from Malcolm Fish of ESI. "He was in charge of this job, was he not?"

"In charge? No, of course not. He held a junior position and even that was as an assistant to someone else. He was in charge of nothing." Geoffrey was adamant. He skimmed through the pages. Craig Stephenson ordered and oversaw the testing. You see..." he pointed to the signature. "It's a big scribble, but I assure you that's his signature, not Malcolm's. Just a moment," Geoffrey buzzed his secretary to ask Craig to join the meeting.

Craig showed Tony his copies. All displayed findings as Beach Sands. The soil was unstable and therefore caisson footings instead of conventional were required – as expected.

"Geoffrey, this is an awkward situation. It seems that your

company – or rather – your company's name may have been involved in a scheme to discredit one of Wallace's valued employees."

"I don't understand."

Tony extended yet another sheet of paper to Geoffrey. This one showed the results to be different.

Geoffrey Fine, as well as Craig Stephenson, was at a loss for words. They could only speculate that Malcolm had somehow sent the incorrect information, but that did not simplify matters for Tony. Even if that was the case and two separate results were submitted, the fact remained that Alex's signature, as well as Craig's scribble, was on both. The only possible way that Alex could be proven innocent was if proof could be found that the results were changed after Alex signed the order. Geoffrey had no forwarding address or number for Malcolm. Tony had hit a brick wall. He knew for certain that Alex was innocent, but he could not prove it. He had nothing concrete to give to Kate, but he had to tell her just the same.

Kate was optimistic. Yes, there was very little evidence, in fact only strange occurrences that only intensified their confusion, but it did raise reasonable doubt of wrongdoings, and that was enough for Kate.

"And what do you intend to do with this piece of information?" This was not the reaction Kate was hoping for from her grandmother.

"Well don't you see? He could very well have been set up!"

"*Could very well have.* We don't know for sure and even if we did, we don't know by whom. You can't even find this Malcolm person! Things are not any clearer with the Gamble and Blaine job!"

Kate sighed and bowed her head, feeling extremely helpless. "Tony spoke to the excavating people. Tony believes they're in the clear."

"There you go. Which would only mean that if your suspicions were true … it would raise the possibility that there is someone in our midst capable of orchestrating such chaos. What do you think Mr. Andrews would say to that? What do you think Liam would do? They should not be told."

"But Gram, it's not right to let everyone think Alex was incompetent."

"I know you'd rather I don't point out the obvious, but that could be the case, Kate."

Kate seemed to ignore her grandmother. "We should tell Alex at least."

"Are you listening to me? Kate!" Abigail waved her hand in front of her granddaughter. "Wake up, lass! What good will that do? We have no proof! This is speculation. How would telling Alex what you *think* may have taken place, help the situation? And telling Liam, of all people. What would be the point to that? We stand to lose not only a large client, but also everything you've worked for – everything your grandfather and I worked for all those years. We're on shaky ground with Liam. Don't you see Kate? Accepting Alex's resignation was the obvious action, but aside from that Liam agreed to continue due to the knowledge of the pending merger. That was our other saving grace. We can't afford to rock the boat with implausible attempts at explanations. It's best to tread very carefully now. We shouldn't do anything to cause them to question our integrity and reliability not to mention our mental stability if we run to them with this 'idea', which in the end proves that we're not to be trusted."

Her grandmother was right – at least this time. Kate had not discovered anything concrete, and unfortunately she didn't have time to play investigator, not with the problems she had been facing lately and with the much-felt absence of Alex, she needed Tony at his post. Her investigator's hat had to return to the shelf for now. One day, however, she would get to the bottom of it.

Kate's latest revelations, or at least possibilities, for what had transpired at Wallace didn't seem to spark a single doubt in her grandmother's mind, and for that, their relationship only continued to deteriorate. Kate refused to admit that the decisions made had been correct, regardless of the seriousness of the matter. She refused to admit that from a business standpoint there was no other alternative. If she would allow herself to admit to the possible necessity of the measures taken, then she'd be admitting that Alex could have indeed been negligent or incompetent and that, she was positive, was not the case.

The little voice in her head scoffed at her rarely illogical behaviour, but still she clung to the possibility that there could have been an alternate plan, one where Alex did not have to pay the price, and thus she resented her grandmother for settling for the quick fix.

Abigail continued to visit the office daily, immersing herself in the business once again, even chairing meetings whenever Kate was called away or had too much to handle. She would relay discussions to her granddaughter, but Kate spoke to her only when necessary, limiting all conversation to business. In fact, to avoid further conversation, Kate stayed late nearly every night, preferring to go home only to sleep.

Sleep. Sleep consisted of, on average, three to four hours and usually not until she'd cried herself to exhaustion or stayed awake fretting over events that she could not possibly change. As time passed other decisions had to be made – personal decisions, as well as preparations. Abigail tried repeatedly to lend an ear or a helping hand, but Kate refused, choosing not to include anyone in her plans.

The thought of leaving did cross Abigail's mind, but she could not. She could not abandon her granddaughter at this crucial time in her life, regardless of Kate's feelings on the subject of her grandmother's departure. There must be something she could do.

Spending countless evenings alone, Abigail had ample time to contemplate Kate's findings and her determination to find the truth. Distressing as it was, there was only one person who could possibly bear ill feelings towards Alex, one person who could have lost a great deal if the relationship between Kate and Alex had flourished. Remembering the results of Tony Picaro's investigative exploits, Abigail confronted Jerry one day regarding Malcolm Fish.

"Jerry, dear," she called towards him as he entered Alex's old office. "I tried to contact Malcolm at ESI, but I've been informed he is no longer employed by them."

Jerry handed her the file she had earlier asked him to retrieve from another department. "Umm … why did you need to speak to him?" he asked innocently.

"I didn't really. I was calling regarding another job and since you had suggested speaking to Malcolm previously…."

"Oh. Well, yes. He resigned recently. He's gone to work for a firm abroad."

Jerry had become decidedly nervous and was quick to change the subject, and Abigail decided that she'd been wrong to expect her granddaughter to place the success of the family business above personal happiness. Trying to relay to Kate her change of opinion, however, would not change the situation on Alex's end, which would only infuriate Kate more. No. She'd give Jerry an ample supply of rope. If she were right, he'd hang himself with it sooner or later. She preferred sooner. Yes, she'd keep her thoughts to herself for now. Actions would speak louder than words in this instance. That – and perhaps divine intervention!

CHAPTER TWENTY-THREE

Things were not much better at the Callahan home.

Alex was hired by another firm within two weeks of his resignation. His would be a senior position, and the salary was comparable, but he'd have to prove himself all over again. He had decided to take an extra few weeks off before beginning with the new company. He wanted to take the opportunity to tackle unfinished chores around the house and possibly planning a little family getaway now that summer vacation approached. Wanting extra time to review his credentials and regain his confidence was another reason for the delay. Blanchart Architectural was happy to have Alex on board and was willing to wait until their new employee was ready to assume his new position.

While between jobs, Alex had much time to spend with his children – and he did. Aside from driving them to and from school, he attended all their soccer games and dance classes. He took them to movies and to the park. The children enjoyed spending this time with their father, but they sensed he was not happy and they behaved extra well so as not to upset him in any way. Alex was aware of their preoccupation, yet he refrained from talking about his feelings.

One Saturday morning several weeks later, Alex had just gone to retrieve a chocolate cake that his mother had baked for the kids, when someone rang the doorbell. The children had been left alone, certain that he'd only be gone for five minutes and certain as well that they would not open the door to anyone except their grandparents, no matter what.

However, upon peeking at the window, Stephanie recognized the visitor as Reginald, Mrs. Wallace's butler.

"You can't open the door, Steph!" Paul whispered loudly. "We're not allowed!"

"I know that!" Stephanie snapped. "But it's Reginald, I wonder what he wants." Stephanie's curiosity was too great to remain indifferent to this particular visitor. She had to find out what he wanted.

"Steph! I'm telling!"

"Oh so what! Go hide in your room if you're so scared."

Paul growled at her and stood his ground, crossing his arms across his little chest as he watched his sister head for permanent grounding.

Stephanie opened the door. "Oh hello, Reginald."

"Good morning Miss Stephanie. How are you?"

"I'm fine thank you, and you?" Stephanie answered politely.

"Quite well, thank you."

Nicholas and Leeza had heard voices and had hurried to the

door as well. Their first reaction was that of dismay at their sister's lack of regard for their father's rule, but then they saw Reginald's familiar form. "Hi," they both greeted the friendly man.

"Hello to you as well. It's so nice to see you again."

"Would you like to come in?" Stephanie invited.

"Is your father home?"

"No, not at the moment—"

Paul looked pointedly towards his older sister. "We're not supposed to open the door if he's not here." He had to relay that information.

"Oh my. I'm so sorry. I hope I haven't caused you to be reprimanded...."

Stephanie shook her head at her brother. "Don't worry about it, Reginald. My Dad will be back in a few minutes. I can give him a message if you like."

Reginald smiled at her proper manners. "Yes, that would be splendid. Mrs. Wallace has asked me to deliver this invitation personally."

"Invitation?" Stephanie asked tentatively.

"Yes, the invitation to Miss Kate's wedding."

"Oh," was all Stephanie could manage.

"The invitation is extended to all of you. Mrs. Wallace would very much like for you to attend. Will you see to it that your father receives it?"

"Yes, all right."

"Good day Miss, children.... " Reginald tipped his chauffeur cap and returned to his car.

Stephanie closed the door and leaned against it. She stared at the cream coloured envelope and let her fingers slide over the elaborate gold calligraphy that spelled their family name.

Paul didn't make further comments about Stephanie opening the door. He watched her quietly for a moment, taking in the strange expression on her face. Neither did Nicholas or Leeza. Everyone seemed concerned with the envelope in Stephanie's hand.

Stephanie didn't hear Alex's truck pull up into the driveway. She didn't realize she was still leaning against the door until her father pushed it open, sending her awkwardly forward.

"Steph? What are you doing?"

"Dad, I didn't hear you."

"Obviously," he chuckled. Then he noticed a strange silence amongst his children and his expression became serious. "What's wrong?"

"Nothing, Dad," Nicholas answered.

"Reginald came to visit us, Daddy." Leeza informed him innocently.

"Reginald?" Alex said curiously, and then, "I thought I told you a million times not to open the door to anyone."

"I told her not to, Dad," Paul offered, and Stephanie sneered at her little brother.

"Steph?"

"I know, Dad," Stephanie sighed as her eyes inspected the ceiling once again. "But I … when I saw it was Reginald, I was curious."

Alex placed the freshly baked cake on the coffee table. "Considering it was Reginald, I would think you would have bolted the door with galvanized steel!" he exaggerated and Stephanie made a face.

"We're invited to Kate's wedding, Daddy!" Leeza exclaimed.

Alex's head turned sharply to his youngest daughter. "What?"

Stephanie handed the envelope to her father. "Mrs. Wallace had Reginald deliver the invitation personally. He said … he said that she'd like us all to go."

The children were silent once again as they waited for their father's reaction. They watched as Alex slowly opened the envelope and read its contents. It read:

Kate Wallace

And

Jerry Kent

Request the honour of your presence

To celebrate together as the two unite…

Replacing the delicate paper in its place of origin, he tried to dismiss the pain that had spread across his chest, the cold sweat that had crept up his spine. It was truly over.

"Daddy, can we go?" Leeza asked excitedly.

"Leeza," scolded Nicholas. "I don't think Daddy wants to go."

"Why not Daddy? I like weddings and I like—"

"Yes, we know – you like Kate!" Stephanie sighed in exasperation. "Change your tune, will you!"

"Stephanie, leave her alone," Alex scolded. "We'll see, Leeza. I'll think about it, okay?"

"Okay, Daddy." Satisfied with his answer, Leeza took her doll into the kitchen for a cup of milk. Paul returned to his building set and Nicholas to his latest school project.

Stephanie remained in the living room, eyeing her father with much interest. "You knew she was going to get married,

Dad. Why do you look so surprised?"

"I'm not surprised. I guess I just hoped she wouldn't go through with it, that's all."

"But she was engaged to him, why wouldn't she marry him?"

Alex closed his eyes and inhaled deeply hoping to disperse the anger he felt. "I know that. I said I hoped she wouldn't."

"Why? Because you wanted to go out with her?"

"Stephanie, I guess it doesn't make much of a difference now, so I'll tell you why," he started. Stephanie's eyes rounded, not in fear of her father, but in fear of what he might say.

Alex glared at his daughter. He was going to tell her exactly what she didn't want to hear, but in compensation, it would make no difference whatsoever. "I loved her. Okay?"

Stephanie digested that piece of information, but her father had more. "In fact, I had been in love with her long before that crazy plan of hers. I had this totally ridiculous idea that I might one day muster enough courage to tell her so and maybe if things worked out, I might have asked her to marry me. Is that a good enough reason, Steph? But, as it happened, it didn't work out, so you don't ever have to worry about it again. I'm sure that by the time I find someone else that I might want to spend my life with, you'll all be married with children of your own. At that time, I'm sure what I do won't matter to you anymore."

"That's not true Daddy," Stephanie said quietly. "I'll always care about what you do."

Alex gave a cynical laugh. "Sure. See me in about three years."

"You hate me, don't you?" Stephanie blurted, tears starting to flow uncontrollably, and Alex instantly regretted being so abrupt.

He took his daughter into his arms. "I don't hate you, Steph.

I love you. I love you so much!"

"But I've given you such a hard time whenever you wanted to go out with someone and then with Kate.... "

"Kate ... Kate was not your fault," he said quietly, and Stephanie cried even more. "That was a no-win situation. I should have known better than to try and compete with someone like Jerry."

"What do you mean? You're a zillion times better than him!"

Alex laughed. "You've never met him. He comes across like a real cool dude."

"So? I don't have to meet him to know that you're better."

"Well, he's rich and has muscles bulging from everywhere – even his ears!"

"So what? You're not rich, but you're kind and good and a perfect father and ... and you're a hunk! You saw all those mothers staring at you at school," Stephanie explained, and Alex shook his head in amazement.

"Why Stephanie, you actually love your old man." Again Stephanie sobbed and Alex hugged her closely. "I love you too."

Guilt was eating her up. Stephanie sneaked a peek at the invitation and learned that the wedding was to take place in two weeks. She felt horrible. She had been the cause for Kate's decision to marry Jerry. She had been the cause for her father's sadness these last few months. Stephanie wanted to make it better, but she didn't know how. There was only one person she could turn to now. Only one person would truly understand how she felt, why she did what she did.

Nicholas and Paul had a soccer game on the following

Saturday morning, so Stephanie suggested that Gramma Gloria would come and sit with Leeza and herself instead of having to tag along or being dropped off at Gramma Mary's. Gramma Gloria was only too happy to oblige. She was there within the hour.

When Alex, Dan and the boys left for the game, and Leeza was deeply enthralled with her cartoons, Stephanie pulled her maternal grandmother into the kitchen.

"Steph?" Gloria was concerned with her granddaughter's peculiar behaviour.

"I have to talk to you Gramma."

"All right," she said slowly. "What happened Stephanie? Are you all right?"

Stephanie started to cry, which only made her grandmother's blood pressure soar to new levels. Still she did her best to remain calm. "Oh dear, what's the matter Stephanie? Tell me what's wrong."

"Gramma, I've made a mess of everything!"

Gloria's heartbeat slowed a little. "Mess of what, honey?"

"Oh, just Dad's life, that's all!"

"What do you mean?"

Between sobs, Stephanie recounted to her grandmother what exactly she had done – what she'd overheard months ago in Kate's office and how she'd remained silent in the hope that the outcome would be the best thing for everyone – especially for her. Trying to stop the flow of tears, she also told her of her conversation with Kate on her veranda. When she was through, Gloria remained silent for quite a while.

"Stephanie.... You shouldn't have been eavesdropping for starters ... but after hearing what they were saying about your dad....

You should have told him. You should tell him now." Gloria shook her head. "Although, I doubt it would make much of a difference now, which brings me to the other piece of information you kept from him."

Gloria sighed and held her granddaughter's hands in hers. "Stephanie, do you love your Grampa? Grampa Dan?"

Stephanie sniffled and looked at her curiously. "Yes. Of course I love Grampa."

"Yes. He's a good man, isn't he?"

"Yes." Stephanie didn't understand this line of questioning.

"Your mom loved him too."

"Well sure, he was her father.... "

"No. No, he wasn't," Gloria admitted quietly.

Stephanie's sob seamed to stop midway, as her mouth dropped open, completely stunned.

"Your Grampa, my husband, was not your mom's father. Her father died when she was very little. She was about five, Leeza's age."

"Did Mom know?" Stephanie's voice came out as a whisper as though this was a secret that her grandmother was entrusting her with.

"Yes, she knew. I met Dan a few years later. At first I thought it was wrong to feel close to someone else. I thought that people would think badly of me. Most importantly I was afraid for my daughter. I didn't know how she would react, but you know what?"

"What?"

"Your mom was the one who pushed me to open my heart to another man. I am so thankful for that. After Julie, I couldn't have another child. He knew this, I told him, but it didn't matter to him. As it happened, Dan loved my daughter as if she were his. I'd say Julie was as much his as her natural father; Dan helped raise her. I was very fortunate. I know things don't always turn out so well when people remarry – hey, things don't always turn out when people marry for the first time either! All I'm saying is that your mom didn't want me to be alone and after what happened … after your mom…. " Gloria's voice tightened. "After my baby girl died, well I'd be alone right now if I didn't have Dan, wouldn't I?"

Stephanie nodded her head. "Does Daddy know?"

"Yes. He's always known. I guess that's why he also knows that we – that I would understand if he would want to remarry. It was my daughter he was married to; my daughter who died, and I know how much he loved her. Your mom wouldn't want him to be alone any more than she wanted me to be alone. I can't tell you how to feel honey, but allowing your father to love another, accepting that woman in his life as well as your own, will never diminish the love you have for your mother – never.

"He loves Kate."

Gloria nodded. "Tell him what you told me, Steph. Tell him what she said."

Stephanie shook her head vigorously. "I can't, I just can't. He'll hate me."

"He won't hate you for telling the truth."

But Stephanie was afraid. She was too afraid.

Stephanie had no fingernails left to speak of. She was so nervous. It was Friday evening. The wedding was tomorrow and still she had said nothing to her father.

While helping with the dishes, she dropped two glasses and a large casserole dish, shattering them into several pieces.

"Stephanie, what's with you tonight? Maybe you should just leave this to me. Mind you, if you'd emptied the dishwasher, we wouldn't be here, would we?" Alex took the salad bowl from her shaking hands. "Go sit down, will you?"

She tried to sit, but she couldn't stay put. She got up again and began to pace.

"Stephanie, you're making me nervous!" her father told her as he continued to gather the larger pieces of the former casserole dish. "Leeza don't walk there, there's glass everywhere. I don't want it crunched under your slippers and scattered throughout the house. Nicholas I told you to get the broom."

Nicholas was wiping down the table. "Paul went to get it."

"I'll sweep it Dad," Paul offered, but his father refused.

Alex swept the remaining pieces into the dustpan that Paul held in place, and securing it all into a double bag, he returned to the dishes. He would vacuum later.

"Dad, can we go to the wedding?" Stephanie blurted suddenly.

"The wedding?" Alex nearly dropped the coffee carafe. "Why?"

"I don't know. Wouldn't you like to go?"

He glared at his daughter in disbelief. "And why would I want to do that?"

"Well," Stephanie felt an idea brewing. "Wouldn't you like to show them that you've not only found a job – a better job, but that you're not upset about … about the wedding?"

"Not really, no." Alex dried his hands and came to stand by his daughter. "Steph? Are you okay?"

"Yes Dad, I'm fine."

"Daddy?" Leeza started and Alex looked heavenward. He knew what she was going to say. "Daddy, can we go the wedding? I'd like to go to the wedding."

"Leeza, honey. Daddy doesn't feel like going."

"Why not?" the tiny voice asked. "Because you're sad?"

He denied Leeza's assumption, and his tone was curt. "I'm not sad."

"Yes you are," Paul told him as he held the refrigerator door open for his brother, who was replacing the jug of juice.

"It's true." Leeza came to take hold of her father's hand. "You don't whistle anymore and we don't have pillow fights…."

"I'm sorry. I didn't realize…."

"Maybe if you go to the wedding, you'll have a nice time, Daddy," Leeza urged.

Alex looked at Stephanie. Watching Kate marry that imbecile was not at all something he wanted to do – in fact major surgery sounded better, but perhaps his daughter had a point. He had to snap out of this slump. Perhaps closure to that part of his life would be the best medicine. "You may be right, Steph. It would certainly put an end to everything. Okay. Do we have outfits or are we going shopping?" he said with a grin.

"Shopping!" Leeza shrieked, bouncing up and down.

They left the cleaned dishes to dry on their own and hurried into the truck for a quick outing to the mall. The boys were not too crazy about their dress shirts and jackets, but Leeza was ecstatic about the little chiffon number with the designer label and price tag to match. Stephanie wasn't too picky. She settled for a simple silk shift dress, the first she saw. Her stomach was in turmoil; she couldn't enjoy her favourite pastime.

It was Saturday morning. Wedding day. Doomsday....

Dressed and ready to go, everyone seemed to stop suddenly at the front door. They all looked at each other in silence. A muscle twitched nervously at Alex's jaw.

"Do you really want to go?" he said suddenly.

"Yes!" Leeza declared. "I have a new dress!"

"So you have," he said, forcing a smile. "Let's go."

CHAPTER TWENTY-FOUR

The wedding ceremony was to be held at Kate's home. Cars lined the long driveway making it awkward to maneuver Alex's large truck through the narrowed passage. He stopped at a clearing where a uniformed young man waited patiently for the four children to climb down from the vehicle.

Alex took a deep breath. Taking Leeza and Paul's hands in his, he made his way around the side of the large house to the backyard.

The garden was beautifully decorated with flowers and ribbons. There were canopies over tables of food and champagne. Musicians were situated in their own little area and waiters attended to the preparation of cocktails and hors d'oeuvres.

A familiar voice called out to him. Tony Picaro made his way towards him, the rest of the office clan close behind. "Alex … buddy … I didn't expect to see you here."

"Neither did I. I mean, I had no intention…. Mrs. Wallace sent the invitation, and … I thought it might be a good idea."

Tony nodded knowingly, before his wife and the others joined the circle. Everyone was happy to see Alex, but his children captivated them. Most of the office employees had never met the Callahan brood. The children were polite as usual, but Stephanie could not join in the small talk. She had other things on her mind. To complicate matters more, she spotted a familiar woman – the woman whom she'd overheard in Kate's office. Stephanie put a hand to her mouth, shocked at the realization she'd made.

Soon someone made his way to stand near the makeshift altar and asked everyone to take their seats.

This was it. Alex followed his friends to the chairs, choosing to sit near the back. Leeza and Paul wanted to sit by the aisle, so Alex allowed Stephanie and Leeza to sit in one row with Angie and Connie and he and the boys sat behind them with Tony and the rest.

Stephanie couldn't bite her nails because there was nothing left to bite. So, she started chewing on the tips of her tender cuticles instead.

The music began to play. Jerry made his way to the raised platform under the canopy covered almost completely with flowers of every shade.

Everyone stood as they waited for the bride to arrive. A woman walked by – the Maid of Honour. She wore a pale lilac dress.

The wedding march. It was time for the bride, but Alex couldn't turn around. Stephanie did, but she watched her father, not the bride. As Kate drew near, walking alone towards the altar, Stephanie's eyes turned to her. It was Kate's wedding day, but she looked far from happy. She looked sad. In fact she looked as though she'd been crying all morning.

Leeza waved excitedly, which drew her father's attention, causing him to turn his eyes to Kate. She wore a simple silk gown; no veil hid her beautiful features. Instead, a few tiny white orchids were arranged in her hair and she looked stunning. Alex managed a strained smile as he looked into her surprisingly strained expression, but he said nothing and Kate continued her walk towards her intended who waited for her arrival.

The ceremony began, but Stephanie couldn't pay attention. Several times she turned to steal a glance towards her father, but Alex kept his eyes lowered as if unable to watch the woman he loved marry another.

Stephanie had heard nothing, but when the Reverend's voice asked if there was anyone there who knew just cause why the two should not be married, to speak now, Stephanie heard him loud and clear.

Abruptly and without thought of consequence, Stephanie jumped up from her chair.

"Wait!"

The guests turned to look at the diminutive person who had just stopped the wedding. So did the bride and groom.

"Stephanie, sit down!" Alex tried to pull his daughter down.

"No, no, let the child speak."

"I'm sorry," Alex apologized, but Stephanie was urged to continue.

"It's quite all right. I did ask the question," the Reverend said, drawing a bit of laughter from the crowd. "Go right ahead, my child."

"Kate, I'm sorry," she blurted. "I treated you really badly, and I shouldn't have. I just didn't want my dad to get close to anyone else." Stephanie began to cry.

"Oh God…." Alex cringed in his seat. "Steph, please sit down…." he pleaded, but his daughter continued.

"I didn't want him to forget my mom. And then, and then … I started to like you, and I didn't want to…. "

"Oh Steph," Kate's voice was barely audible. Alex's eyes were glued to Stephanie's back, as if willing her to sit down, willing her to shut up!

"I was afraid that if I liked you, then maybe I would forget my mom and I just can't – I won't forget my mom. But … but I was being selfish because my dad … when we get older … my dad will be alone and that's not fair to him. He's been so sad … like when my mom died and now – I mean before … he had started to look happy again, like when my mom was alive," she sobbed. "I was jealous of that, but I was wrong. I'm sorry…. "

"Stephanie, please!" Alex stood now, taking hold of Stephanie's hand. "You could have written her a note! This is Kate's wedding day!" He looked up to the bride and groom. "My apologies again. We're going to leave now—"

"No! Dad, you don't understand!" she implored, pulling away from him. "She came to the house. Kate came to talk to you that Sunday when Mrs. Wallace was supposed to leave. She told me that she didn't care about the company or anything. She said that she wanted you – and all of us—"

Alex's former co-workers, who had been dabbing at their eyes, now gasped in delighted surprise. Tony nodded knowingly. His heart was breaking for this young girl who desperately wanted to keep her mother's presence alive, yet he felt no less for Alex, whose life had been manipulated by his fourteen-year-old daughter.

"Steph!" Alex said between clenched teeth, his voice low. "It was a mistake. I spoke to Kate afterwards. She had been upset because Jerry had gone away, that's all. She was confused when she came over. We all got carried away, but he came back and everything went back to normal. They're getting married, Steph, the way they were supposed to, understand?"

Stephanie accepted this confusing piece of information, but she hadn't finished, there was more.

"But Dad, there's ... there's something else. You have to know something! Kate too. I'm sorry, I should have told you when I first overheard, but I thought ... I thought it would be for the best—"

Alex couldn't believe there was more, but what was the point in trying to stop her now?

Stephanie turned to the bride. "Kate, the day ... the day after you came over to work with my dad ... I was at my dad's office. I overheard a woman talking to someone in your office about my dad being a liability, that he could ruin everything for them because you depended too much on my dad." Stephanie paused to catch her breath as Kate watched and listened in horror.

People were mumbling and whispering and the groom was getting edgy, but Stephanie pushed forward. "Then the man said he'd found the perfect way to get rid of my dad. He said that what he had in mind was sure to get him fired."

Alex's lips contorted to form a cynical smile. He knew exactly what happened now. So did Tony!

"I didn't say anything because after meeting you I was so

afraid that you and my dad … I thought if he didn't work there anymore, if he didn't see you anymore … I was wrong. I'm sorry."

Kate spoke now, her voice quiet, strained. "Stephanie, do you know who they were?"

"I couldn't see the man, but the woman … that's her right there," Stephanie pointed. "The woman with the pink … I mean … red hair."

Everyone gasped. Kate turned angry, knowing eyes towards her mother. She should have known.

Debra's face nearly matched her hair, but it was the only indication of nervousness. Other than that she simply sat there in exaggerated shock at the accusation, dumfounded that her daughter could even consider believing those lies!

Alex took hold of his daughter's hand. "Stephanie … it's time to go now."

Stephanie looked to Kate and then back at her father. "But …"

"It's all right, I promise," he assured her. "I think we need a change of scenery. Please excuse the interruption," he said to guests. "Come on, kids…. "

Tony stood, allowing more room for Alex to pass. He patted his friend on the shoulder, but didn't follow him. He needed his privacy now.

Kate watched them leave. She continued to stand in silence as if in a trance. Alex hadn't said anything. The proof that he was innocent didn't seem to faze him. Kate's visit to his home and declaration of love, his daughter's public announcement of her acceptance of Kate, had made no difference to him. Kate felt a hand constricting her heart. But Alex had been wronged in more ways than one. It was time to make the proper adjustments.

"That was truly pathetic!" spat Jerry. "I thought I told you not to invite them!"

Abigail Wallace stood. "I invited them."

Kate ignored her fiancé. She turned and stepped down from the raised platform where the Reverend watched with concern. "I'm sorry, Reverend Boon, I just need to catch my breath," she said quietly. "Mother, I'd like a word with you." She walked down the path to the safety of her living room, away from the bewildered stares of the gathered guests.

Jerry's face became the shade of a wonderfully ripened tomato as panic set in. "Sweets?" he called after his bride-to-be. "Sweets, where are you going?"

Abigail followed the bumbling groom, while Debra turned to address her guests.

"Everyone, if you'll just excuse us for a tiny a moment," she said with a bright smile, although her little laugh was nervous. She signaled to the waiters. "Please enjoy some refreshments in the meantime, but we won't be long – I promise!" Debra hurried along the path after her daughter as Gregory Kent started with a speech of his own.

Jerry caught up to Kate and took hold of her arm. "Sweets! What are you doing?" He tried to sound flip, as if what had just happened – hadn't happened at all. "Sweets, this is our wedding day. Let's get back—"

"The wedding's off, Jerry."

"You don't mean that. Come on, let's go back."

"I think not. I think you'd better start explaining."

Jerry was indignant. "I beg your pardon! I don't know what you're talking about."

Her mother had just entered the room and Kate turned to her. "But *you* do, don't you?"

"Kate, don't you tell me that you're going to believe the ranting of an obviously disturbed little snot!"

Abigail stomped her cane on the floor. "You watch your mouth! That little girl has more integrity than both of you put together. She was frightened and confused, that's all she's guilty of – unlike the two of you!"

Jerry turned to look at Abigail. He wasn't pleased with her choice of words, her accusations. "Really Gram, I don't know what are you're talking about," he said with a tight smile.

"*Mrs. Wallace,*" Abigail corrected.

Jerry huffed. "Mrs. Wallace … I think we've had enough enlightenment for one day. This is our wedding day. I don't particularly like all these interruptions!"

Abigail laughed incredulously. "Interruptions? Is that what you call this? Are you on drugs lad? What do you take me for? I knew you're involved in this somehow! I just couldn't prove it! You and that hussy set out to destroy a man's reputation for your own personal gain! Do you honestly think this wedding is going to take place? I apologize to you Kate," she said to her granddaughter, "if I hadn't persuaded you into stopping your investigation, you'd have arrived at the truth a fair bit sooner. We could have avoided this charade of a wedding! And as for you," she turned accusing eyes to her ex-daughter-in-law, "I've never known anyone to be more greedy than you! You are a poor excuse for a human being. You disgust me!"

"Naturally, what would I expect from you, you old crone!"

"Don't you dare speak to my grandmother like that! Gram

is right! You, Mother, are guilty as sin, and you," she turned to her ex-fiancé, "are up to your steroid enhanced neck in this! You will pay for this, I promise you – both of you!"

"Sweets, don't include me in this! I had nothing to do with it. You heard the girl. She didn't see who your mother was speaking to. It wasn't me, I tell you!"

Debra nearly lunged towards Jerry. "You little weasel! This is why I wanted the old biddy to come while you were away! Now, don't you try to worm your way out of this! It was your idea to get Malcolm to change those results and those drawings!"

Jerry's role had been exposed. His face red, his brow beaded with sweat, he lashed back, blindly. "Yeah, because you kept saying that he was a threat. I don't see how that was possible since the marriage was only supposed to last long enough to make us both some money—" Jerry stopped short, realizing he'd just revealed more than he had intended. And Kate smiled.

"You idiot!" Debra hissed.

"It was all her idea, you know," he nodded as he looked from Abigail to Kate. "She wanted me to talk to my father, to get him to talk to you about joining forces. She figured I would come into the picture later, so that you wouldn't be suspicious. Our pre-nup would naturally have been advantageous to me since I would have shares in both companies, securing my future. The plan was to divorce you soon afterwards, and we," he motioned to Debra and himself, "we would split the profits, so to speak...."

Debra almost snorted, her face distorted. "You bastard, I should have left you in Africa!"

If Jerry hadn't returned, things would have been different. Yes, their plan to discredit Alex had been set in motion, but she and Alex would have been together, they would have found a way to work things out.... All of Kate's questions were being answered. In fact, she was being given answers to questions she hadn't even voiced. "You arranged for Gram to come while he was away because you must have known he'd screw up somehow, that Gram would not have liked him, didn't you? And then you called him back when you realized your plan might be in jeopardy. That doesn't surprise me either."

"Naturally I called him, you were starting to enjoy playing house! You were falling all over yourself over that – that man, whom you seemed to have forgotten was merely your employee by the way – and his entire brood! I couldn't let you throw away your life! I had to do something!"

"Throw away my life? How would I be doing that by being with a man I loved? You wanted me to marry *him*," she pointed at Jerry with contempt. "A parasite with no integrity, who has never personally earned one penny of his family's fortune, who conspired and carried out a plan to destroy another human being, with the intent to marry me – not for love, but for my money to line your pockets; to secure your futures!" Kate took a breath. "I suppose that would have been the right thing to do!" Kate pulled off the flowers from her hair and turned to her fiancé. "I must have been in a daze ... I can't believe I was actually going to marry you for the good of the company! Perhaps I should thank you – your elaborate plan turned out to be the best thing that could have happened to me. I got to know a man, a caring man, an honourable man; one who puts his family first. He awakened me from a deep sleep; I'm wide-awake now. I have truly come to my senses. Know this: even if I hadn't learned about your intentions, your carefully laid out plan, simply realizing that I might have a chance with Alex, I would never have married you," she stated calmly.

"Huh!" Debra let out a cynical laugh. "And just who is it you intend to marry – Alex Callahan? That was a sappy speech that little runt performed, but what are you so happy about? What did it reveal to you? All *I* learned is that his daughter is a conniving little bitch—"

"—Don't you dare call her names!" Kate shook with anger.

"What's the matter, can't face reality? I didn't hear anything about her father having any possible feelings towards you, did *you*? You are fooling yourself if you think he is in love with you!"

"That's enough!" Abigail declared.

"Would someone please fill me in on what just transpired out there?" Gregory Kent's voice thundered loudly, turning all heads in his direction.

Jerry's face was now ashen in colour. Things had definitely soured and he looked as though he was about to faint.

Abigail faced the new arrival to their private party, her chin raised, her cane tapping the floor. "Mr. Kent. I just hope your innocence is real and not just a successful cover-up!"

"My innocence? What is going on?"

"Then listen carefully. You're about to be enlightened." Abigail turned to Jerry, who actually took a step backward. "Did you honestly believe that you would get away with that scheme of yours?" He didn't answer so she glared towards Debra. "Well?" Debra huffed and puffed, but nothing escaped her blood red lips. "My ex-daughter-in-law seems to have lost her voice momentarily. Jerry, would you like to fill him in?"

Jerry couldn't speak.

"No? Very well. They have been busy little bees, the both of them. They've doctored laboratory results as well as blueprints, costing us a substantial amount of money and all to discredit Alex Callahan, so that he would be fired or resign, which is exactly what he did, because he is an exceptional individual who placed others above himself."

Kate's heart swelled at the realization that her grandmother truly cared for Alex.

Gregory Kent was incredulous. "This is ridiculous! Why would they do this? How was Mr. Callahan a threat?"

"I suppose they were both insecure and Alex's obvious ability and value to the company made the feasibility of attaining their ultimate goal less than clear. I suppose Jerry wanted to, should we say … cement his foundations in the business. To do so, he had to get rid of Alex."

Gregory shook his head in disappointment. "Jerald Augustus Kent. I've always known you to be selfish, and in fact a schemer, but to set out to destroy a person's reputation – his livelihood! This happened because I'd capped your spending! I suppose in a way I'm to blame for your actions – actions that are going to be addressed, rest assured!"

"Look, there's no way in hell I'm going to take the fall for this. It was *her* idea, *her* plan!" Jerry declared.

Debra lashed out, warning her partner in crime. "You bastard. You're going to regret the day you met me."

It was Kate's turn to glare at her mother, as did Gregory, his mouth open in utter dismay. Abigail simply watched with sincere satisfaction. "He's right, you're both going to pay, *mother.*"

"Are you going to listen to *him*? Don't you see? He's been caught! He's only trying to pass the buck!"

"You double crossing bitch!" Jerry spat.

Gregory Kent threw up his arms, and made to leave only to quickly turn to his son. "You are not my son. I don't know you. Kate, Mrs. Wallace, I offer my sincere apologies. I'll go and speak to our respective guests. Frankly, I don't want to hear another word."

"Just one more thing, Mr. Kent," Abigail spoke calmly. "I believe under the circumstances you understand that our business dealings will have to be rethought."

"Yes. Yes, I understand. I assure you we'll speak again in private."

"Kate, darling, you're not going to listen to a child's obvious delusions and … and to this raving lunatic, are you? I'm your mother…." Debra used an uncharacteristically sweet and loving tone.

"My *mother*? And when exactly did you start being a mother to me?"

"Why Kate, how can you say that?" Debra played the part of the injured party.

"All you ever did for me, was give birth to me – and even that was something that I know for a fact you'd had no intention of doing. You never wanted me. I complicated your life – not that it showed, mind you. Having a child never interfered with your outings, with your social life!" Kate's voice shrilled even in her own ears. She was aware of her mother's shallow personality, but this new revelation had been a shock, even for her. "Stop denying what you've done – both of you! It only makes you more detestable, what you've done more deplorable. I want both of you to leave – immediately!"

"But Kate, where will I go?" Debra started to panic.

"I don't care. You can move in with Jerry. You seem to be made for each other."

Debra didn't move. She stood like a statue, as did her co-conspirator.

"*Now* Mother!"

Debra decided to assume an air of indifference. "Well, I have to pack," she shrugged.

"No. I will send your things to his place. I want you to leave – now."

Debra finally unglued herself from the Persian rug and started towards the door. She pushed Jerry to walk ahead of her, but Jerry suddenly turned to Kate once again.

"I want that ring back. It cost me a fortune!"

"Yes, of course, your precious ring. Actually, Jerry, I'm sure it cost *me* a fortune."

Kate slipped off the ring and threw it at him. "But you can have it. I don't want anything that even remotely reminds me of you. Think of it as my gift to both of you. Having no other means of income, you'll have to live on whatever that ring will get you!"

Abigail gathered her granddaughter into her arms, but Kate held her at arm's length. "Gram, can you handle the guests? I have to get out of this dress…. "

Stephanie sat on the white wrought iron bench at the far end of their backyard. Everyone had gone inside to change, but Stephanie needed a few minutes to be alone, a few minutes to gather her thoughts.

On the ride home, Alex had reached over to his daughter and taken her hand. "Are you okay Steph?" he'd asked softly. Stephanie could only nod her head. The other children had remained quiet. It was not a time for idle conversation.

Her family joined her at the bench a little while later. Leeza came to sit beside her; the boys stood alongside their father. Her brothers watched her intently; they were worried.

"I'm sorry Daddy," she sniffed.

Alex squatted down in front of her. "Steph … you shouldn't have been listening at Kate's door, although I'm glad to know the truth, but regardless … her mother plotting against me has no bearing on what happened with Kate and me. I believe things happen for a reason. If something's meant to be, it'll happen regardless of the circumstances. This thing with Kate … was not meant to be. So, don't fret about it. Besides, I'm sorry that I involved you in a scheme that I knew could only result in disaster. I obviously wasn't thinking clearly."

"But I lied to you."

Alex sighed. "Yes you did. But, you may have saved me from making a fool of myself. She decided to marry Jerry anyway."

"But only because of what I said to her."

"We don't know that. Today didn't seem to change anything."

"Maybe it did," Nicholas said suddenly, looking towards the side of the house.

"It's Kate!" exclaimed Leeza in a loud whisper.

Alex straightened out. A frown creasing his brow, his eyes didn't leave her as she drew near. The wedding gown was gone; the two-carat diamond was gone.

"Hi," she said simply.

The children responded. Alex was too surprised to speak.

"Alex … I apologize for what was done to you. In my heart I knew you were innocent, I even tried to investigate, but I came up with nothing. I should have stood my ground … I'm so sorry. Your name will be cleared, I promise."

Alex shrugged. "Don't worry about it." He wasn't quite sure what to make of her visit. What happened to her wedding?

"Well I do…. " Kate watched him for a moment longer, but Alex said nothing more and she turned to the petite girl with the tear-stained face, sitting quietly on the bench. "Stephanie, are you okay?" she asked, concern in her voice.

Stephanie started to sob again, and Alex held her against him.

"Steph?" Kate spoke softly.

Stephanie pulled herself from her father's dampened T-shirt and turned towards Kate. "I ruined you wedding!" she cried.

Kate smiled. "No, you didn't. You saved my life," she told her, coming to sit next to her.

"What?" Steph tried to wipe her tears.

Alex stared at his former boss, his heartbeat accelerating, but still he said nothing. He needed to hear more.

"I couldn't marry him," Kate said in a loud whisper. He didn't really love me, he loved my family's money and I've grown to really dislike him – a lot!" she smiled as she wiped a tear from Stephanie's cheek.

"But you were going to marry him because of what I said before."

"And I didn't … because of what you said today – and because the man that my mother was speaking to that day in my office … it was Jerry. So, thank you."

Kate gathered Steph into her arms. "Do you think we can be friends?"

Steph nodded. "I'm sorry."

"I know you are. You were just frightened. I understand."

"You can marry my dad," Stephanie blurted suddenly, pulling away from Kate's embrace. "I don't mind anymore, honest!"

Suddenly, Alex felt a tremendously heavy black curtain lifted from his heart. He filled his lungs with fresh clean air, feeling as though he'd stopped breathing months ago.

Kate's eyes rounded in surprise. "That's very generous of you," she laughed, "but where did you get the idea that your dad might want to marry *me*?"

Kate finally found the nerve to raise her eyes to Alex, who had now taken a lazy stance, hands in pockets, head slightly tilted, his eyes sparkling and a hint of a smile tugging at the corner of his mouth.

"Did he say something to you?" Kate turned to Stephanie and the other kids. They all shook their heads, a grin adorning their faces. "He's never said anything to me – in fact I'm not even sure that he likes me all that much and—"

Alex's fingers clamped down on her wrist suddenly and pulled her to her feet.

"Did I ever tell you that you talk too much?" he said as he held her against him.

"Well, you never said…. "

"Neither did you."

"No, I guess I didn't…. If someone told me this was going to happen … I would have dismissed that person as crazy. Gram said that this entire substituting scheme I concocted … well, she thinks that subconsciously I wanted to have the opportunity to know you better, to get close to you."

"Really."

"I think she was right. That day …that day of Leeza's dance recital … it was as though a light bulb was switched on and I finally saw you. Every day I spent with you since then … I didn't want it to end. Working together, I'd come to care about you – quite a bit actually," she said as if just now realizing just how much, "but during all this … I fell in love with you. I love you, Alex," she declared.

Alex exhaled a slow breath, as if he'd been unable to breathe until she confirmed her feelings. She did, and now he could finally tell her. "I love you too. I have for quite a while."

"And I never realized…. "

"No, you didn't." Alex shook his head. "You know, for such an intelligent woman, you were oblivious to quite a bit," he smiled.

"I know, I'm sorry…. "

He gazed into her eyes, his voice taking on a more seductive tone, albeit a quiet one, "I guess you'll just have to make it up to me."

"I plan to …" she returned. And his lips covered hers in a gentle kiss; a kiss he had thought he would never experience again.

His children gathered around, embracing the two, happy to be part of the beginning of a new family.

THE END

Don't miss

Services Rendered

THE NEXT SCINTILLATING ROMANCE NOVEL

by

J.E. D'Angelo

Hair & Make-up by Phases

J.E. D'Angelo's active imagination was fostered through childhood years spent watching and discussing thousands of movies and dozens of operas with a creative father who inspired her passion for storytelling. It wasn't long before she began to re-imagine personal versions of these stories, which finally led to creating her own. Ms. D'Angelo is a member of the Canadian Authors' Association, Toronto Romance Writers, and Romance Writers of America. Visit her on the web at:

www.jedangelo.com